MW01178874

10/9a

Halifax:
A Literary Portrait

Edited By John Bell

With a Foreword by Robert MacNeil

Pottersfield Press
Lawrencetown Beach
Nova Scotia

Canadian Cataloguing in Publication Data
Main entry under title:

Halifax: a literary portrait

  Includes bibliographical references.
  ISBN 0-919110-65-3

1. Halifax (N.S.) --Literary Collections. 2.
Halifax (N.S.) in literature. I. Bell, John,
1952-

FC2346.1H34 1990 971.6'225 C90-097610-1
F1039.5.H17H34 1990

Cover painting by Elizabeth Nutt: *Winter, George Street,*
Halifax, N.S. (1935) courtesy of The Public
Archives of Nova Scotia

Published with the assistance of The Nova Scotia
Department of Tourism and Culture
and The Canada Council

  Pottersfield Press
  Lawrencetown Beach
  R.R. 2, Porters Lake
  Nova Scotia B0J 2S0

For acknowledgements, see p.227

CONTENTS

FOREWORD

What is it that makes a city romantic? I think it is being made the subject and setting of literature.

Romantic things happen in all cities, in small towns, in villages. Romance comes with the human condition. To any of us individually, a romantic city is one where we fell in love or had an affair, got engaged or spent our honeymoon; had an adventure, were in danger and escaped; a city which gave us a moment of feeling intensely alive, an existential moment when our own life became a story.

Halifax has given me such moments. I can remember spring evenings, those moist, thick evenings in May, when the very green fog smelt of romance. Play the right popular song (circa 1949-51), get the right halo of mist around the street lights under the fresh-leafed trees, add the moan of a foghorn and I can re-live it all. In those memories, Halifax is a place of romance to me. It is, as it has been for hundreds of thousands of people, a city of personal romance.

But I would not then have called Halifax a romantic city. Romantic cities were London, New York, Paris, Bombay, St. Petersburg, Moscow, Dublin, Edinburgh — the cities of Dickens, Runyon, Sartre, Kipling, Dostoevsky, Tolstoy, Joyce, Stevenson. They were the settings for books. They were the places of adventure and romance. They were where stories happened, where writers wrote. They were more real to my imagination when I was young than the actual world around me, Halifax and other parts of Nova Scotia.

The Frisian Islands off the coast of Germany have nothing remarkable in the way of natural beauty: they are sandy and flat, not a patch on thousands of islands in Nova Scotia. Yet your heart will probably swell at their mention if, as I, you have loved Erskine Childer's *The Riddle of the Sands*, or Isak Dinesen's story "Deluge at Norderney," one of those islands. In fact the

Frisian Islands can probably boast no more in the way of real life adventure than the coast of Nova Scotia, with its rich lore of piracy, smuggling, privateering, and buried treasure. But the power of Childer's imagination created a psychic reality greater than fact. He made the Frisian Islands romantic.

Every city — Rawalpindi, Pakistan, or Cedar Rapids, Iowa — is a power station for human energy. The currents of that energy course through the collective life, generation after generation. But it dissipates; it flies off into the ether; it is consumed in living and disappears. Writers magically reunite that spiritual energy by making books like storage batteries that can perpetually recharge a city with that forgotten human energy. Thus the extraordinary power of curiosity in men like Samuel Pepys, James Boswell and Arnold Bennett constantly recharges Londoners, as do the fictions of Charles Dickens, Virginia Woolf and many others. Writers create a greenhouse effect with the human energy they collect and prevent from escaping.

Dublin, however drab and scabby in reality, in the sour spilt-beer fug of its pubs, reeks of Joyce; as Paris does of Proust, or Gide, or whomever you like. Rouen, as unprepossessing a provincial city as I can think of, will be haunted for ever by the sexuality of Emma Bovary, lost in the toils of love in a carriage driven all day.

It is an unlucky city that has no writers to seize and preserve that energy so that present citizens can be charged and inspired by it. Although surrounded by books, I grew up thinking Halifax had simply not been written about, which translated too easily into not being worth writing about. In middle age I fell upon Charles Ritchie's *The Siren Years* like a starved man.

People do the same things everywhere on earth, the things people like to read about — even in Halifax: make love and give birth; quarrel and fight; find life ridiculous or terrifying; dare or shrink from daring; conquer or surrender to life; feel pride, shame, honour, courage, cowardice; are pious or not; toil and prosper or envy those who do; fear and hate; sicken and recover, age and die. But when I was growing up all that powerful stuff got converted into literature somewhere else, far away; so that this callow Haligonian got the idea that the real juice and nectar of life could be tapped only from trees that grew in more exotic places.

That is why this collection is so fascinating to me and why I wish the literature it samples (to the extent it existed then) had been stuffed into me in my impressionable years.

No one told me when I was a child growing up in Halifax that the great Rudyard Kipling, author of *The Jungle Book* and *Kim* and *Stalky & Co*, had written a verse about Halifax. It never entered my head, as I recited his "Recessional" at Tower Road School, that Kipling had the slightest idea that Halifax existed. No one told me that Charles Dickens, of *Great Expectations* and *David Copperfield*, had actually been to Halifax and written about it — that his pen had written down the name!

What makes a city is the collective sense of community, sometimes oppressive, mostly stimulating, of many humans busy together. Cities create propinquity and promiscuity — in all senses, naughty and nice. When that is recorded, each citizen draws something from it, becomes more worldly, has a heightened sense of where and when he is living. Newspapers do it for today, but they are forgotten. Books must do it for yesterday and for tomorrow and for the hidden reality of today. I have no doubt that people who live in Toronto will have a deeper sense of the psychic reality of their city from reading the early childhood chapters of Margaret Atwood's *Cat's Eye*.

Canada has been a long time creating its own sense of identity, its national romance. As one of Robertson Davies' characters observed, Canadians have often felt like strangers in their own land. It has not been healthy for the national psyche for that sense of exile to linger so long. Eventually one generation had to stand and say: "we know who we are and this is where we belong." That psychological development probably began with the First World War. It has been slow, decent and slow, because it suits Canadians to evolve in small increments. Every writer has to overcome a certain autobiographical squeamishness. So, perhaps, does an emerging people. Slowly now, but with a quickening pace, Canada has begun to tell itself the stories long unrecognised.

This book fits into that process of accumulating increments of awareness, to create the humus which will fertilize future awareness, perhaps nourish a great imagination.

Like Canada in all its parts, Halifax always deserved to be written about more. Perhaps this welcome collection will start some young writer's juices flowing. He never needs to think, as I mistakenly did, that it is all happening somewhere else.

Perhaps he will make Halifax for the rest of the world the romantic city it is to some of us personally.

Robert MacNeil

INTRODUCTION

"Whether you love Halifax or not, you must admit that she has character."

Hugh MacLennan

Halifax is very much a writer's city not only because it has long been one of Canada's major literary centres, but also because of the richness of its history and architecture, as well as the appeal of its strong sense of community and tradition. It is a place that native, resident, and visiting writers have found to be a source of fascination and inspiration for more than two centuries. In fact, even before Halifax became a British colonial settlement in 1749, the physical beauty of the harbour and its environs was celebrated by the French poet and botanist Dièreville in his *Relation du voyage du Port Royal de l'Acadie, ou de la Nouvelle France* (1708).

As an important focus of English-language literary activity, Halifax has been rivalled by few Canadian cities. In 1752, John Bushell of Halifax edited and published the *Halifax Gazette*, the first newspaper in what would eventually become Canada. In the three decades which followed, the town witnessed the publication of a number of significant books and pamphlets, including several works by the New Light preacher Henry Alline. One of the first literary visitors to record his impressions of Halifax, Alline was distressed by what he saw during his brief sojourn in the seaport in January 1783, lamenting in his journal that "the people in general are almost as dark and as vile as in Sodom."

Not long after Alline's visit, the town was transformed by the arrival of masses of Loyalist refugees, including a large number of educated and professional people — former members of the New England elite — who brought with them not only a desire for newspapers, schools, and other cultural institutions, but also an established literary tradition. Although many of the best Loyalist writers were located outside of Halifax, the Nova Scotia capital continued to be a leading colonial publishing centre. In addition to the first Canadian literary periodical, *The Nova-Scotia Magazine* (1789-92) edited initially by William Cochran and then by its publisher, John Howe, the town saw the publication of the first separate volume of poetry issued in Canada, *Annapolis Royal: A Poem* (1788) by Roger Viets of Digby.

The literary achievements of the pre-Loyalist and Loyalist eras were, however, dramatically eclipsed by those of the three decades which followed the end of the Napoleonic Wars in 1815. It was during these years of unparalleled economic, political, and cultural change that a distinct Nova Scotian identity emerged together with many of the institutions that would shape the province's future. While Halifax poet Oliver Goldsmith and the Pictou educator Thomas McCulloch were the first important writers of the period, the central figure of this time of ferment was Halifax's Joseph Howe.

At the end of 1827 Howe became the publisher and editor of the *Novascotian* and soon transformed the paper into the leading journal in British North America. In its pages he strove to promote colonial culture, publishing many local authors, like Thomas C. Haliburton, Lawrence O'Connor Doyle, Captain John Kincaid, and Dr. William Grigor, all members, with Howe, of the Halifax-based literary coterie the Club. In 1835 the *Novascotian* began running a series of satirical sketches by Haliburton, the era's greatest writer, under the title "Recollections of Nova Scotia." The following year these tales about the Yankee peddler Sam Slick were reprinted in book form by Howe in the volume *The Clockmaker*. The collection soon became the first Canadian international best seller and confirmed Halifax's place as the principal literary community in British North America, a position that was reinforced by the appearance in the city of periodicals like *The Acadian Magazine* (1826-28), *The*

Halifax Monthly Magazine (1830-31), *The British North American Magazine* (1831), and Howe's *The Pearl* (1837-40).

Howe's involvement with literary pursuits, however, began to decline by the late 1830s as he threw himself increasingly into the struggle for responsible government. By the time of Charles Dickens' visit to Halifax in 1842, Howe, who served as the English writer's host, was the Speaker of the Assembly. He would eventually become premier, then a federal cabinet minister, and finally the lieutenant-governor of Nova Scotia.

Among the other figures active in the Halifax literary milieu during the 1814-45 period were the poets Grizelda Tonge and Andrew Shiels, the editor and novelist Sarah Herbert, and the writer Douglas Smith Huyghue, who contributed poetry to *The Halifax Morning Post* while living in the city in 1840-41. Also resident in the city about the same time as Huyghue was the Quebec writer Philippe-Ignace-François Aubert de Gaspé, the author (with some help from his father, Philippe-Joseph Aubert de Gaspé) of the first French-Canadian novel, *L'Influence d'un livre* (1837). The younger Aubert de Gaspé died at Halifax in March 1841.

In the years after 1845 the era of Howe and Haliburton gave way to a new period in Halifax's literary history, one that was characterized by both the increasing importance of the novel as a literary form and the appearance of a number of significant women writers. The new era began in earnest during the early 1850s with the publication in Halifax of two ambitious literary periodicals: the *Mayflower* (1851-52), edited by Sarah Herbert's half-sister, Mary Eliza Herbert, and the *Provincial, or Halifax Monthly Magazine* (1852-53), edited by Mary Jane Katzmann. While neither magazine lasted beyond 1853, both writers continued to make their mark in the local literary milieu — particularly Herbert, who published two collections of poetry and prose-sketches and three novels, including *Belinda Dalton; or Scenes in the Life of a Halifax Belle* (1859).

The same year that *Belinda Dalton* appeared, Halifax had a major European literary visitor — the French diplomat, historian, and novelist, Comte Joseph-Arthur de Gobineau.

Gobineau's account of his trip later appeared in his *Voyage à Terre-Neuve* (1861). Not long after Gobineau's visit, another French literary figure, Victor Hugo's daughter Adèle, came to the garrison town in pursuit of her lover, the British officer Albert Pinsen. Her story was later told in the François Truffault film *L'Histoire d'Adèle H.* (1975).

By the mid-1860s as the careers of Herbert and Katzmann were tapering off, that of James De Mille, the most accomplished Haligonian writer of the period immediately after Confederation, was just beginning. A native of St. John, New Brunswick, De Mille arrived in Halifax in 1865 to assume a position as a professor of rhetoric and history at Dalhousie College. Over the course of the next fifteen years, until his death in 1880, he would emerge as one of the most popular writers in North America, producing more than twenty books in a variety of genres. Also an accomplished poet and scholar, De Mille is best remembered for a posthumous novel, the classic dystopian satire *A Strange Manuscript Found in a Copper Cylinder* (1888). It was with his career that Dalhousie University began to play a role as one of the chief literary centres within the city.

The first decade of the next period in the history of literature in Halifax — the years 1880 to 1920 — marks a slight ebb in Haligonian literary activity, although the era did begin with a bit of a stir when Oscar Wilde gave two lectures in the city in October 1882. Writing from Halifax, Wilde commented "I am having charming audiences ... but it is a great fight in this commercial age to plead the cause of Art." The same year that Wilde visited Halifax, another Irish writer, Francis Blake Crofton, moved to the city to become the province's Legislative Librarian. An active member of the Halifax literary community for more than twenty years, Crofton was the author of the popular Major Mendax stories for children.

As was the case during the preceding decades, these years saw the emergence of a number of important Halifax-based women writers. Chief among them were Marshall Saunders, the author of the classic animal story *Beautiful Joe* (1894); Alice Jones, a prolific romantic novelist whose father was

Lieutenant-Governor Alfred Gilpin Jones; the novelist Susan Jones, the sister-in-law of Alice Jones; and Maria Amelia Fytche, who is best remembered for the novel *A Kerchief to Hunt Souls* (1899). Another major woman author, Lucy Maud Montgomery, also spent some time in Halifax during this period, attending Dalhousie University from 1895 to 1896 and then later returning to the city to work on the *Echo* from 1901 to 1902.

Among the other writers connected with the city during the era were Basil King and James MacDonald Oxley, both of whom pursued their literary careers after leaving Halifax, and Arthur Wentworth Eaton, who co-authored a collection of Halifax short stories, *Tales From a Garrison Town* (1892), with the New Brunswick writer Craven Longstreth Betts. Eaton also later wrote a history of the city which was serialized in the Boston journal *Americana*. In 1918, a lesser-known writer, F. Mc-Kelvey Bell, published *A Romance of the Halifax Disaster*, the first work of fiction to portray the terrible explosion which devastated Halifax on December 6, 1917.

Perhaps the most important Haligonian writer of the period, though, was the academic who served as the official historian of the Explosion — Archibald MacMechan. A professor of English at Dalhousie from 1889 to 1931, MacMechan was one of Canada's leading men of letters. In addition to being an influential scholar and critic, he was an essayist, a local historian, and a sometime poet and small-press publisher. As a result of the breadth of his activities and the length of his tenure at Dalhousie, MacMechan represented a link between the era of De Mille and that of the writers who would come to prominence in the post-1920 period. Among his students were Lucy Maud Montgomery, Kenneth Leslie, Hugh MacLennan, and Charles Ritchie.

In fact, until his death in 1933, MacMechan remained a major presence in Halifax for much of the 1920-40 period, a time of increasing economic, political, and cultural marginalization for the Atlantic region. The other leading Haligonian literary figure during these troubled decades was the journalist and

5

poet Andrew Merkel, whose house on South Park Street served as a meeting place for resident and visiting writers for close to thirty years. During the late twenties and early thirties, Merkel was at the centre of the Song Fishermen, an informal poetry group and the city's first major coterie since Howe's group the Club of a century before. Among the members of the Song Fishermen were the Cape Bretoners Stuart McCawley and James D. Gillis and such well-known summer visitors as Charles G. D. Roberts, Bliss Carman, and Robert Norwood. The group also included several writers more closely connected with Halifax, like Kenneth Leslie, Charles Bruce, Joe Wallace, John D. Logan, Eliza Ritchie, and Elizabeth Nutt. In addition to issuing the group's mimeographed journal, *The Song Fishermen's Song Sheet* (1928-30), Merkel launched a small literary imprint, Abanaki Press. The most important literary publication of the period, though, was the university-based journal *The Dalhousie Review*, which was founded in 1921.

A number of notable fiction writers were also active in Halifax at various times during the twenties and thirties, such as Edith Archibald, whose first and only novel, *The Token* (1930), appeared when she was in her late seventies; the popular-fiction writer Benge Atlee; and the prolific novelist and short-story writer Will R. Bird, who moved to the city in the late thirties. It was during this period as well that Margerie Bonner, who grew up in Halifax, wrote two novels set in Nova Scotia, *Rainbow at Night* (1936) and *A World of Our Own* (1937).

In some respects, the next era in Halifax's literary history, comprising the years from 1940 to 1965, marks a low point in the city's literary evolution. Although Andrew Merkel and Will R. Bird remained active and *The Dalhousie Review* continued to be an important cultural force, the city's national role was in decline. Furthermore, even within the region, Fredericton, New Brunswick supplanted Halifax as the major Atlantic Canadian literary centre. Curiously, at the same time, two former Haligonians were making their mark on the national literary scene, producing some of the best writing ever about the city. In 1941 Hugh MacLennan published the book which many regard as *the* Halifax novel — *Barometer Rising*. The next year, the city figured as a significant setting in *His Majesty's Yankees*, the first of many Halifax-related novels by the country's greatest historical novelist, Thomas H. Raddall. (Although a resident of Liverpool, Raddall spent a good deal of time in his home town, particularly at the Public Archives of Nova Scotia.)

It is also worth noting that a number of significant literary figures attended university in Halifax during the fifties and the first half of the sixties. Among the most important were Robert MacNeil, Simon Gray (who launched a short-lived literary magazine), Douglas Barbour, Ray Smith, and Fraser Sutherland. Most of these writers would later make some use of their Halifax years in their writing.

As the sixties ended, however, changes were evident in the Halifax literary milieu that would lead to the reestablishment of the city as a major regional and national literary centre. Many of these developments could be traced to two related factors: the growth of the literary small-press movement and increasing government support for the arts. Probably the first writer to personify the new direction in Halifax literary activity was Rick Rofihe. Now a contributor of short fiction to *The New Yorker*, during the early seventies Rofihe was involved with the launching of two Halifax literary presses, Straw Books and An-der-bo Books. Another important editor and publisher during these years was the playwright Paul Ledoux, the founder of the underground paper *Gandalf* (1971-72) and the magazine *We People* (1972). Also active in the city during the period was the poet Bill Howell.

Not long after these first signs of the arrival of a new generation of Halifax writers, a number of literary organizations established offices in Halifax: the Writers' Federation of Nova Scotia, the Atlantic Publishers Association, the *Our Books Atlantic* project, and the Canadian Book Information Centre. *The Atlantic Provinces Book Review* was also launched during this period. In addition, several new publishers emerged, including Wooden Anchor Press, Abanaki Press (co-founded by Andrew Merkel's grandson Scott Thompson), Nimbus Publishing, and

Pottersfield Press. While the latter has, since its inception in 1979, been located in Lawrencetown, it should nonetheless be viewed as a vital part of the Halifax literary milieu. Lesley Choyce, who founded and still operates Pottersfield, has also been active as a leading writer and as the host of the television programme *Choyce Words* (formerly *East Coast Authors*).

Among the other writers who have been connected at some time with the Halifax literary scene during the past decade and a half are Susan Kerslake, Fred Ward, Jim Lotz, Andy Wainwright, George Elliott Clarke, Maxine Tynes, Joe Blades, Elizabeth Jones, Tony Foster, and Bill Gaston. As well, Malcolm Ross, Malcolm Parks, Alan Kennedy, Patricia Monk, and other important Canadian literary scholars have pursued their careers in the city.

The late seventies and the eighties also saw the emergence of several Halifax-based literary magazines, such as *Borealis, Skylight, The Pottersfield Portfolio, Fathom,* and *Poetry Halifax Dartmouth*. Furthermore, during much of this period Halifax came to be seen as a major centre for Canadian science fiction. In part, this was due to the presence in the city of one of Canada's leading science-fiction writers, Spider Robinson. However, not only were other Haligonians active in the genre, but in 1980 the city hosted the first national science-fiction convention, at which the Canadian Science Fiction and Fantasy Award was inaugurated. And while the fact that the old seaport had become a focal point for science fiction seemed like an unlikely development to some, it was simply one more indication that by the early eighties Halifax was once again a major Canadian literary centre.

In addition to its distinguished tradition of literary activity, Halifax has figured as a significant setting for, and subject of, literature. Charles Bruce, in an epigraph to his classic novel *The Channel Shore* (1954), noted that there are two Nova Scotias, one the actual place and the other "the image of that land.... a country of the mind." This same duality applies, of course, to the province's capital city and the other Halifax — the city of the mind — when expressed in literature also forms an important part of Halifax's literary heritage.

In fact, it is the depiction of the city in literary works — poetry, fiction, essays, and memoirs and travel accounts by creative writers — that is the focus of *Halifax: A Literary Portrait*. Needless to say, in documenting the literary portrayal of Halifax, the anthology inevitably reflects to some degree the history of literature in the city, so that many of the major authors who have both lived and written in Halifax are found in the book: Oliver Goldsmith, Joseph Howe, Marshall Saunders, Archibald MacMechan, and Will R. Bird.

On the other hand, because *Halifax* is concerned with the literary representation of Halifax itself, a number of the city's most important resident writers are not included, because, surprisingly, they either did not write about the city or if they did, the image of Halifax encountered in their work is not particularly strong or sustained. For this reason, authors like James De Mille, Alice Jones, and Susan Kerslake are not found in the book.

The absence of such leading Haligonian literary figures in the anthology is offset by the presence of two other categories of writers: first of all, visitors who left some record of their contact with Halifax and secondly, those who lived in the city for a substantial period of time and then left, later drawing on their former home as a source for their writing. The first group includes writers like Charles Dickens, Richard Henry Dana, Jr., Rudyard Kipling, L. M. Montgomery, and Earle Birney. The second group embraces such figures as Kenneth Leslie, Thomas H. Raddall, Hugh MacLennan, and bill bissett, all of whom grew up in the city. Also represented in the book is one writer, the British novelist and playwright Israel Zangwill, who apparently never saw the city but was able to utilize other sources to depict a Halifax that was not remembered but imagined.

Taken together, the thirty-one selections in *Halifax: A Literary Portrait* afford a multi-faceted portrait of Nova Scotia's capital. And while the depictions of Halifax found in the anthology are not always complimentary, they are, it is hoped, diverting, and shed light on both the city's historical development and its changing identity. Through the eyes of many different writers, the reader will see Halifax in various guises: garrison town, naval station, major East Coast port, and centre of commerce, government, and education. Not surprisingly, a number of crucial events in the city's history are depicted or reflected, including the arrival of Loyalist refugees, the Explosion of December 6, 1917, and the destruction of the Black community of Africville. As well, many of the landmarks which have contributed to Halifax's distinctiveness are in evidence, such as the harbour, the Citadel, the Town Clock, Government House, and Point Pleasant Park. In a sense, *Halifax* is a book with one character but thirty-one authors, all of whom delineate different aspects of that character's identity.

However, while all the poems, stories, and other pieces in *Halifax* were chosen primarily for the image of Halifax which they offer — whether it occupies the foreground or the background — each selection reveals as much about its author as it does about the city. For some writers, Halifax represents a welcome haven, for others a way station to be quickly abandoned. Where one author sees a vibrant metropolis, another sees a cultural backwater. What is a quaint outpost of Empire to one, is an imposing fortress to another. Whatever the approach to Halifax, the portrayal of the community presented in each selection is obviously coloured by its author's attitudes and also, in many instances, by the circumstances which brought him or her to the city. In addition to these differences in perception, there is naturally a variety of forms and styles evident throughout the anthology. Some writers rely on matter-of-fact realism to convey their impressions of Halifax, while others are intent on more lyrical explorations of the city's heart and soul.

For this reason, readers will find it interesting, as they work their way through the anthology, to compare the various views of Halifax that it contains. In some cases they will discover not divergences but intriguing echoes. Readers might also reflect on the creative process itself, whereby the city affects the writer and then is, in turn, reshaped in literature. Hopefully, this process will also encompass the book's readers, who might find that their perceptions of the city are transformed and enriched to some degree by the representations found in *Halifax: A Literary Portrait*, so that their contact with Halifax becomes, in part, an encounter with Dickens, Kipling, Raddall, bissett, and the many other contributors to the anthology.

Whatever the case, it should be noted that despite its variety, *Halifax* does not, by any means, exhaust the rich vein of writing about Halifax that is found in Canadian, British, American, and, to some extent, French literature. Many important writers who have dealt with the city are not included, for a host of reasons, including editorial balance and more mundane concerns such as space and, in one instance, copyright problems. Furthermore, since there is only one selection from each contributor, a difficult choice had to be made when it came to writers like Raddall (probably the author who has written more about the city than anyone else), MacLennan, Howell, Clarke, and bissett, all of whom have produced a number of strong works relating to the city. Some effort was also made, without sacrificing quality, to uncover selections that were not readily available elsewhere. For this reason, Hugh MacLennan is represented not by an excerpt from *Barometer Rising*, but rather, a less familiar piece — the Christmas story "An Orange from Portugal."

The anthology's introduction, headnotes, and appendix (see "Further Reading," p. 223) are all intended to direct readers to many of the other literary works pertaining to Halifax, both by the anthology's contributors and by writers not included in the book. The headnotes should also provide readers with sufficient bio-bibliographical information to situate each selection in the context of its author's career and work.

Whenever possible, complete stories and poems have been used. However, in some instances an excerpt was the only or the best choice to represent an author. As much as possible these excerpts are self-contained. In terms of arrangement, the book is largely chronological, but with reference not to the date of publication, but instead to the period of Halifax's history with which each selection is concerned. For this reason, the anthology ends with a passage from Spider Robinson's near-future novel *Mindkiller*.

For me, a Haligonian living in Ottawa (which is presently home to Halifax literary expatriates like Charles Ritchie and George Elliott Clarke), compiling *Halifax: A Literary Portrait* was a labour of love, one that permitted me to spend more than a year revisiting in print the streets of my home town. Assisting me on my many literary journeys back to Halifax were a number of people without whom the anthology couldn't have been completed. In particular, I would like to thank the staff of the National Library in Ottawa and the following individuals: Charles Armour, Jim Burant, George Elliott Clarke, George Henderson, Bill Howell, Lewis Jackson, Douglas Lochhead, Nadine McInnis, Brian Murphy, Malcolm Parks, Peter Rogers, Suanne Rogers, Bill Russell, Pat Townshend, and Rena Van Dam.

I am also extremely grateful to Robert MacNeil, who kindly agreed to prepare a foreword to the anthology. His memoir *Wordstruck* (1989), which was nominated for a Governor-General's Award, is one of the finest works linking Halifax and literature. I want to acknowledge as well my debt to my friend and publisher Lesley Choyce, who strongly believed in the anthology and provided much encouragement.

Halifax: A Literary Portrait is for all those who have been touched by Halifax and have what Charles Bruce called "the remembering blood" flowing in their veins, including those who live away but still, from time to time, hear the fog horns in the harbour or the echo of the noon gun, or close their eyes and walk the shaded paths of Point Pleasant Park or stand at the top of Citadel Hill and drink it all in: the city of Howe, Saunders, MacMechan, Leslie, Bird, Raddall, MacLennan, and so many other voices — a literary capital like no other.

John Bell
Ottawa, April 1990

SIEUR DE DIÈREVILLE

*   *   *   *   *   *   *

Sieur de Dièreville was born in France, possibly at Pont-l'Evêque in the department of Calvados. His date of birth is unknown, although it has been suggested that it was likely about 1670. He apparently studied surgery at the Hôtel-Dieu in Paris and is known to have contributed poetry to the Mercure galant. *In August 1699 he sailed for Acadia, where he spent nearly a year investigating the people, geography, and flora of the region. The year after his return to France he became a surgeon at Pont-l'Evêque. A recognized expert on the plants of Acadia, in 1708 he published an account of his trip to the New World,* Relation du voyage du Port Royal de l'Acadie, ou de la Nouvelle France. *The narrative was originally written entirely in verse; however, Dièreville's friends convinced him that the book would be better received if he alternated prose and poetry. This advice seems to have been sound, as the revised text became something of a best seller, appearing in three editions in 1708. A condensed English translation was published in 1714. And while very little is known about Dièreville either before or after his voyage to Acadia, his work remains a classic of Acadian literature.*

The following excerpt is from the Champlain Society's English-language edition of Dièreville's account. Entitled Relation of the Voyage to Port Royal in Acadia or New France *(1933), the book was translated by Mrs. Clarence Webster and edited by John Clarence Webster. Dièreville's description of his visit to the abandoned French fishing station at the place known to the Micmac as* Chebooktook *("great harbour") provides us with a fascinating glimpse of the site of Halifax fifty years before the arrival of British colonists under Edward Cornwallis.*

*   *   *   *   *   *   *

from **Relation of the Voyage to Port Royal in Acadia or New France**

When day had come, we saw a vast wooded Country & we followed along the Coast until Noon; we were sailing well, but a gale, which would have intimidated the hardiest Navigators, forced us to seek a good anchorage & take shelter from its blast. We were, furthermore, beginning to run short of Wood & Water; we were cooking enough food at a time to last us for a week, good reasons for dropping anchor; too many dangers threatened our lives at once; we had, quite by chance, been driven to Chiboüetou, Bayesenne on the Chart, on the Shores of Acadia, where we soon obtained the succor we needed.

> This Harbour is of great extent,
> And Nature has, herself, formed there
> A splendid Basin, and around about
> Green Fir-trees, which afford the eye
>
> A pleasant prospect; at its edge
> A Building used for drying Cod;
> That such construction is not known
> To Mansard, is quite possible.

It was half as long, & quite as wide as the Mall in Paris, built on a fine Beach along the River, at a distance which permitted the water to pass under it at high tide & carry away the refuse of the Cod. Imagine a wooden Bridge, built over the land, of large trees driven well in on the side facing the water; at their extremities, other pieces of wood placed crosswise & securely clamped; imagine the same construction on the land side, but not so high because it was on a Slope; over all this, young Fir trees, long enough to rest on either edge, laid evenly, one alongside the other, & well nailed at both ends to the wooden supports, & you will then know what this Contrivance, which is called by the Fisherman a Dégras, is like. The Cod, carefully split, are spread upon it during the summer, & turned & re-turned continually, so that they may dry & attain the proper state, the one familiar in a thousand places in the World to which they are easily transported. This Station was uninhabited; it had been made before the last war by French Fishermen, who had established themselves there in the name of a Company which did not prove profitable.

No sooner anchored, than I had myself
Transferred to Land; and thus, I disembarked
After so much delay. Wild Geese
And Cormorants aroused in me
The wish to war on them, but all
In vain I ran in their pursuit;
They fled with even greater speed,
Or in Amphitrite's bosom hid;
My steps were all superfluous.
But I consoled myself with shots
At the small Game along the Shore;
In this Vicinity, a noise like that
Startles the Indians; unwittingly
I ran some risk, for, as I roamed about,
I passed a Hut, which might have served
As ambush for a member of this Tribe.

The Indians have not such cruel hearts; our Sailors, going to the Spring for water one evening, met two of these People who appeared very gentle; they were, however, armed with Musket & Hatchet. I had doubtless alarmed them, & they feared that they might be taken by surprise & were therefore on the defensive; who would not have done the same under the circumstance? They maintained a kind & resolute attitude in the presence of our Men, who had no sooner made themselves known as French, than the Indians lowered their arms.

I think they meant to indicate thereby,
That they were subject to our own great King;
Though not a word was understood, they talked
Together thus, and parted best of friends.

Early the following morning, three of their Chiefs came in a little bark Canoe, to pay us a visit; their address was brief & yet I could find nothing to say in reply.

I showed them such a friendly face
That with it they appeared content;
It does not seem Uncivilized
To visit People in this way.

In order to offer them more adequate entertainment, which was perhaps that for which they had come, I gave them a good breakfast of Meat & Fish & they munched Biscuit with the best appetite in the world, & drank Brandy with relish & less moderation than we do; they have a craving for it & I think that they would have emptied my Cellar without becoming intoxicated. I observed with much edification an action on their part; it was, that on sitting down to table, they said their Prayer devoutly & made the Sign of the Cross, &, when they had finished, they gave thanks with the same piety.

Each had a Rosary around his neck
Worn in the manner of a Scapular,
And a small Reliquary sewn inside
A piece of Cloth or Druggetting.
They had received Baptism, and were
Of their original sin thus purged
By a most zealous Priest, who had
I went that very day; I saw at once
His Tomb of stakes, covered with bark
Been taken from them since by death.
With Signs they made us understand
That he was buried in a Wood nearby;

And there, by curiosity impelled,
Arched, cradle-shaped, and rather long
Than round; while covering his clay
Small Stones, instead of Marble, were
Neatly arranged upon the ground.
They left our Ship at last, well pleased,
To show us their delight and happiness,
They fired a shot which rang across the waves.
Little enough; someone might say there should
Have been three Salvos; but they had
One Musket only, how could they do more?

I had given them ammunition in order that they might bring me some Game, & they doubtless would have done so, but the wind on the following night become favourable for leaving this Haven, in which we had secured all we required, so we hoisted sail at dawn to continue on our way.

JACOB BAILEY

*   *   *   *   *   *   *

Jacob Bailey was born at Rowley, Massachusetts in 1731. Following his graduation from Harvard in 1755, he worked briefly as a teacher before becoming a Congregationalist minister and later an Anglican priest. In 1760 he assumed a parish at Pownalborough, Maine, where he remained until the American Revolution forced him to seek refuge in Nova Scotia. After his arrival in Halifax in 1779, he served as a parish priest, first at Cornwallis and then at Annapolis Royal. At the time of his death in 1808, Bailey left a large body of writing, including letters, journals, fiction, and poetry. Selections from his correspondence and journals were eventually published in W.S. Bartlet's The Frontier Missionary: A Memoir of the Life of the Rev. Jacob Bailey, A.M. *(1853). More recently, some of his poetry appeared in* Narrative Verse Satire in Maritime Canada, 1779-1814 *(1978) edited by Thomas B. Vincent.*

The following passage is from Bailey's "Journal of a Voyage from Pownalboro' to Halifax, with Notices of Some Events in the Latter Place," which was first published in Bartlet's The Frontier Missionary. *In this excerpt, Bailey describes his arrival, with his family, in Halifax, on June 21, 1779, following a terrible twelve-day voyage from Maine. While Bailey betrays a certain degree of apprehension concerning his new home, it is clear that for him, like many Loyalists, the town represented a haven.*

*   *   *   *   *   *   *

from **Journal of a Voyage from Pownalboro' to Halifax, with Notices of Some Events in the Latter Place**

June 21st. No sooner did the morning light begin to soften the horrors of darkness, than I arose and took possession of the deck to observe the weather and to survey the adjacent country. I found that we were overtaken by a dead calm, and the heavens were covered with rolling volumes of black and dismal clouds which shed a dark and dejecting gloom over all the surrounding scenes of nature. But if I was inspired with melancholy sentiments at this dusky prospect, I was perfectly shocked when I turned my eyes towards the land which stretched along the western quarter. The shore which now engages my attention is the famous Jebucto Head, a most enormous congress of rocky ledges running with a lofty and impregnable front into the sea, while the surface is inexpressibly rugged and broken, covered with shrubby spruce, fir and hemlock, which by their starving and misshapen appearance sufficiently indicate the severity of the climate and the barrenness of the soil. But notwithstanding the unpleasing aspect of this strange region, I could not forbear the returns of gratitude to Providence for safely conducting me and my family to this retreat of freedom and security from the rage of tyranny and the cruelty of oppression. The wind beginning to blow softly as the light increased, we weighed anchor, displayed the canvas and got under way. The sun being risen we perceived that the land on the eastern side of the harbour was in comparison extremely agreeable; the beach was covered with small pebbles, the banks, which were moderately high, resembled the colour of deep burnt bricks, and the trees of various species, tall and well shaped. And what added to the beauty and cheerfulness of the prospect, the forest was in many cases discontinued and finely interspersed with patches of cleared ground, adorned with a lively verdure.

But we were again sadly disappointed in our expectations, for we fondly imagined that upon our entrance into the harbour we should have the whole metropolis in open view, and a number of lofty buildings rising in conspicuous glory, with a respectable part of the Royal Navy lying at anchor before the town. Instead of which flattering instances of power, grandeur and magnificence, we could observe no edifices except the citadel and two or three scattered habitations; and as to shipping we saw only two sail of armed vessels and three or four sail at Major's Beach, for we were ignorant that both the town and the proper harbour were concealed by the interposition of St. George's Island and certain aspiring eminences to the northward. As we sailed slowly up the harbour, the next object which invited our attention, was a large fleet of Indian canoes, coasting along the Jebucto shore and filled with multitudes of the native Micmacs, and at the same time we espied several of these copper-faced sons of liberty either landing on the margin of a little bay, or climbing up the stupendous precipices. We took notice upon this occasion, that artificial ways were formed up these steepy cliffs for the conveniency of ascending or conveying down timber, which is frequently cut on the summit of these ridges for the public works at Halifax. As we advanced still further from the ocean, the town began gradually to open, and we had in prospect several strong fortifications, as the Eastern Battery, George's Fort, and strong ramparts upon the neighbouring heights, with all their terrible apparatus of cannon and mortars. When we arrived near the above-mentioned Island of St. George's, we had a most advantageous, striking view of this northern capital, stretching a mile and a half upon the eastern ascent of an extensive hill, while a large collection of shipping lay either contiguous to the wharves, or else were riding, with the Brittanic colours flying, in the channel, a sight which instantly inspired us with the most pleasing sensations. We expected to be hailed as we passed St. George's Fort, but the people, conceiving our vessel to be some coaster from Malagash, we were suffered to proceed without any inquiry.

We were now all upon deck, contemplating with infinite wonder and satisfaction the various objects about us, but we must however except John Hoffman from this agreeable employ, who was so affected with alternate joy and concern at the sight of his native place, that he retired into the cabin, there to indulge in solitude these conflicting passions. I perceived, that though he was highly rejoiced to behold the country where he was born and educated, yet he was seized with a prevailing anxiety of heart, lest he should find his tender mother, who had long mourned his absence, departed to the shades of death.

These uneasy apprehensions rendered him unfit for company, and threw him at length into visible confusion and distress. We were now indulging in a thousand pleasing reflections as we approached near the centre of the town, and this situation reminded us that it was proper to explore some convenient place to secure a landing, but previous to this agreeable event it was concluded to investigate the Commodore's ship, and to solicit the naval commander for liberty to go on shore. A boat passing by this instant hailed us and demanded, as they were going swiftly under sail, from whence we came? We replied, from Kennebeck. This answer occasioned a visible surprise in the company, who continued repeating: "Kennebeck! Kennebeck!" Seeing a number of men on board a sloop, we desired them to point out the Commodore, and received immediate information that there was no such officer in the harbour. This intelligence determined us directly to make towards a wharf, which happened to be near the Pontac. We were now plainly sensible that our uncouth habits and uncommon appearance had, by this time, attracted the notice of multitudes, who flocked towards the water to indulge their curiosity. These inquisitive strangers threw us into some confusion, and to prevent a multitude of impertinent interrogations, which might naturally be expected by persons in our circumstances, I made the following public declaration, standing on the quarter deck: "Gentlemen, we are a company of fugitives from Kennebeck, in New England, driven by famine and persecution to take refuge among you, and therefore I must entreat your candour and compassion to excuse the meanness and singularity of our dress."

I that moment discovered among the gathering crowd Mr. Kitson, one of our Kennebeck neighbours, running down the street to our assistance. He came instantly on board, and after mutual salutations, helped us on shore. Thus, just a fortnight after we left our own beloved habitation, we found ourselves landed in a strange country, destitute of money, clothing, dwelling or furniture, and wholly uncertain what countenance or protection we might obtain from the governing powers.

THOMAS MOORE

* * * * * * *

*Thomas Moore was born in Dublin, Ireland in 1779 and attended
Trinity College. In 1803 he was appointed admiralty registrar in Ber-
muda, a position that he soon transferred to a deputy. His first book of
poetry,* The Poetical Works of the Late Thomas Little, *appeared in 1801.
A talented song-writer and musician, his* Irish Melodies *(1807-35) established him as Ireland's national bard. As a result of financial problems,
Moore was forced to leave England for Italy for several years, returning
to England in 1822. In 1835 he received a literary pension and in 1850 a
civil list pension. Among his major works are* Lalla Rookh *(1817),* The
Loves of the Angels *(1823), and biographies of Sheridan (1825), Byron
(1830), and Lord Edward Fitzgerald (1831). A close friend of Byron,
Moore took it upon himself to destroy Byron's memoirs in 1824. After
Moore's death in 1852 his own memoirs were edited by Lord John
Russell.*

*The following lines are from the opening of Moore's 56-line ode "To
the Boston Frigate, on Leaving Halifax for England, October, 1804,"
which was first published in his collection* Epistles, Odes, and Other
Poems *(1806). Written at the end of his fourteen-month visit to North
America in 1803-1804, the poem is so pervaded by the poet's overwhelming desire to quit Halifax and the continent, that nowhere in evidence are
the "cordiality and kindness" which, according to a letter Moore wrote
to his mother from Windsor, Nova Scotia, greeted him everywhere during
his trip. In fact, Moore later qualified his unflattering depiction of Nova
Scotia in a note appended to* Epistles, Odes, and Other Poems: *"Sir John
Wentworth, the Governor of Nova-Scotia, very kindly allowed me to
accompany him on his visit to the College, which they have lately
established at Windsor, about forty miles from Halifax, and I was indeed
most pleasantly surprised by the beauty and the fertility of the country
which opened upon us after the bleak and rocky wilderness by which
Halifax is surrounded. I was told that, in travelling onwards, we should
find the soil and the scenery improve, and it gave me much pleasure to*

know that the worthy Governor has by no means such an 'inamabile regnum' as I was, at first sight, inclined to believe." King's College, which is now located in Halifax, still possesses the copy of Lucian that Moore signed to mark the occasion of his visit.

* * * * * * *

from **To the Boston Frigate, on Leaving Halifax for England, October, 1804**

With triumph this morning, O Boston I hail
The stir of thy deck and the spread of thy sail,
For they tell me I soon shall be wafted in thee
To the flourishing isle of the brave and the free,
And that chill Nova Scotia's unpromising strand
Is the last I shall tread of American land.

OLIVER GOLDSMITH

*   *   *   *   *   *   *

Oliver Goldsmith was born at St. Andrews, New Brunswick in 1794 and grew up in the Annapolis Valley and Halifax. After working for a number of years, Goldsmith briefly attended the Halifax Grammar School before joining the commissariat of the British Army at Halifax in 1810. He later held various positions in the commissariat, serving at Saint John, Hong Kong, Newfoundland, and Corfu. Following his retirement in 1855, he lived with his sister in Liverpool, England, where he died in 1861. The namesake of his great-uncle, the Anglo-Irish author of The Vicar of Wakefield *(1766) and* The Deserted Village *(1770), Goldsmith published* The Rising Village, *a long narrative poem about colonial settlement, in 1825. The first volume of verse by a native-born Canadian, the work was reissued together with a few lyrics in 1834. Goldsmith's only other literary work was his autobiography, which Rev. Wilfrid E. Myatt edited for publication in 1943. A second edition of the book, with a foreword by Phyllis Blakeley, was published in 1985 by Lancelot Press.*

The following passage is from The Autobiography of Oliver Goldsmith. *Completed by Goldsmith in December 1855, the memoir sheds light on some of the adversities which the poet confronted both in his personal life and in his short-lived literary career. For the modern reader, the most striking part of the narrative will likely be Goldsmith's matter-of-fact description of his 160-day voyage from Liverpool to Halifax in 1817–18.*

*   *   *   *   *   *   *

from **The Autobiography of Oliver Goldsmith**

I remember very little of my earliest Years. My Mother taught me to read, my father to write and cypher. My recollections of any importance commence from my first introduction into life, at the early age of eleven years.

My father had a small Income, and a large family, and like other parents was, no doubt, anxious to provide for his Boys as soon and as well as possible. With this view I was placed in the Dispensary and Surgery of the Naval Hospital at Halifax. I suppose my parents thought it would be a very pleasing thing to have another Doctor Oliver in the family, for I can imagine no other reason, why a boy so young and so unfit, should have been placed in such a Position. Nevertheless, I commenced my professional career with becoming propriety. I mixed up Pills, made Poultices spread Sticking Plaster, attended the Surgeon with the Tray through the different sick Wards, was present at the cutting off [of] sundry extremities of the Body corporal. It was war time; such things were common and of little moment. During my Medical Labours I performed a little also in the Church Line. There were no naval Chaplains in those days, and at the request of their Messmates, I read the Burial Service over two sailors who died in the Hospital, and were buried in a piece of ground in the Neighbourhood. I was becoming very discontented with my situation, which I did not like, and a circumstance soon happened to crown my disgust, and sicken me with the Profession. In the Court Yard of the Hospital I saw a Sailor tied up to a grating, and his Back scourged with four Dozen Lashes! The first time, such a sight makes the boldest Heart shudder; mine almost ceased to beat. I cried and was quite sick. I went no more to the Hospital.

My next step in civilization was as Boy in an Ironmonger's Shop. Here I weighed out Nails of all Sorts, Pots and Pans, Swedes' Iron, and other ferruginous Articles which compose *a*

Store. But Master thought I was too young, or too idle, or I know not what else, but I was sent Home.

My next essay was a literary One. As my first attempt failed in making me a Doctor, perhaps it was thought this would succeed in making me a Poet. I entered a Bookseller's Shop, where I learned to fold paper, stitch pamphlets, and do a trifle in the Binding Line. This was of short Duration, and I do not now remember why I was removed, but a second time I was restored to the paternal roof.

As I was, doubtless, supposed to have picked up some scraps of knowledge in these several trials, my next attempt was in a Lawyer's Office. I was employed in copying old Parchments, writing Pleas, filling up Writs, and, at my leisure Hours, I was directed to read and study three works, Blackstone's Commentaries, Coke upon Littleton and Tidd's Practice.

My Master's Cognomen was Savage, and his temper was like his Name. I happened to ask him for an explanation of some Latin Phrases. "Why, don't you know Latin?" — "No, Sir." — "Nor Greek?" — "Nor, Sir." — I knew as much of either as the last of the Mohicans. — "My young Lad, you won't do for my office; return to your father and go to School." He was right.

My father was discouraged at these failures; but, at length, a Merchant, a connexion of my Mother, offered to take me young as I was into his Employ. He was extensively engaged in a Wholesale Business of British and East India Cotton and Wollen Goods &ca. I joined his Establishment as the youngest clerk. Here I dealt in large Parcels only, was employed in various duties, was diligent, attentive, and gave satisfaction. I dined at my Master's House every Sunday, and went to Church with his family. I was pleased and contented with my Situation.

But Childhood has its Clouds, as well as the years of Manhood, and the paternal Roof again received me. My kind and good Master had become involved in his Business, which ended in Bankruptcy; his Establishments were broken up, and my Hopes and Prospects were ruined.

My father now began to think, like my savage Master, that before I entered on any future occupation, it would be best to

give me a little schooling. I was accordingly sent to Halifax
Grammar School. Boys generally remember school days with
pleasure, but I must confess nothing agreeable is connected
with my stay at this Seminary of "teaching the young Idea how
to Shoot." An antiquated Latin Grammar was put into my
Hands, with the Bible, and the Church Catechism. I was obliged
to attend to the last two, but an utter indifference was observed
as to my progress in the Irish Dog Latin. I was learning. The
Master was an Irishman. I never looked into Greek, and
Hebrew was, in truth, a dead language to me. I was assiduous,
however, in acquiring a knowledge of figures. I made some
advance in the Mathematics and Algebra, which Branches of
Instruction were confided to the Second Master. But the time
approached when my Irish Tutor and I were to separate, he to
continue his worthless Instruction, and I to enter on a new
Sphere.

But a few months were now to elapse when I should be 16
years of age, and in the Autumn of the year 1809, my father
determined I should go into the Army. His eldest Son, Henry,
was a lawyer, his second Son, Hugh Colvill, a Lieutenant in the
Royal Navy, and his fourth Son, Charles, a Midshipman, in the
same service, so it was decided that I, his third Son, should be a
Soldier, and I was devoted to the glorious Profession of Arms.

The 7th and 23rd Fusileers were stationed at this time at
Halifax, and with the Commanding Officers of those Corps,
Colonels Pakenham and Ellis, my father was on a friendly
Footing, and they had promised him if he succeeded in obtaining a Commission for me in either Regiment, they would take
care I was duly instructed in the art of shooting, and properly
looked after. Through the Interest of the Duke of Kent I was
nominated to an Ensigncy, not, however, in either of the Corps
anticipated and sought for, but in the Nova Scotia Fencibles, a
fencible Regiment then stationed in Newfoundland. My father
considered this Corps unsuitable, as there was no Half Pay for
the Officers belonging to it at this Period, and when the order
arrived from Brigadier General Skerrett for me to join the

Regiment, the Ensigncy was resigned without hesitation. I was destined not to wear Scarlet, and smell Powder.

In the month of May 1810, the Charge of the Commissariat developed temporarily on my father, who was the next Senior Officer, and he thought it a good opportunity for me to enter that Department as a Volunteer, in the hope that I should secure in it ultimately a permanent position. I accordingly bade Adieu to the Irish Dog Latin on the 3rd June 1810, and prepared to enter on a race which was not soon to terminate. It was during this temporary Charge, then, that on the 5th June, 1810 not quite Sixteen Years of age, I entered the Commissariat at Halifax as a Volunteer.

On the 25th September 1810, I was made Clerk and Issuer at 5s. per day, and placed on the Establishment. I wrote a good Hand, was well acquainted with Figures, and my assiduity and attention gained me, during the summer of 1811, I forget the precise date, a Treasury Clerkship.

As I continued to meet the approbation of my Superiors, in the summer of 1814, I was made an Acting Deputy Assistant Commissary General, and confirmed in that Appointment by Commission bearing date the 17th Decem. 1814.

At the end of the year 1816 a great Reduction was effected in the Commissariat. A long war had just terminated, and the probabilities of a long Peace was apparent. I was one of the unlucky and was named for the Half-Pay List. I had the option of remaining in the Colony, or of going to England, but as my Mother had removed to Plymouth after the Death of my father, I availed myself of the opportunity of joining her. I felt that I had served long enough in the Province, and I was desirous of going to some other Station, if I should be so fortunate as to obtain future employment.

I must confess that I was much grieved at being selected for Half Pay in preference to a Junior Officer. I had worked very hard during the whole period of the American War, and, though not in the Field, I could not have been more usefully employed that I was at Headquarters. It was then, I thought, an act of injustice on the part of Mr. D., who subsequently endeavoured to repair it, as he supposed, by an application to have me sent back to the Station; but I was doubly injured: first, in being removed; and next, in being sent back without any wish expressed on my part or the least solicitation. However, as the step promised me the pleasure of seeing England, and, perhaps, giving me the chance of seeing more of the World, and obtaining a more agreeable station, I made ready for my departure.

I left Halifax on the 6th January 1817, and arrived at Liverpool on the 6th February. I remained three days at "The Star and Garter" Hotel, and then the "Umpire" Post Coach, in thirty-one hours, put me down at the "Golden Cross," Charing Cross, in the grand and gloomy city of London! What a change since that time; now the same distance is performed in six hours!!

I presented myself at Great George Street, and had an Interview with Mr. Archer. I was told that the Pay due to me and my Travelling Expenses would be paid, and in the meantime I was to wait until I received further Orders.

After paying all my Expenses, I found that I was in possession of One Half Crown. I was to remain in town for an indefinite period. I was at an expensive Hotel. I knew nobody in London, nobody knew me. Here was a dilemma! What was I to do? A man in town without Money is very small Beer. I had only one resource to relieve me from my embarrassments, the Spout, so it was three to one against me. I left the Hotel and took a Lodging in Henrietta street, near the Foundling Hospital.

Having nothing now to do I literally wandered about the Streets, up one and down another, losing myself or finding myself all right as it may have happened. I may truly say that I saw the whole exterior of London; as to the interior my slender purse forbade the gratification of my Curiosity. Nevertheless, this Street Knowledge was afterwards very useful.

A week had elapsed in the Month of March when I received an Official. It informed me that I was placed on Half Pay at the end of One Month from the date of my arrival, the 6th February, and that my Pay and Expenses would be issued on application. I at once received my Money, took a seat in the Post Coach outside, and about the Middle of March, 1817, I embraced my Mother at Plymouth.

My Mother, two Brothers, and two Sisters, were now at Plymouth, and I remained with them until the latter end of July, when I was ordered to town and employed under Mr. Manby, in relation to his Accounts, with which I was well acquainted. This duty commenced on the 1st August, and at the end of the Month Mr. Hill sent for me and informed me that an application had been made by the Earl of Dalhousie, Commanding at Halifax, and requesting that I should be sent again to that Station. The following is a Copy of the Letter.

Halifax 2d June 1817

Sir,

I request you will do me the Honor to state to the Lords Commissioners of Her Majestys Treasury, my wish that Mr. Goldsmith, deputy Assistant Commissary General, may be sent out to this Province should it be in the contemplation of their Lordships to retain that Officer on full Pay, and his employment in Nova Scotia not materially interfere with their Arrangements.

Mr. Goldsmith having served for some time in this Province, where he had been found very useful in a Confidential situation, it is the wish of the deputy Commissary General to place him again in a similar one near himself.

A selection being made by Mr. Damerum in this instance may probably appear the more reasonable, in consideration of the reduced number of Officers allotted for the duties of the Commissariat in this Command.

  I have &ca
  (Signed) Dalhousie
George Harrison Esqr.
  Secretary to the Treasury

I must say I was much astonished at this application, for I had not even hinted a wish to return to Halifax, and I exhausted all my oratory in trying to persuade Mr. Hill against this determination. I represented to him that I had just come away from Nova Scotia, intentionally, and with the view and in the hope of employment at some other Station, that I had served there already six years, and was most desirous of going else-where, and that I would gladly accept any place whatever it might be rather than return. But his reply to everything was: "You have been asked for; it is a great compliment to so young a man, and unless you can urge more cogent reasons I would *advise* you not to offer any further objections." There was an end of the Matter.

I remained with Mr. Manby about Six Weeks, and having received my Orders at the end of the Month of September 1817, I repaired to Liverpool to take a passage to Halifax.

When I reached the Port of Liverpool, all the vessels for Nova Scotia had previously sailed. I sought for one to Boston, the nearest Port, but without success, and my last Refuge was in a Ship bound to New York, and the last for the Season.

Here, thought I, at the very threshold of my departure is a warning against my return to America. The attempt was, however, to be made, and on the 9th October 1817, I embarked in the ship "Protection" and sailed the same day. What a difference then and now! At this time you may obtain a Ship for America almost every Hour!

The Commencement of the Voyage was very prosperous, as we reached the Banks of Newfoundland in 18 days, but from that time we encountered a succession of gales of Wind and heavy seas. One man was lost overboard, the Decks were swept, and the Boats carried away. The crew were violent and mutinous, and a short allowance of food and water rendered the Voyage still more disastrous. At the end of 10 weeks we anchored in the Harbor of New York!

My first care on landing was to search for a vessel going to Halifax. To my sad disappointment I found that the British Packet, and also a Schooner, had sailed the day before. This seemed a second Warning. As there was no probability of another Vessel until Spring of the next Year, I was obliged to take the Land Route to Boston. I was detained at New York for some days, as a Witness on the Trial between the Master and Crew of the "Protection" in the Marine Court, but as soon as I was released, I started for Boston, a long and severe Journey of nearly 300 Miles, which, as well as I remember, occupied a week before I arrived.

It was late at night when I got to Boston, but my first act early the next morning was to seek a conveyance to Halifax. I went to a Merchant to whom I was referred, and, Oh! bitter disappointment, the last vessel for the season had just sailed! I was too late and missed the Train. I walked down to the end of the Long Wharf, and through a Mist of Tears, I saw in the Distance the flowing sail that would have borne me, in four or five days at furthest, to my Destination.

The prospect before me was now gloomy indeed. The Route by Land from Halifax, setting aside the expense, was almost impracticable in the Winter, and I must therefore wait until something favorable offered. In a few days this presented itself in a British Schooner that was going to the Eastport. I embraced the opportunity with alacrity, and I left Boston on the 1st February 1818. "Once more unto the Breach, dear friends, once more." At the end of Six days the prospect of a speedy termination to the voyage was most favorable. Grand Manan was in sight, and there were only a few miles more to run, when a Snow Storm came on, drove the vessel to leeward, and all human exertions powerless, she was cast ashore at daylight on Hat Island, one of the Outer Islands which fringe the Coast of Maine, and was uninhabited. I was washed from the Deck on the top of a wave which carried me to the Shore, and I managed to cling to a rock whilst the wave receded, and before another returned I had scrambled into a place of Safety. I was much bruised and my hands were cut by the Barnacles. I lost everything I had with me. The Master and crew were all saved. The Island was small and well wooded. I commenced to beat down a path where the snow was nearly two feet deep, and here I trotted backward and forward to keep myself warm as I was quite wet, and this plan was adopted by all until the gale abated.

After a search in the wreck for the proper materials, some powder and some tow, a fire was fortunately made, and but for that every one would that night have perished for the excessive cold. It would be too long to give all the Details of this Shipwreck. Suffice it to say that the Wreckers discovered us, obtained assistance for us, and a small schooner came and took us all to Eastport. Thence I made a passage to Saint John; thence I crossed the Bay of Fundy to Digby, in a coaster, as there were no Steamers in those Days; thence I pursued my Route to Annapolis Royal, and finally reached my destination on the 18th March 1818, worn out in body and mind, just 160 days after my exit from Liverpool.

I was very soon put into Harness after my arrival. I commenced again my public Duties on the 1st April, and applied myself with assiduity and attention to their performance. As I always possessed an ardent love of reading, I now devoted every leisure Hour to Study. I felt most bitterly how deficient had been my education, and I endeavoured as far as possible to repair the defect. I commenced my old Dog Latin to which I added Greek, but after a short period I found I could make no progress without a Master, and I also considered of how little advantage would be the acquisition of those languages in my present pursuits, and I therefore turned my attention from the dead to the living and studied French and Spanish, and by the aid of a Master soon acquired a knowledge of them. I read many useful and practical Works, and entered *con spirito* into the Regions of Poetry.

At the commencement of the Year 1822 "a change came o'er the spirit of my dream." Some Ladies and Officers of the Garrison established an "Amateur Theatre" of which I became a member. I played many parts, and among others that of "Tony Lumpkin" in "She Stoops to Conquer," rather a curious circumstance. When the Poet saw his Play performed at Covent Garden, little did he imagine that in the course of time a grand-nephew would play, even as an Amateur, his Tony in a far distant Land, and at no great remove from the Spot,

"Where wild Oswego spreads her swamps around"
"And Niagara stuns with thundering Sound."
It was at this time also [that] that Spirit of Poetry fired my breast. An opening address was solicited and among others I made an attempt and wrote one. I believe it was as good as any other, but it was not accepted. However, the ice was broken. I had made the plunge, and determined on a future effort. Encouraged by some friends I wrote a poem called the "Rising Village," which was published by John Sharpe in 1825 in London. The celebrated Author of the "Deserted Village" had pathetically displayed the Anguish of his Countrymen, on being forced, from various causes, to quit their native plains, endeared to them by so many delightful recollections, and to seek a Refuge in regions at the time but little known.

"Good Heavens! What sorrows gloomed that parting Day.
"That called them from their native walks away:
"When the poor Exiles, every pleasure passed.
"Hung round the bowers, and fondly look'd their last,
"And took a long Farewell and wished in vain
"For Seats like those beyond the Western Main."

In my humble poem, I, therefore, endeavoured to describe the sufferings they experienced in a new and uncultivated Country, the Difficulties they surmounted, the Rise and progress of a Village, and the prospects which promised Happiness to its future possessors.

I had better have left it alone. My unfortunate Bantling was torn to Shreds. My first effort was criticized with undue severity, abused, and condemned, and why? Because I did not produce a poem like the great Oliver. Alas! Who indeed could do so? Whatever merit it possessed in itself was disowned because the genius that wrote it did not equal that of his great predecessor. I had, however, the approbation of the "judicious few," who thought it an interesting Production. It was very fortunate for me that it was the occupation of leisure Hours. My living did not depend on my poetical talent, lucky fellow, and in this respect I had the advantage of the immortal Poet. After this essay I abandoned the Muses, and I have not had the pleasure of any further intercourse with the lovely ladies. I passed the Years I remained in Halifax in social intercourse with the Inhabitants. I made many friends, and endeavoured to deserve and secure their good Opinion.

CAPTAIN FREDERICK MARRYAT

*   *   *   *   *   *   *

Frederick Marryat was born in Westminster in 1792. Educated at private schools, he tried several times to run away to sea before his father finally arranged for him to join a Royal Navy frigate in 1806. His naval career lasted until 1830 and saw him serve with distinction on a number of stations, including Halifax. Marryat's retirement from the navy permitted him to commit himself full-time to literature. The author of more than twenty novels, he is best remembered for such classic tales of the sea as Peter Simple *(1834),* Mr. Midshipman Easy *(1836), and* The Phantom Ship *(1839), as well as for children's books like* The Settlers in Canada *(1844) and* The Children of the New Forest *(1847). The editor of the* Metropolitan Magazine *from 1832 to 1835, Marryat toured the United States and Canada during 1837 and 1838. He died at Langham, his small farm in Norfolk, England in 1848.*

The following chapter is from Marryat's first novel, an autobiographical work entitled The Naval Officer; or, Scenes and Adventures in the Life of Frank Mildmay *(1829), in which, he later admitted, "we had sowed all our wild oats." In subsequent editions, the title of the book was shortened to* Frank Mildmay. *Marryat fondly referred to Halifax in a number of his works, but nothing else he wrote about the town compares with this hilarious account of the young Mildmay's encounter with the unforgettable Sir Hurricane Humbug.*

*   *   *   *   *   *   *

from **The Naval Officer; or, Scenes and Adventures in the Life of Frank Mildmay**

Bell. You have an opportunity now, Madam, to revenge yourself upon him for affronting your squirrel.
Belin. O, the filthy, rude beast.
Aram. 'Tis a lasting quarrel

Old Bachelor

We sailed the next day, and after one month more of unsuccessful cruising, arrived safe at Halifax, where I was informed that an old friend of my father's, Sir Hurricane Humbug, of whom some mention has already been made in this work, had just arrived. He was not in an official character, but had come out to look after his own property. It is absolutely necessary that I should here, with more than usual formality, introduce the reader to an intimate acquaintance with the character of Sir Hurricane.

Sir Hurricane had risen in life by his own ingenuity, and the patronage of a rich man in the South of England: he was of an ardent disposition, and was an admirable justice of peace, when the *argumentum baculinum* was required, for which reason he had been sent to reduce two or three refractory establishments to order and obedience; and, by his firmness and good humour, succeeded. His tact was a little knowledge of everything (not like Solomon's, from the hyssop to the cedar), but from the boiler of a potato to the boiler of a steam-boat, and from catching a sprat to catching a whale; he could fatten pigs and poultry, and had a peculiar way of improving the size, though not the breed of the latter; in short, he was "jack of all trades and master of none."

I shall not go any farther back with his memoirs than the day he chose to teach an old woman how to make mutton-broth. He had, in the course of an honest discharge of his duty, at a certain very dirty sea-port town, incurred the displeasure of the lower orders generally: he nevertheless would omit no opportunity of doing good, and giving advice to the poor, gratis. One day he saw a woman emptying the contents of a boiling kettle out of her door into the street. He approached, and saw a leg of mutton at the bottom, and the unthrifty housewife throwing away the liquor in which it had been boiled.

"Good woman," said the economical baronet, "do you know what you are doing? A handful of meat, a couple of carrots, and a couple of turnips, cut up into dice, and thrown into that liquor, with a little parsley, would make excellent mutton-broth for your family."

The old woman looked up, and saw the ogre of the dockyard; and either by losing her presence of mind, or by a most malignant slip of the hand, she contrived to pour a part of the boiling water into the shoes of Sir Hurricane. The baronet jumped, roared, hopped, stamped, kicked off his shoes, and ran home, d—ning the old woman, and himself too, for having tried to teach her how to make mutton-broth. As he ran off, the ungrateful hag screamed after him, "Sarves you right; teach you to mind your own business."

The next day, in his magisterial capacity, he commanded the attendance of "the dealer in slops." "Well, Madam, what have you got to say for yourself for scalding one of his Majesty's Justices of the Peace? don't you know that I have the power to commit you to Maidstone gaol for the assault?"

"I beg your honour's pardon, humbly," said the woman; "I did not know it was your honour, or I am sure I wouldn't a done it; besides, I own to your honour, I had a drop too much."

The good-natured baronet dismissed her with a little suitable advice, which no doubt the good woman treated as she did that relative to the mutton-broth.

My acquaintance with Sir Hurricane had commenced at Plymouth, when he kicked my ship to sea in a gale of wind, for fear we should ground on our beef bones. I never forgave him for that. My father had shown him great civility, and had introduced me to him. When at Halifax, we resided in the same house with a mutual friend, who had always received me as his own son. He had a son of my own age, with whom I had long been on terms of warm friendship, and Ned and I confederated against Sir Hurricane. Having paid a few visits *en passant*, as I landed at the King's Wharf, shook hands with a few pretty girls, and received their congratulations on my safe return, I went to the house of my friend, and, without ceremony, walked into the drawing-room.

"Do you know, Sir," said the footman, "that Sir Hurricane is in his room? but he is very busy," added the man, with a smile.

"Busy or not," said I, "I am sure he will see me," so in I walked.

Sir Hurricane was employed on something, but I could not distinctly make out what. He had a boot between his knees and the calves of his legs, which he pressed together, and as he turned his head round, I perceived that he held a knife between his teeth.

"Leave the door open, messmate," said he, without taking the least notice of me. Then rising, he drew a large, black, tom cat, by the tail, out of the boot, and flinging it away from him to a great distance, which distance was rapidly increased by the voluntary exertion of the cat, which ran away as if it had been mad, "There," said he, "and be d—d to you, you have given me more trouble than a whole Kentucky farm-yard; but I shall not lose my sleep any more, by your d—d caterwauling."

All this was pronounced as if he had not seen me — in fact, it was a soliloquy, for the cat did not stay to hear it. "Ah!" said he, holding out his hand to me, "how do you do? I know your face, but d—n me if I have not forgot your name."

"My name, sir," said I, "is Mildmay."

"Ah, Mildmay, my noble, how do you do? how did you leave your father? I knew him very well — used to give devilish good feeds — many a plate I've dirtied at his table — don't care how soon I put my legs under it again; — take care, mind which way you put your helm — you will be aboard of my chickabiddies — don't run athwart hawse."

I found, on looking down, that I had a string round my leg, which fastened a chicken to the table, and saw many more of these little creatures attached to the chairs in the room; but for what purpose they were thus domesticated I could not discover.

"Are these pet chickens of yours, Sir Hurricane?" said I.

"No," said the admiral, "but I mean them to be pet capons, by and by, when they come to table. I finished a dozen and a half this morning, besides that d—d old tom cat."

The mystery was now explained, and I afterwards found out (every man having his hobby) that the idiosyncrasy of this officer's disposition had led him to the practice of neutralising the males of any species of bird or beast, in order to render them more palatable at the table.

"Well, sir," he continued, "how do you like your new ship — how do you like your old captain? — good fellow, isn't he? — d—n his eyes — countryman of mine — I knew him when his father hadn't as much money as would jingle on a tombstone. That fellow owes every thing to me. I introduced him to the duke of—, and he got on by that interest; but, I say, what do you think of the Halifax girls? — nice! a'n't they?"

I expressed my admiration of them.

"Ay, ay, they'll do, won't they? — we'll have some fine fun — give the girls a party at George's Island — hay-making — green gowns — ha, ha, ha. I say, your captain shall give us a party at Turtle Cove. We are going to give the old commissioner a feed at the Rockingham — blow the roof of his skull off with champagne — do you dine at Birch Cove to-day? No, I suppose you are engaged to Miss Maria, or Miss Susan, or Miss Isabella — ha, sad dog, sad dog — done a great deal of mischief," surveying me from head to foot.

I took the liberty of returning him the same compliment; he was a tall raw-boned man, with strongly marked features, and a smile on his countenance that no modest woman could endure. In his person he gave me the idea of a discharged life-guardsman; but from his face you might have supposed that he had sat for one of Rubens' Satyrs. He was one of those people with whom you become immediately acquainted; and before I had been an hour in his company, I laughed very heartily at his jokes — not very delicate, I own, and for which he lost a considerable portion of my respect; but he was a source of constant amusement to me, living as we did in the same house.

I was just going out of the room when he stopped me — "I say, how should you like to be introduced to some devilish nice Yankee girls, relations of mine, from Philadelphia? and I should be obliged to you to show them attention; very pretty girls, I can tell you, and will have good fortunes — you may go farther and fare worse. The old dad is as rich as a Jew — got the gout in both legs — can't hold out much longer — nice pickings at his money bags, while the devil is picking his bones."

There was no withstanding such inducements, and I agreed that he should present me the next day.

Our dialogue was interrupted by the master of the house and his son, who gave me a hearty welcome; the father had been a widower for some years, and his only son Ned resided with him, and was intended to succeed in his business as a merchant. We adjourned to dress for dinner; our bed-rooms were contiguous, and we began to talk of Sir Hurricane.

"He is a strange mixture," said Ned. "I love him for his good temper; but I owe him a grudge for making mischief between me and Maria; besides, he talks balderdash before the ladies, and annoys them very much."

"I owe him a grudge too," said I, "for sending me to sea in a gale of wind."

"We shall both be quits with him before long," said Ned; "but let us now go and meet him at dinner. To-morrow I will set the housekeeper at him for his cruelty to her cat; and if I am not much mistaken, she will pay him off for it."

Dinner passed off extremely well. The admiral was in high spirits; and as it was a bachelor's party, he earned his wine. The next morning we met at breakfast. When that was over, the master of the house retired to his office, or pretended to do so. I was going out to walk, but Ned said I had better stay a few minutes; he had something to say to me; in fact, he had prepared a treat without my knowing it.

"How did you sleep last night, Sir Hurricane?" said the artful Ned.

"Why, pretty well; considering," said the admiral, "I was not tormented by that old tom cat. D—n me, Sir, that fellow was like the Grand Signior, and he kept his seraglio in the garret, over my bed-room, instead of being at his post in the kitchen, killing the rats that are running about like coach-horses."

"Sir Hurricane," said I, "it's always unlucky to sailors, if they meddle with cats. You will have a gale of wind, in some shape or another, before long."

These words were hardly uttered, when, as if by precon-certed arrangement, the door opened, and in sailed Mrs Jel-lybag, the housekeeper, an elderly woman, somewhere in the latitude of fifty-five or sixty years. With a low courtesy and contemptuous toss of her head, she addressed Sir Hurricane Humbug.

"Pray, Sir Hurricane, what have you been doing to my cat?"

The admiral, who prided himself in putting any one who applied to him on what he called the wrong scent, endeavoured to play off Mrs Jellybag in the same manner.

"What have I done to your cat, my dear Mrs Jellybag? Why my dear Madam" (said he, assuming an air of surprise), "what *should* I do to your cat?"

"You *should* have left him alone, Mr. Admiral; that cat was my property; if my master permits you to ill-treat the poultry, that's his concern; but that cat was mine, Sir Hurricane — mine, every inch of him. The animal has been ill-treated, and sits moping in the corner of the fire-place, as if he was dying; he'll never be the cat he was again."

"I don't think he ever will, my dear Mrs Housekeeper," answered the admiral, drily.

The lady's wrath now began to kindle. The admiral's cool replies were like water sprinkled upon a strong flame, increas-ing its force, instead of checking it.

"Don't dear *me*, Sir Hurricane. I am not one of *your dears* — *your dears* are all in Dutchtown — more shame for you, an old man like you."

"Old man!" cried Sir Hurricane, losing his placidity a little.

"Yes, old man; look at your hair — as grey as a goose's."

"Why, as for my hair, that proves nothing, Mrs Jellybag, for though there may be snow on the mountains, there is still heat in the valleys. What d'ye think of my metaphor?"

"I am no more a *metafore* than yourself, Sir Hurricane; but I'll tell you what, you are a *cock-and-hen* admiral, a dog-in-the-manger barrownight, who was jealous of my poor tom cat, because —, I won't say what. Yes, Sir Hurricane, all hours of the day you are leering at every young woman that passes, out of our windows — and an old man too; you ought to be ashamed of yourself — and then you go to church of a Sunday, and cry, 'Good Lord, deliver us.' "

The housekeeper now advanced so close to the admiral, that her nose nearly touched his, her arms akimbo, and every preparation for boarding. The admiral, fearing she might not confine herself to vocality, but begin to beat time with her fists, thought it right to take up a position; he therefore very dexterously took two steps in the rear, and mounted on a sofa; his left was defended by an upright piano, his right by the breakfast-table, with all the tea-things on it; his rear was against the wall, and his front depended on himself in person. From this commanding eminence he now looked down on the housekeeper, whose nose could reach no higher than the seals of her adversary's watch; and in proportion as the baronet felt his security, so rose his choler. Having been for many years Proctor at the great universities of Point-street and Blue-town, as well as member of Barbican and North Corner, he was perfectly qualified, in point of classical dialect, to maintain the honour of his profession. Nor was the lady by any means deficient. Although she had not taken her degree, her tongue from constant use had acquired a fluency which nature only concedes to practice.

It will not be expected, nor would it be proper, that I should repeat all that passed in this concluding scene, in which the housekeeper gave us good reason to suppose that she was not quite so ignorant of the nature of the transaction as she would have had us believe.

The battle having raged for half an hour with great fury, both parties desisted, for want of breath, and consequently of ammunition. This produced a gradual cessation of firing, and by degrees the ships separated — the admiral, like Lord Howe on the first of June, preserving his position, though very much mauled; and the housekeeper, like the Montague, *running down* to join her associates. A few random shots were exchanged as they parted, and at every second or third step on the stairs, Mrs Margaret brought to, and fired, until both were quite out of range; a distant rumbling noise was heard, and the admiral concluded, by muttering that she might go —, somewhere, but the word died between his teeth.

"There, admiral," said I, "did not I tell you that you would have a squall?"

"Squall! yes —d—m my blood," wiping his face; "how the spray flew from the old beldam! She's fairly wetted my trousers, by God. Who'd ever thought that such a purring old b—h could have shown such a set of claws! — War to the knife! By heavens, I'll make her remember this."

Notwithstanding the admiral's threat, hostilities ceased from that day. The cock-and-hen admiral found it convenient to show a white feather; interest stood in the way, and barred him from taking his revenge. Mrs Jellybag was a faithful servant, and our host neither liked that she should be interfered with, or that his house should become an arena for such conflicts; and the admiral, who was peculiarly tenacious of undrawing the strings of his purse, found it convenient to make the first advances. The affair was therefore amicably arranged — the tom cat was, in consideration of his sufferings, created a baronet, and was ever afterwards dignified by the title of *Sir H. Humbug*; who certainly was the most eligible person to select for god-father, as he had taken the most effectual means of weaning him from "the pomps and vanities of this wicked world."

It was now about one o'clock, for this dispute had ran away with the best part of the morning, when Sir Hurricane said "Come, youngster, don't forget your engagements — you know I have got to introduce you to my pretty cousins — you must mind your P's and Q's with the uncle, for he is a sensible old fellow — has read a great deal, and thinks America the first and greatest country in the world."

We accordingly proceeded to the residence of the fair strangers, whom the admiral assured me had come to Halifax from mere curiosity, under the protection of their uncle and aunt. We knocked at the door, and the admiral inquired if Mrs M'Flinn has at home; we were answered in the affirmative. The servant asked our names. "Vice Admiral Sir Hurricane Humbug," said I, "and Mr Mildmay."

The drawing-room door was thrown open, and the man gave our names with great propriety. In we walked; a tall, grave-looking, elderly lady received us, standing bolt upright in the middle of the room; the young ladies were seated at their work.

"My dear Mrs M'Flinn," said the admiral, "how do you do? I am delighted to see you and your fair nieces looking so lovely this morning." — The lady bowed to this compliment — a courtesy she was not quite up to — "Allow me to introduce my gallant young friend, Mildmay — young ladies, take care of your hearts — he is a great rogue, I assure you, though he smiles so sweet upon you."

Mrs M'Flinn bowed again to me, hoped I was very well, and inquired "how long I had been in these parts."

I replied that I had just returned from a cruise, but that I was no stranger in Halifax.

"Come, officer," said the admiral, taking me by the arm, "I see you are bashful — I must make you acquainted with my pretty cousins. This, Sir, is Miss M'Flinn — her christian name is Deliverance. She is a young lady whose beauty is her least recommendation."

"A very equivocal compliment," thought I.

"This, Sir, is Miss Jemima; this is Miss Temperance; and this is Miss Deborah. Now that you know them all by name, and they know you, I hope you will contrive to make yourself both useful and agreeable."

"A very pretty sinecure," thinks I to myself, "just as if I had not my hands full already." However, as I never wanted small talk for pretty faces, I began with Jemima. They were all pretty, but she was a love — yet there was an awkwardness about them that convinced me they were not of the *bon ton* of Philadelphia. The answers to all my questions were quick, pert, and given with an air of assumed consequence; at the same time I observed a mode of expression which, though English, was not well-bred English.

"Did you come through the United States," said I, "into the British territory, or did you come by water?"

"Oh, by water," screamed all the girls at once, "and *liked* to have been eaten up with the nasty roaches."

I did not exactly know what was meant by "roaches," but it was explained to me soon after. I inquired whether they had seen a British man-of-war, and whether they would like to accompany me on board of that which I belonged to? They all screamed out at same moment —

"No, we never have seen one, and should like to see it of all things. When will you take us?"

"To-morrow," said I, "if the day should prove fine."

Here the admiral, who had been making by-play with the old chaperon, turned round and said:

"Well, Mr Frank, I see you are getting on pretty well without my assistance."

"Oh, we all like him very much," said Temperance; "and he says he will take us on board his ship."

"Softly, my dear," said the aunt: "we must not think of giving the gentleman the trouble, until we are better acquainted."

"I am sure, aunt," said Deborah, "we are very well acquainted."

"Then," said the aunt, seeing she was in the minority, "suppose you and Sir Hurricane come and breakfast with us to-morrow morning at eleven o'clock, after which, we shall all be very much at your service."

Here the admiral looked at me with one of his impudent leers, and burst into a loud laugh; but I commanded my countenance very well, and rebuked him by a steady and reserved look.

"I shall have great pleasure," said I, to the lady, "in obeying your orders from eleven to-morrow morning, till the hour of dinner, when I am engaged."

So saying, we both bowed, wished them a good morning, and left the room. The door closed upon us, and I heard them all exclaim — "What a charming young man!"

I went on board, and told the first lieutenant what I had done; he, very good-naturedly, said he would do his best, though the ship was not in order for showing, and would have a boat ready for us at the dock-yard stairs at one o'clock the next day.

I went to breakfast at the appointed hour. The admiral did not appear, but the ladies were all in readiness, and I was introduced to their uncle — a plain, civil-spoken man, with a strong nasal twang. The repast was very good; and as I had a great deal of work before me, I made hay while the sun shone. When the rage of hunger had been a little appeased, I made use of the first belle to inquire if a lady whom I once had the honour of knowing, was any relation of theirs, as she bore the same name, and came, like them, from Philadelphia.

"Oh, dear, yes, indeed, she is a relation," said all the ladies together; "we have not seen her this seven years, when did you see her last?"

I replied that we had not met for some time; but that the last time I had heard of her, she was seen by a friend of mine at Turin on the Po. The last syllable was no sooner out of my mouth, than tea, coffee, and chocolate was out of theirs, all spirting different ways, just like so many young grampuses. They jumped up from the table and ran away to their rooms, convulsed with laughter, leaving me alone with their uncle. I was all amazement, and I own felt a little annoyed.

I asked if I had made any serious lapsus, or said any thing very ridiculous or indelicate; if I had, I said I should never forgive myself.

"Sir," said Mr M'Flinn, "I am very sure you meant nothing indelicate; but the refined society of Philadelphia, in which these young ladies have been educated, attaches very different meanings to certain words, to what you do in the old country. The back settlements, for instance, so called by our ancestors, we call the western settlements, and we apply the same term, by analogy, to the human figure and dress. This is a mere little explanation, which you will take as it is meant. It cannot be expected that *'foreigners'* should understand the niceties of our language."

I begged pardon for my ignorance; and assured him I would be more cautious in future. "But pray tell me," said I, "what there was in my last observation which could have caused so much mirth at my expense?"

"Why, Sir," said Mr M'Flinn, "you run me hard there; but since you force me to explain myself, I must say that you used a word exclusively confined to bedchambers."

"But surely, Sir," said I, "you will allow that the name of a celebrated river, renowned in the most ancient of our histories, is not to be changed from such a refined notion of false delicacy?"

"There you are wrong," said Mr M'Flinn. "The French, who are our instructors in every thing, teach us how to name all these things; and I think you will allow that they understand true politeness."

I bowed to this dictum, only observing, that there was a point in our language where delicacy became indelicate; that I thought the noble river had a priority of claim over a contemptible vessel; and, reverting to the former part of his discourse, I said that we in England were not ashamed to call things by their proper names; and that we considered it a great mark of ill-breeding to go round about for a substitute to a common word, the vulgar import of which a well bred and modest woman ought never to have known.

The old gentleman felt a little abashed at this rebuke, and, to relieve him, I changed the subject, hoping that the ladies would forgive me for this once, and return to their breakfasts.

"Why, as for that matter," said the gentleman, "the Philadelphia ladies have very delicate appetites, and I dare say they have had enough."

Finding I was not likely to gain ground on that tack, I steered my own course, and finished my breakfast, comforting myself that much execution had been done by the ladies on the commissariat department, before the "Po" had made its appearance.

By the time I had finished, the ladies had composed themselves; and the pretty Jemima had recovered the saint-like gravity of her lovely mouth. Decked in shawls and bonnets, they expressed much impatience to be gone. We walked to the dockyard, where a boat with a midshipman attended, and in a few minutes conveyed us alongside of my ship. A painted cask, shaped like a chair, with a whip from the main yard-arm, was let down into the boat; and I carefully packed the fair creatures, two at a time, and sent them up. There was a good deal of giggling, and screaming, and loud laughing, which rather annoyed me; for as they were not my friends, I had no wish that my messmates should think they belonged to that set in Halifax in which I was so kindly received.

At length, all were safely landed on the quarter-deck, without the exposure of an ancle, which they all seemed to dread. Whether their ancles were not quite so small as Mr M'Flinn wished me to suppose their appetites were, I cannot say.

"La! aunt," said Deborah, "when I looked up in the air, and saw you and Deliverance dangling over our heads, I thought if the rope was to break, what a 'squash' you would have come on us: I am sure you would have *paunched us*."

Determined to have the Philadelphia version of this elegant phrase, I inquired what it meant, and was informed, that in their country when any one had his bowels *squeezed* out, they called it "*paunching*."

"Well," thought I, "after this, you might swallow the Po without spoiling your breakfasts." The band struck up "Yankee Doodle," the ladies were in ecstacy, and began to caper round the quarter-deck.

"La! Jemima," said Deborah, "what have you done to the western side of your gown? it is all over white."

This was soon brushed off, but the expression was never forgotten in the ship, and always ludicrously applied.

Having shown them the ship and all its wonders, I was glad to conduct them back to the shore. When I met the admiral, I told him I had done the honours, and hoped the next time he had any female relatives, he would keep his engagements, and attend to them himself.

"Why, now, who do you think they are?" said the admiral.

"Think!" said I, "why, who should they be but your Yankee cousins?"

"Why, was you such a d—d flat as to believe what I said, eh? Why, their father keeps a shop of all sorts at Philadelphia, and they were going to New York, on a visit to some of their relatives, when the ship they were in was taken and brought in here."

"Then," said I, "these are not the bon-ton of Philadelphia?"

"Just as much as Nancy Dennis is the bon-ton of Halifax," said the admiral; "though the uncle, as I told you, is a sensible fellow in his way."

"Very well," said I; "you have caught me for once; but remember, I pay you for it."

And I was not long in his debt. Had he not given me this explanation, I should have received a very false impression of the ladies of Philadelphia, and have done them an injustice for which I should never have forgiven myself.

The time of our sailing drew near. This was always a melancholy time in Halifax; but my last act on shore was one which created some mirth, and enlivened the gloom of my departure. My friend Ned and myself had not yet had an opportunity of paying off Sir Hurricane Humbug for telling tales to Maria, and for his false introduction to myself. One morning we both came out of our rooms at the same moment, and were proceeding to the breakfast parlour, when we spied the admiral performing some experiment. Unfortunately for him, he was seated in such a manner, just clear of a pent-house, as to be visible from our position; and at the same time, the collar of his coat would exactly intersect the segment of a circle described by any fluid, projected by us over this low roof, which would thus act as a conductor into the very pole of his neck.

The housemaid (these housemaids are always the cause or the instruments of mischief, either by design or neglect), had left standing near the window a pail nearly filled with dirty water, from the wash-hand basins, &c. Ned and I looked at each other, then at the pail, then at the admiral. Ned thought of his Maria: I of my false introduction. Without saying a word, we both laid our hands on the pail, and in an instant, souse went all the contents over the admiral.

"I say, what's this?" he roared out. "Oh, you d—d rascals!"

He knew it could only be us. We laughed so immoderately, that we had not the power to move or to speak; while the poor admiral was spitting, sputtering, and coughing, enough to bring his heart up.

"You infernal villains! no respect for a flag-officer? I'll serve you out for this."

The tears rolled down our cheeks; but not with grief. As soon as the admiral had sufficiently recovered himself to go in pursuit, we thought it time to make sail. We knew we were discovered; and as the matter could not be made worse, we resolved to tell him what it was for. Ned began.

"How do you do admiral? you have taken a shower-bath this morning."

He looked up, with his teeth clenched — "Oh, it's you, is it? Yes, I thought it could be no one else. Yes, I have had a shower-bath, and be d—d to you; and that sea-devil of a friend of yours. Pretty pass the service has come to, when officers of my rank are treated in this way. I'll make you both envy the tom-cat."

"Beware the housekeeper, admiral," said Ned. "Maria has made it up with me, admiral, and she sends her love to you."

"D—n Maria."

"Oh, very well, I'll tell her so," said Ned.

"Admiral," said I, "do you remember when you sent the — to sea in a gale of wind, when I was midshipman of her? Well, I got just as wet that night as you are now. Pray, admiral, have you any commands to the Misses M'Flinn?"

"I'll tell you when I catch hold of you," said Sir Hurricane, as he moved up stairs to his room, dripping like Pope's Lodona, only not smelling so sweet.

Hearing a noise, the housekeeper came up, and all the family assembled to condole with the humid admiral, but each enjoying the joke as much as ourselves. We however paid rather dearly for it. The admiral swore that neither of us should eat or drink in the house for three days; and Ned's father, though ready to burst with laughter, was forced in common decency to say that he thought the admiral perfectly right after so gross a violation of hospitality.

I went and dined on board my ship, Ned went to a coffee-house; but on the third morning after the shower, I popped my head into the breakfast parlour, and said, "Admiral, I have a good story to tell you, if you will let me come in."

"I'd see you d—d first, you young scum of a fish pond. Be off, or I'll shy the ham at your head."

"No, but indeed, my dear Admiral, it is such a nice story; it is one just to your fancy."

"Well then, stand there and tell it, but don't come in, for if you do —"

I stood at the door and told him the story.

"Well, now," said he, "that is a good story, and I will forgive you for it." So with a hearty laugh at my ingenuity, he promised to forgive us both, and I ran and fetched Ned to breakfast.

This was the safest mode we could have adopted to get into favour, for the admiral was a powerful, gigantic fellow, that could have given us some very awkward squeezes. The peace was very honourably kept, and the next day the ship sailed.

THOMAS CHANDLER HALIBURTON

* * * * * * *

Thomas Chandler Haliburton was born in Windsor, N.S. in 1796 and was educated at King's College. Called to the bar in 1820, he practised law in Annapolis Royal. After serving as a member of the legislative assembly from 1826 to 1829, he became a judge of the Inferior Court of Common Pleas. In 1841 he was promoted to the Supreme Court of Nova Scotia. One of Nova Scotia's greatest writers, he published a two-volume history of the province in 1829. He was also a member, with Joseph Howe and others, of the Club, a literary group which contributed to Howe's the Novascotian *from 1828 to 1831. A few years later, the paper began publishing Haliburton's sketches about a Yankee clock peddler named Sam Slick. In 1836 Howe issued a volume of the stories under the title* The Clockmaker; or The Sayings and Doings of Sam Slick, of Slickville. *The book earned Haliburton an international reputation and was soon followed by a second Sam Slick series in 1838 and a third in 1840. Haliburton's other works include* A Reply to the Report of the Earl of Durham *(1840),* The Old Judge; or, Life in a Colony *(1849), and* The English in America *(1851). A staunch Tory, he retired from the bench in 1856 and moved to England, where, in 1859, he became a member of parliament. He died at Isleworth, Middlesex in 1865.*

"A Ball at Government House" was published first in Fraser's Magazine *(December 1847) and then in Haliburton's two-volume collection of tales,* The Old Judge; or, Life in a Colony, *in which, according to his preface, he sought to delineate the "habits, manners, and social conditions" of the people of Nova Scotia. Several pages of extraneous introductory material, on the role and nature of colonial governors, have been cut to make the story a little more palatable to modern readers. The only other deletion is indicated by ellipses (...). Narrated by old Judge Sanford, one of three narrators found in* The Old Judge, *the story is a satiric* tour de force *that encompasses a multitude of different voices as it*

ranges episodically through the crowd that has assembled for a New Year's ball at Government House during the administration of the fictional governor Sir Hercules Sampson.

*   *   *   *   *   *   *

A Ball at Government House

"It is some years since I was at a ball at Government House. My age and infirmities render them irksome to me, and, of course, unfit me for enjoying them. The last time I was there, was during the administration of Sir Hercules Sampson. I need not describe him, or his lady and daughter, or his two aides, Lord Edward Dummkopf and the Honourable Mr Trotz... It was on the first day of January, there was a levée in the morning, a dinner party in the afternoon, and a ball in the evening. A custom prevailed then, and still does, I believe, at Halifax, as well as elsewhere in the country, for the gentlemen to call that day on all the ladies of their acquaintance, who are expected to be at home to receive visitors, to whom cake and wine are offered. Of course, there is at every house a constant succession of people, from mid-day till the hour of dinner; and, at the time I am speaking of, these morning libations to the health of the fair sex increased not a little towards afternoon the difficulty that always exists in winter, in walking over the slippery and dangerous streets of the town. Although generally considered a very troublesome ceremony, it is not without its beneficial effects, inasmuch as it induces or compels a renewal of relations that have suffered from neglect or misunderstanding during the preceding year, and affords a good opportunity for reconciliation without the intervention of friends, or the awkwardness of explanations. Indeed it is this consideration alone that has caused this rural practice to survive the usages of the olden time.

"Many absurd anecdotes are in circulation relating to the accidents and incidents of the 'New Year's Calls,' among the drollest of which is the sudden irruption into a house of the greater part of those persons who had attended the governor's levée, and their equally sudden departure, amid shrieks of affright and roars of laughter, as the cracking of the beams of the floor gave notice of the impending danger of a descent into the cellar, and the subsequent collective mass of fashionables in one confused and inextricable heap at the foot of the very icy steps of the hall door. Ah, me! those were days of hilarity and good-humour, before political strife had infused bitterness and personality into every thing. *We were but too happy before we became too free.* The dinner was an official one; the guests were the various heads of departments in the place, and it passed off much in the same manner as similar ones do elsewhere.

"Of the ball, it is difficult to convey to you a very distinct idea, such entertainments being so much alike everywhere. There may be more fashion and more elegance in one assembly than another; but if the company are well-bred people, the difference is one of appearance, and not of character; and even when the company is mixed and motleyed, as on the occasion I am speaking of, still, when the greater part of them are gentry, the difference between it and one more exclusive, though perceptible to the eye, well defined and clearly distinguishable, is one of colouring; and if, in delineating it, the shades are made too strong, it becomes a fancy sketch rather than a faithful picture, and the actors appear in caricature, and not in natural and faithful portraiture. To give you the proprieties would be insipid, as all proprieties are, and to give you only the absurdities would be to make them too prominent, and lead you to suppose they were samples of the whole, and not exceptions. You must bear this in mind, therefore, or you will think the account exaggerated, or the party more exceptionable than it really was.

"When I first knew Government House, the society to be met with there was always, as I have before said, the best in the place. In time, each succeeding Governor enlarged the extent of his circle; and at last, as a corrective, two were formed for evening entertainments: one that was selected for small parties, and for frequent intercourse with the family; and a second designed for public nights only and rare occasions, and so arranged as to embrace all within, as well as most people beyond, the limits of the other. The effect of this arrangement was, to draw the two classes apart, to create invidious distinctions, and to produce mutual dislike. Subsequently the two have been merged into one, which has consequently become so diluted as to be excessively unpalatable. The best part have lost their flavour without imparting it to others; and the inferior, being coarser and stronger, have imbued the rest with as much of their peculiarities as to neutralize their effect, while they have retained enough to be as disagreeable and repulsive as ever.

"The evening to which I allude being a public one, the invitations were very numerous, and embraced the military, navy, and staff, the members of the legislature, which was then in session, and all the civilians whose names were to be found on the most extended list that had been formed at the time. Having dined at the palace that day, I happened to be present at the arrivals. The guests were shown into the drawing-room, and courteously, though ceremoniously, received by the Governor, his lady, and staff. Those who were wholly unknown, and the least acquainted with the usages of society (as is always the case with awkward people), arrived long before the rest, and were not a little surprised and awed at finding themselves alone in the presence of the 'royal party.' The ladies were unable or afraid to be at ease, or to appear at home, and sat on the edges of their chairs, stiff, awkward, and confused. The utterance of the gentlemen, who were no less conscious of being out of their element, was thick, rapid, and unintelligible; while they appeared to find hands and feet an intolerable nuisance. The former felt into every pocket of their owners for a secure retreat, but were so restless, they had hardly secreted themselves before they made their escape into another hiding-place, when they put a bold face on the matter, advanced and clasped each other in agony in front, and then undertook the laborious task of supporting the skirts of the coat behind. The latter, like twin-brothers, entered the room together, and stood on a footing of perfect equality; but it was evident ambition was at work among them, for the right first claimed precedence, and then the left, and then they rudely crossed before each other, and, at last, as if ashamed of this ineffectual struggle, when their master sat down, hid themselves under the chair, or embraced each other lovingly on the carpet.

"Lord Edward could not, and Trotz would not, talk. Sir Hercules, with great good humour, tried every topic; but he no sooner started one than it fled in affright at the cold and repulsive monosyllable 'Yes,' or 'No,' and escaped.

" 'How very icy the streets are!' he said; 'they are really quite dangerous.'

" 'Very, sir.'

" 'Does your harbour ever freeze over?'

" 'No, sir — O yes, often sir! — that is, very rarely — when the bar rises, sir....'

" 'Perhaps, madam, some of these prints would amuse you! Here are some of the latest caricatures, they are capital....'

" 'No, thank you, Sir Hercules — not any, sir.'

" 'Are you fond of driving in a sleigh?'

" 'Some, sir.'

" 'Do you play?'

" 'I never touch cards, sir.'

" 'No, but upon the piano?'

" 'No, but my Anna Maria does; and master says she has a most grand ear, sir.'

" 'Perhaps you would like to hear some music? If so, Lady Sampson will have great pleasure in playing for you.'

" 'For *me*! O dear, no — not for the world! I couldn't think of it for *me*, sir.'

" 'What a pity it is there is no theatre at Halifax!'

"Yes, sir — very, sir — for them as sees no harm in 'em, sir — yes, sir.'

"The Governor gave it up in despair, and offered me a pinch of snuff, with an air of resignation that would have done honour to a martyr. They were afraid of him, and knew not how to address him; and, besides, who could talk amid general silence, and subject their chit-chat to the critical order of strangers?

"Announcements now became more frequent, and relieved the embarrassment of both parties. Major and Mrs Section; Mrs and the Misses de Laine; the Hon. Mr Flint (a privy councillor); Mr Steel (the Speaker), Mrs and Miss Steel, and Miss Tinder; Colonel Lord Heather; Vice-Admiral Sir James Capstan; Lady Capstan; Captain Sheet; Lieutenant Stay; and so on. The room was soon filled, and it was amusing to witness the effect this reinforcement had on the spirits of the advanced party, who had hitherto sustained, unaided and alone, the difficult conversation, and to watch the eagerness with which they recognised and claimed an acquaintance with whom they could be at ease and talk freely. An incipient attack of the gout compelling me to take a chair, I sat down near the table on which were the prints and caricatures, but soon became more interested in the scene before me than in those over-drawn pictures of life, and was excessively amused at the scraps of conversation that reached me from detached groups in my neighbourhood.

" 'Ah, Mrs Section!' said Trotz, as he gave her, very condescendingly, one finger, 'how do you do? And how is my friend, the major?'

" 'The major is poorly, thank you,' she replied; 'he caught a bad cold in going those 'orrid grand rounds last night.'

" 'Ah,' said Trotz, 'he should have had a fourpost bedstead put upon runners, and driven in that manner to visit the posts! The orderly could have accompanied him, turned out the guards for him, and, when all was ready, opened the curtains.'

" 'How very good,' said Lord Edward.

" 'What a droll fellow Trotz is!' observed the lady to her neighbour: 'but those grand rounds really are a great nuisance, and I get dreadfully frightened when Section is out. Last night I wanted to have Sergeant Butter to sleep in the 'ouse; but the major said, "Enrietta, don't be foolish!' So I put my maid Hann in the dressing-room. Presently I 'eard a noise, and called to Hann, and we examined every place — and what do you think it was? an howl tapping against the heaves of the 'ouse!'

" 'I am afraid,' said the Admiral to his flag-captain, 'that Sampson will find himself in a scrape this winter. I don't see how he is to get over the rupture of the last session; where it was tongued then, it has again given way, I understand, and nothing holds it now but the cheeks and back fish.'

" 'Dear me, Sir James,' said Mrs Section ' 'ow very 'orrid! do, pray, recommend to him 'Olloway's 'Ealing Hointment — it's hexcellent! But what did you say it was that hung by the governor's cheeks?'

"Their sense of the ludicrous overcame their sense of propriety, and they both laughed heartily; when the Admiral said —

" 'Nothing, my dear madam — nothing in the world but his whiskers!'

"Moving a little further off, their place was soon supplied by another set, among whom was the pretty Mrs Smythe.

" 'Ah, Mrs Section, how do you do to-night? You really look charmingly! Let me introduce dear Mrs Claverhouse to you! ... How glad I am to see you, Mrs Schweineimer! When did you come to town? Has your father taken his seat in the council yet? — Stop, my dear, there is nobody looking just now; your dress is unhooked at the top; let me fasten it. What a lovely complexion! I would give the world for such a colour as you have. I suppose you ride a great deal a-horseback in the country?'

" 'No, I never ride; father hasn't a beast fit for the side-saddle.'

" 'Call it a horse, dear; we call nothing a beast in Halifax, dear, but Colonel Lord Heather, who won't allow his band to play at private parties. Do you know Lady Capstan? I will introduce you.'

" 'Oh dear, no, not for the world, before so many folks! I shouldn't know whether I was standing on my head or my heels, if you did.'

" 'Don't talk of standing on your head, dear; women never do it here, except at a circus.'

" 'It's allowable to have one's head turned a little sometimes, though, ain't it?' retorted the young lady. 'But who is that old fellow at the table?'

" 'Don't call him a fellow, dear — fellows are only found at colleges and workhouses: call him 'gentleman,' and leave the word 'old' out: nobody is old here but the devil. It is Judge Sandford, dear. Shall I introduce you? I think he knows your father.'

" 'Oh no, pray don't; he looks so horrid cross and grumpy!'

" 'Who is to be the new Legislative Councillor?' inquired a member of the Assembly of another.

" 'Morgan, I believe.'

" 'Morgan! why, he can't write his name! You don't mean to say they intend to put in Morgan? Why, he ain't fit to be a doorkeeper — and, besides, his character is none of the best, they say!'

" 'It will conciliate all the clergy of ...'

" 'Conciliate the devil! Well, you do astonish me! Did you get your vote through for the Shinimicash Bridge?'

" 'Yes.'

" 'I wish you'd help me, then — log-roll mine through, for an over-expenditure I have of five hundred pounds.'

" 'I will, if you will support the academy in my county. I was put in on that interest.'

" 'Done!' and the parties shook hands, and separated.

"As they turned to depart, one of them struck his elbow against a musical instrument, that gave out a loud and long-continued sound.

" 'What's that?' he asked.

" 'They call it a harp,' was the reply.

" 'The devil it is! I wonder if it is like the harp of Solomon!'

" 'Well, it's much of a muchness, then, for I never saw it; so we are about even, I guess.'

" 'I say, Bill, that's a devilish pretty craft with a rainbow on her catheads, ain't she? — there, that one with pink streamers and long-legged gloves,' said one little middy to another. 'I'm blowed if I don't go and ask her to dance with me!'

" 'Why, Black, what are you at, man? You haven't been introduced to her.'

" 'The uniform's introduction enough to her; there's no harm in trying it, at any rate. So I'm off in chase of the strange sail, and will speak her, at all events.'

" 'How was dry cod at Berbice?' inquired a little, cold, calculating man, of another (who, from his enormous bulk, appeared to have fed upon something much better than his favourite export) — 'how was cod, when the brig Polly left Berbice? And lumber — was the market good? What a grand government contract Longhead got for the supply of the army and navy! That fellow don't entertain the commissary people for nothing; that's a fact! There's no use to tender where he's concerned.'

" 'How late the officers of the 10th are in coming to-night!' whispered a very pretty young lady to her companion. 'There is nothing but those horrid black coats here, and they look like ill-omened birds. I can't bear them; they take up so much room, and, I fancy, soil my gloves.

" 'I can't say I have any objection to them,' said the other; 'but I wish they were not so fond of dancing. But just look at Ann Cooper, what a witch she has made of herself; she actually looks like a fright! I wonder what Captain Denham can see in her to admire. Come this way; there is that horrid Lawyer Galbanum seeking whom he can devour, for the next quadrille: I shall say I am engaged.'

" 'So shall I, for I have no idea of figuring with him. Look at Major Mitchell, how he is paying court to Lady Sampson! They say he is attentive to Miss Sampson. They are moving this way; let us go over to Mrs Section, she always has so many people about her that one knows.'

" 'What a magnificent screen!' exclaimed Major Mitchell to the great enchantress, Lady Sampson. 'How beautifully it is executed! It is the most exquisite piece of embroidery I ever saw. I am at a loss which most to admire — the brilliancy of the colouring and delicate shading, or the skilful way in which it is worked in; for it has a richer and softer effect than any thing of the kind I ever beheld. Where in the world did you get it?'

" 'I hardly like to tell you, after such extravagant praise; but it is the joint production of myself and daughter. One has to resort to some such occupation to pass the time in this horrid country, and,' looking round cautiously, and lowering her voice, 'among such horrid carriboos of people, too.'

" 'Exactly,' said the major; 'I know how to pity you.'

" 'When I was in the West Indies I used to amuse myself by embroidering by way of killing time. The weather was so extremely hot, it was impossible to use any exercise.'

" 'Got this place made a free port, you see, Sir Hercules,' said a man, who appeared to have had an interview on some occasion at the Colonial and Home Office. 'I told the Secretary of State refusal was out of the question, we must have it; and threatened to have a committee moved for on it in the House of Commons — regularly bullied him out of it. The Chancellor of the Exchequer, who is a particular friend of mine, told me before I went it was the only way at Downing Street. Bully them, says he, and you'll get it. But Peel, he said, was a different man: self-created — a new man — important — feels himself — stands before the fire with his back to it, and his hands in his pockets. He knows who he is, and so must you appear to know. I took the hint, pitched into him about the confidence of the colonies in his great grasp of intellect, comprehensive mind, and so on. Don't say another word, my good fellow, it shall be done. *I* say it, you know, and that's enough. I had a conversation with John Russell, too; and, between you and me, they tell me his lordship is a rising man. Plumbstone, said he, Halifax is a very important place — a very important place, indeed. I really had no idea of it, until you explained to me its capabilities; and then, tapping me on the shoulder, he said, and it has some very important men in it, too! — a handsome compliment, wasn't it? And then he quoted some Latin; but I've grown so rusty — hem! — so long since I've had time — hem! — I couldn't follow him.'

" 'Stop a minute, Sarah; let me pull out your flounce, and fix your sleeves and braids for you,' said an anxious mother to her daughter. 'There, now, that will do; but hold yourself up, dear. In a ball-room, people look shorter than they are and must make the most of themselves; and don't dance with those horrid little midshipmen, if you can find any other partners.'

" 'Why, ma?'

" 'Exactly,' said Mrs Smythe, who appeared to be endowed with ubiquity, 'your mother is right. Do you know Captain Beech, or Lieutenant Birch of the Jupiter? I will introduce them to you; they are both well connected, and have capital interest. Take my arm, but don't look at those country members, dear, and then you won't have to cut them, for Sir Hercules don't like that. Appear not to see them, that's the most civil way of avoiding them. Recollect, too, that walls have ears — especially when they are covered with flowers, as they will be to-night. Now, I'll tell you a secret, dear; Major Macassar is engaged in England, so don't waste your time in talking to him this evening. Keep close to me, now, and I'll take you among the right set, and introduce you to good partners, for I see preparations making for moving out.'

"Here Sir Hercules gave his arm to Lady Capstan, Lord Heather following with Lady Sampson, and led the way to the ball-room. It was a large and handsome apartment, tastefully decorated, and well-lighted; and the effect produced by the rich and various uniforms of the military and navy was gay, and even brilliant — more so, indeed, than is generally seen in a provincial town in England; for the garrison consisted of three regiments, and the greater part of the fleet upon the station was in port at the time. At the upper end of the room were the Governor, Lady Sampson, the Admiral and his lady, and the heads of the civil and military departments of the place and their families. Those next in rank adorned the sides of the room; and groups of those who made no pretension to that equivocal word 'position' occupied and filled the lower end.

"The indiscriminate hospitality that had thus assembled together people of the same community, wholly unknown to each other except by name, had the effect of causing a restraint in the manner of the upper class, in a vain and weak desire not to be thought on a footing of equality with those beneath them; and, on the other side, a feeling that this difference was purposely rendered palpable, and maintained, if not with incivility, at least with a total want of courtesy. Where such was the condition of things, the whole naturally suffered from the conduct of a few individuals; and those who exhibited or assumed airs of superiority, on the one part, or resented them coarsely, on the other, naturally involved the right-thinking people of both in the censure that belonged peculiarly to themselves.

" 'Who is that beautiful girl?' asked a person near me of a lady belonging to the place.

" 'I don't know her.'

" 'And that extremely interesting young lady?'

" 'I am not aware; I never met her before; she is not of our set.'

"And yet it was manifest she knew her name; had seen her frequently, though not, perhaps, in the same room; and was well acquainted with the condition and respectable character of her parents. If any allowance could be made for this absurd fastidiousness, some extenuation might be found for female vanity in the fact, that what the lower end of the room lost in station was more than compensated for in beauty. Trotz, who had observed this littleness, did not fail to use it to the annoyance of those who had been weak enough to exhibit it. He affected great astonishment at their not knowing people so distinguished for beauty, ease of manner, and agreeable conversation. The lower they were in the scale of society, the more he extolled them for these qualities, and pronounced them decidedly the finest women in the country.

"In a short time the quadrilles were formed, and all (that is, all the younger part of the company) were in motion; and, whatever the under-currents and unseen eddies of feeling might have been, all appeared gay and happy. Indeed, some of the young ladies from the country danced with a vigour and energy that showed their whole hearts were engaged in displaying what they considered most valuable qualities — exertion and endurance. The effect of the sudden cessation of music in a ball-room is always ludicrous, as the noise compels people to talk louder than usual; and, when it terminates, the conversation is continued for a while in the same key.

" 'My heart is as free as the eagle, sir,' were the first words I heard from a fair promenader.

" 'Father is shocked at a waltz. I must wait till he goes in to supper.'

" 'Ma says she's a sheep in lamb's clothing; she recollects her, forty years ago, dancing with a boy as she is tonight.'

" 'I say, Bill, look at the old ladies a-starboard there, how they haul in their claws like lobsters when the promenading commences!'

" 'Hush, there's Captain Sheet!'

" 'I hope he's not in the wind! Who is that he has got in tow? She looks like a heavy sailer.'

" 'Hush, he'll hear you!'

" 'It's a great shame, now, to wear spurs in a ball-room! Major Macassar has torn my dress, and scraped my ancle dreadfully. I'm really quite lame. The gold wire, too, has made my neck smart, as if it was stung with nettles.'

" 'Well, if it's any satisfaction to retaliate, you have certainly punished that Highland officer nicely, for the beetle-wing trimming on your dress has scratched his knees most unmercifully! But, oh, Sarah! look at Captain Denham! if his epaulette hasn't drawn off a false curl, and there he carries it suspended from his shoulder as a trophy! Well, I never! He needn't think it will ever be claimed! I wonder who in the world it belongs to? How glad I am it isn't the colour of my hair!'

" 'Oh, sir, if you haven't seen Cariboo Island, sir, near Pictoo, you haven't seen the prettiest part of Nova Scotia! I never beheld any thing so lovely as Cariboo Island. We have such pleasant clam-parties there, sir, especially when the timber-vessels arrive.'

"Lady Sampson had but one topic which, though it had lasted since October, was likely to endure through the winter season.

66

She had visited the Falls of Niagara in the autumn, and was filled with wonder and amazement. She was now describing them to a circle of admiring friends.

" 'It was a mighty cataract!' she said.

" 'It might be removed by couching,' remarked a deaf staff-doctor, who thought she was talking of her eyes, which were greatly distended at the time with the marvellous story.

" 'The Falls!' she said, raising her voice.

" 'Ah! the effect of a fall — that will render the operation doubtful.'

" 'Water-fall!'

" 'Ah, exactly, the lachrymal gland is affected.'

" 'Ni-ag-a-ra!' she said, raising her voice still higher, and pronouncing the word slowly.

" 'I beg your pardon madam,' he replied, putting his hand to his ear, and advancing his head much nearer; 'I beg your pardon, but I didn't hear.'

" 'Trotz! do, pray, take that horrid man away, and explain to him,' said the lady, and then continued. 'I saw the pool at the foot of the rock where the Indian warrior rose after going over the Fall, and was whirled round and round in the vortex for a great many days, in an upright position, as if he were still alive! They say it was a fearful sight; at last the flesh dissolved, and the frame parted and sunk!'

"She then led the way to the drawing-room, to show a sketch of Niagara, that the military secretary had prepared for her. Trotz detained the doctor a minute behind, and I heard him say, —

" 'Though the cataract was not, that story of the Indian really was, 'all in my eye.'

" 'So I should think,' was the reply.

"The anterooms through which we passed were filled with persons playing cards, or taking refreshments. At a small table sat my friend, the midshipman, with the little strange sail with pink streamers, to whom he had given chase in the early part of the evening, and, as he said, brought to. They were just commencing a sociable game of chess.

" 'Suppose,' said the jolly tar to his fair friend — 'suppose that we strip as we go? It's great fun.'

" 'I don't understand you,' said the young lady, with an offended toss of her pretty head.

" 'What! not know what strip as we go is?'

" 'I don't know what you mean, sir!'

" 'Why, this is the rule. Any thing you *can* take, you are *bound* to take, and strip the board as you go on. It shortens the game amazingly.'

"Lady Sampson now opened a large book containing the promised sketch, and unfolded and extended out a narrow strip of paper of immense length, painted green, and resembling an enormous snake, and explained it all in detail.

" 'There is the Gulf of St. Lawrence,' she said; 'and there's Quebec; and there's Montreal, and there are the lakes; and there — just there — no, not there — a little higher up — just between your thumb and finger — is Niagara — vast, mighty, and grand Niagara! Don't you see the grand Falls, Mrs Section? There, that little white speck — that's it! It's so mighty, that neither the eye nor the mind can take it all in at once! Captain Howard drew it! Ain't it beautifully done? He draws so well! He can draw any thing!'

" 'I must introduce him to you,' whispered Mrs Smythe to Miss Schweineimer.

" 'Yes,' said Trotz to Lord Edward, 'he can draw any thing — a long bow, a long cork — any thing but a bill, and that he won't draw for any one!'

" 'How very good!' replied Lord Edward.

" 'Here is an epitome of it — an abridgement — the idea, as it were, itself, though not developed;' and she exhibited a very good and accurate sketch taken by her daughter, infinitely better done; and more intelligible, than the other. 'What do you think, Mrs Smythe, of my transferring this to embroidery — working it for a screen or a cushion? No, a cushion wouldn't do, either; it's inconvenient to have to rise every time you wish to show it. But for a screen, eh?'

"Another party, an exploring one, that was reconnoitering what was going on in the drawing-room, now arrived; and the loud prolonged sound of Niagara was again heard in the distance, amidst the confused hum of many voices, as I returned to the ball-room. The dancing being about to be resumed, I took a seat near a Mrs Blair, an old lady who came for the purpose of chaperoning her daughter that evening. I had known her in her youth, but had not met her of late years, and was shocked to see the change that time had effected both in her appearance and disposition. The playful humour, for which she was remarkable when young, had degenerated into severe sarcasm; the effects, probably, of ill health, or of decreased fortune.

" 'Who would have thought of seeing you here, Judge?' said she.

" 'The truth is, my dear Mrs Blair,' I replied, 'I have not been at a ball for many years, and probably never shall be again; and as I dined here to-day, and was in the house when the company arrived, I thought I would stay and take one long last look at a scene which recalls so many recollections of bygone days; and, besides, it always does me good to see happy faces about me.'

" 'Happiness in a ball-room!' she ejaculated, with some bitterness of feeling; 'I thought you were too much of a philosopher to believe in such a deception! Look at that old wall-eyed colonel, now (excuse the coarseness of the expression, but I have no patience with people of his age forgetting their years) — look at that wall-eyed colonel, with an obliquity of vision, and the map of Europe traced in red stains on his face! Happy fellow, is he not? See, he is actually going to dance! It will puzzle those two sisters to know which he is addressing.'

"She had scarcely uttered the words, when both the young ladies rose at once, each thinking he had asked for the honour of her hand.

" 'How happy he must feel,' she continued, 'in having such an ocular proof of the want of unity or expression in his eyes! Oh! look at that old lady with a flame-coloured satin dress, and an enormous bag hanging on her arm, with tulips embroidered on it, and a strange-looking cap with a bell-rope attached on one side of it, fanning a prodigious bouquet of flowers in her belt, as if to keep them from fainting with the heat, and losing their colour! Oh, observe that member woman, that 'lady from the rural districts,' habited in a gaudy-coloured striped silk dress, trimmed all over with little pink bows, having yellow glass buttons in the centre; a cap without a back, stuffed full of feathers, like Cinderella's godmother; and enormously long gloves, full of wrinkles, like the skin of an elephant! They are both happy, but it is the happiness of fools! Happiness in a ball-room! Ah, Judge, you and I are too old for such twaddle! I wish you had been here when the yellow-fever was raging! In a garrison town, the young ladies have the scarlet-fever all the year round; but last year the yellow-fever predominated; for, you know, two diseases cannot exist in the constitution at one time. At a sale of wrecked goods, a fashionable milliner bought a lot of maize-coloured satins so cheap as to be able to sell them for a mere trifle; but disposed of them skilfully, by exhibiting only a few at a time. The consequence was, a great number of young ladies made their appearance here in what each one considered a rare fabric; and, to their horror, found the room full of them! I christened it then, and it has ever since been known as 'the bilious ball.' Do you suppose those maize-coloured satins covered happy hearts that night? There is Ella M'Nair, now dancing with her awkward country cousin, whom she is afraid to refuse, yet unwilling to accept as a partner, alarmed for the horror of Lord Heather, the sneers of Trotz, and the triumph of the Shermans. Sweet girl! how joyous she looks, does she not? Oh, look at that supercilious little fellow near the fireplace, whose elbow is resting on the mantlepiece! The education his foolish father gave him spoiled him for the kitchen, without fitting him for the parlour. Instead of being a cheerful, thrifty tradesman, he has been metamorphosed into a poor, shabby, discontented gentleman. He looks like a grasshopper on half-pay!

" 'You see the same thing everywhere. Observe that very pretty and remarkably well-dressed lady opposite. She is a widow of large fortune and good connexions. Her affections are all absorbed by that lout of a boy she is talking to, who is her only child. His bent knees and stooping shoulders give you the idea of a ploughboy, while his fashionable dress would lead you to suppose he had clothed himself, by fraud or mistake, from his master's wardrobe. She is beseeching him to stand properly, and behave like a gentleman; and, above all, to dance; to all which he is becoming more and more rebellious; and now he has jerked away his arm, and is diving into that crowd of men near the fire, to escape from her importunities and the observation of others. Her wealth and station have given her but little happiness, and her maternal cares and devoted affection are the torment of her son. Did you use that word happiness, therefore, Judge, as a commonplace phrase, or did it express what you really meant?'

" 'I meant what I said,' I replied. 'Happiness is rather a negative than positive term in this world, and consists more in the absence of some things than in the presence of others. I see no harm in assemblies where they are not the business, but the relaxation of life, as they certainly are in the country. People come together for the purpose of pleasing and being pleased, of seeing and being seen, to be amused themselves and to contribute their share to the amusement of others. They come with a disposition and a hope to be happy. Music and dancing exhilarate the spirits, hilarity is contagious, and, generally speaking, people do enjoy themselves, and I derive great gratification in witnessing their happiness. That was what I meant, for I never supposed there could be an assemblage of two or three hundred people, without there being some individuals unable or unwilling to partake of the gaiety about them.'

"Just then Miss Schweineimer, the young lady that called her horse a beast, and myself an ugly old fellow, passed, hanging on the arm of a subaltern officer, into whose face she was looking up with evident satisfaction, while listening to his flattering accents.

" 'Oh, charming!' she said. 'If I haven't enjoyed myself tonight, it's a pity, that's all! How do you feel? I feel kind of all over. It's the handsomest party I ever saw in all my life! How I like

Halifax! I wish father lived here instead of the Blueberry Plains!'

" 'There, madam,' I said, 'let us abide by the decision of that unsophisticated girl. I forgive her nasal twang and her ignorance, for the simplicity and truthfulness of her nature,' and I effected my escape from my cynical companion.

"Conversation such as hers is depressing to the spirits, and lowers one's estimate of mankind. It puts you out of sorts; for such is the mysterious effect of sympathy, that a discontented person soon infuses a portion of his own feeling into the mind of his auditors. I did not, however, derive much benefit from change of place, for the gentleman who next accosted me was imbued with much of the same captious spirit.

" 'I have been pitying you for some time, Judge,' he said. 'How could you think of remaining so long with that bitter specimen of humanity, Mrs Blair? She speaks well of no one, and has been amusing herself by feeling the silks and satins of her neighbors this evening, so as to find fault with their texture, if thin, and the extravagance of their owners, if otherwise. She has been grumbling to every one that the room is so badly lighted, good dresses are lost in the dim and gloomy apartment. I shall propose to Sir Hercules to have shelves put up on the wall for those old chaperons, with chandeliers in front of them to show off their velvets to the best advantage; when they will be out of all danger themselves from heels and spurs, and be deprived of the power of annoying others. Capital idea, isn't it? A very vulgar party this, Judge? When the guests that are invited do come, it's not fair to send to the highways and byways for others. In the olden time, we are told, it was only when a man's friends declined, that a press-warrant issued to man the tables with the first poor devils that could be found going to bed supperless.'

"The party now began to move towards the supper-room, which generally presents more attractions to persons who stand less in need of refreshments than those who have been fatigued or exhausted with dancing. The tables were tastefully and beautifully arranged: but the effect was much injured by the profuse and substantial character of some of the viands, which the number and quality of the guests rendered necessary. Whatever doubt there might have been as to the possibility of a ball conferring happiness, there could be none as to the enjoyment derived from the supper. In approving or partaking, nearly all seemed to join; few claimed exemption from age, and no one objected to a *vis-à-vis*; and, if some had danced with all their hearts, an infinitely greater number ate and drank with as much relish as if eating and drinking were as unusual a thing as waltzing.

"I looked, but in vain, for my cynical companion, Mrs Blair, to draw her attention to my friend, the midshipman, who had evidently made a prize of the strange sail, and was behaving with the utmost generosity and kindness to the vanquished. He insisted upon filling her plate with everything within reach; and when it could hold no more, surrounded it with tenders, deeply laden with every variety of supply. Nor did he forget champagne, in which he drank to the fair one's health, to their better acquaintance, and to a short cruise and speedy return; and then protesting it was all a mistake to suppose he had already done so, apologized for his neglect, and repeated the draughts till his eyes sparkled as bright as the wine. He cut the large cake before him, and helped his partner to a liberal share, complaining all the time that the knife was desperately dull; that it was the severest cutting-out service he was ever employed in; and vowed that the steward ought to have three dozen for his carelessness. He succeeded, however, at last in effecting the incision, and brought away several folds of a three-cornered piece of napkin, exactly fitting the slice, which had impeded the progress of his knife. As he deposited this trophy of his skill and strength on the plate, he said, in an under-tone, 'It only wanted a ring to make it complete;' whereat the young lady's face was suffused with blushes and smiles, and, holding up her glass, she said, 'A very little wine, if you please.' Complying with this request, and filling his own, they pledged each other again; and something was looked, and something was thought, and something was felt, though not expressed on that occasion, that, notwithstanding Mrs Blair's theory to the contrary, looked to me uncommonly like happiness.

"Miss Schweineimer was no less pleased, though she thought that the sandwiches were rather bitey; and the little red things in the pickles, to which Trotz had helped her, the hottest, not to be a fire, she had ever tasted, for they burned her tongue so as to make tears trickle down her cheeks.

" 'Do look!' said a young lady near me to Mrs Smythe — 'do look at that strange creature covered with pink bows, and yellow glass buttons in them; she is actually eating her supper backwards! She began with fruits, and then proceeded to confectionary and jellies, and so on, and is now winding up with the breast and leg of a turkey! Who is she, and where does she come from?'

" 'Her name is Whetstone; I will introduce you to her, by and by.'

" 'No, thank you; I'd rather not.'

" 'The place is unpronounceable. It is Scissiboo-goomish-cogomah, an Indian word, signifying The Witch's Fountain.'

" 'Ah, indeed! she is a fit representative.'

"The inventor of shelves for the chaperons now accosted me again.

" 'I should have liked, Judge, to have had the pleasure of taking wine with you, but really Sampson's wine is not fit to drink; he seems to have lowered his standard of taste to suit the majority of his guests. Did you ever see any thing so disgusting as the quantities of things with which the tables are loaded, or the gross appetites with which they were devoured? It is something quite shocking! He is ruining the state of society here. These people realize our ideas of the harpies: —

Diripuuntque dapes, contactuque omnia fœdant
In mundo.

By the way, a little man, with a face like a squeezed lemon, has done me the honour to notice me once or twice to-night, with a half familiar and half obsequious nod, whom I have been at a loss to make out. The supper-table has betrayed him at last, for its resemblance to his own counter (for he keeps a confectionary-shop in the country) put him at ease in a moment. He is the most useful person here.'

"A message from Sir Hercules to his aide, Mr Trotz, brought him to his feet, muttering, as he rose, his discontent in very audible tones. The renewal of the music in the ball-room at the same time intimated that the last dance was about to be commenced.

" 'You ain't going, Mr Trotz, are you?' said Miss Schweineimer, who had unconsciously been the object of many impertinent remarks during the last half-hour. 'Pray try one of these custards before you go; they are so good! Do, just to please me. You know I ate those fiery pickles, because you asked me,' and she handed him a liquid one contained in a small circular glass.

"To the astonishment of every body, he complied with her request; but, being in a hurry to attend to the governor's wishes, drank it off without the aid of a spoon, and replaced the glass on the table. In a moment he became dreadfully pale, and, putting his handkerchief to his face, exclaimed —

" 'Good heavens, the mustard-pot!' and left the room in convulsive agony from the effects of this powerful emetic, and disappeared amid the malicious laughter and uproarious delight of all those whom he had at one time or another annoyed by his insolence.

" 'Well, I never!' said the young lady: 'it looks as like a custard-glass as two peas, don't it? and it's the identical colour, too! I am sorry it's done, but I'd rather it had happened to him than any one else; for I believe in my soul he gave *me* the red hot pickles a-purpose. I am up sides with him, at any rate.'

" 'So would I, my dear,' said Mrs Smythe, 'but don't say so; here you must always appear to be sorry for an accident. Let me introduce you to Mr Able, assistant surgeon of the Jupiter; for this is the last dance, and he'll tell you where the red pickles grow. I really love you for putting that trick upon that horrid Trotz.'

" 'I assure you it was a mistake ...'

" 'That's right, dear, look innocent, and say it was a mistake.'

" 'But I assure you ...'

" 'Oh, of course! you really do it very well. You are a capital scholar!'

"The last dance lasted for a long time; for the termination of everything agreeable is always deferred to the utmost moment of time. At length the band played 'God save the King!' which was the signal for parting, and the company took leave and disappeared in a few minutes, with the exception of the awkward squad that first arrived. Owing to their having made a mistake in the hour, or forgotten to give orders as to the time their carriages were to come for them, they were again doomed to annoy the gubernatorial party, and to be no less perplexed and bored themselves.

"Such were my last reminiscences of Government House, and, from what I hear, it has not at all improved of late years. Don't let me be misunderstood, however. I do not give you this as a sketch of society at Halifax, but of a promiscuous ball at Government House: nor are the people whom I have described samples of the whole company; but some of them are specimens of that part of it who ought never to have been there."

JOSEPH HOWE

*   *   *   *   *   *   *

Joseph Howe was born in Halifax in 1804. At the age of thirteen he became an apprentice in his father's printing and newspaper business. Late in 1827 he took over the Halifax journal the Novascotian *and soon transformed it into Nova Scotia's leading newspaper, as well as a major vehicle for the promotion of local literature. In 1836 Howe was elected to the legislative assembly, becoming a leading spokesman for responsible government, which was achieved in Nova Scotia in 1848. The premier of Nova Scotia from 1860 to 1863, he was a staunch opponent of Confederation, but eventually joined the federal government as a cabinet minister. In May 1873 he was appointed lieutenant-governor of Nova Scotia. He died the following month at Government House, Halifax. The year after his death, his literary contributions to local newspapers were collected in* Poems and Essays. *His speeches and public letters were first edited by William Annand in 1858. A more comprehensive edition, prepared by Joseph Andrew Chisholm, was issued in Halifax in 1909. "Eastern Rambles" and "Western Rambles," two Nova Scotia travel accounts which Howe serialized in the* Novascotian *between 1828 and 1831, were finally published in book form in 1973.*

"To the Town Clock" first appeared in the Novascotian *(October 12, 1836) and was later collected in Howe's* Poems and Essays *(1874). In keeping with his desire to promote local culture, Howe wrote a number of poems celebrating various aspects of his native province. In this ode he exalts one of Halifax's best-known landmarks, the Town Clock that was completed in 1803 for the town's garrison on the orders of Prince Edward, the Duke of Kent. The Halifax broadcaster and writer William C. Borrett, who reprinted part of the poem in his* More Tales Told Under the Old Town Clock *(1943), saw his own books of tales about Nova Scotia as the fulfillment of Howe's prophecy, in the fifth stanza of the poem, that "No Book would sell so well/About the town" as a volume recording all that the clock had seen and heard.*

To The Town Clock

Thou grave old Time Piece, many a time and oft
    I've been your debtor for the time of day;
And every time I cast my eyes aloft,
    And swell the debt — I think 'tis time to pay.
Thou, like a sentinel upon a tower,
    Hast still announced "the enemy's" retreat,
And now that I have got a leisure hour,
    Thy praise, thou old Repeater, I'll repeat.

A very *striking* object, all must own,
    For years you've been, and may for years remain,
And though fierce storms around your head have blown,
    Your form erect, and clear and mellow tone,
Despite their violence, you still retain.

A "double face," some foolishly believe,
    Of gross deception is a certain sign;
But thy *four faces* may their fears relieve,
    For who can boast so frank a life as thine.
You ne'er disguised your thoughts for purpose mean,
    You ne'er conceal'd your knowledge from the crowd,
Like knaves and asses that I've sometimes seen,
    But what you knew with fearlessness avow'd.

Time, with his scythe, could never mow you down,
    Though you could cut him up in fragments small —
Showing his *halves* and *quarters* to the town,
    Old *Quarter* Master General for us all.
Though unambitious, still the highest place
    All ranks and classes cheerfully resign,
And "looking up to thee," feel no disgrace
    If to "look down on them" thou dost incline.
While some the Graces seek,
    And others love the Muse's rosy bowers —
Thou art content from week to week,
    To revel with the ever fleeting Hours.

How many curious scenes and odd displays
    You've gazed upon, since first you took your stand;

How many sad, how many brilliant days,
    You've had a *hand* in — Oh! that you could hand
        Your knowledge down —
Your Log — your Album — all your observations,
    Jokes and remarks, on what you've heard and seen;
If besides "note of time," your cogitations
    On all the doings that in time have been
        You had recorded,
No book would sell so well
        About the town,
 Nor any author be so well rewarded.

What various feelings, in the human heart,
        Thy tones have stirred ; —
How hast the Lover curs'd thee, when he heard
Thy voice proclaiming it was time to part.
        With what a start
    Of quick delight, about to be set free,
The schoolboy heard you say that it was *three*;
But then, next morning, how he'd sigh and whine
When you as frankly told him it was *nine*;
Oh! cruel Clock! thus carelessly to shout it,
        If e'er you'd play'd
At Ball, or By the Way, on the Parade,
You never would have said one word about it.

To wretch, condemn'd for flagrant crimes to swing,
What horrid anguish would thy clear tones bring,
        Telling his hour!
But, to the pilloried scoundrel, placed on high,
Round whom stale fish and rotten eggs did fly —
        A fearful shower!
Whose dodging shoulders, and averted eye,
Half uttered prayer, or sharp and piercing cry,
        Betray'd his fears;
Who thought "his hour" would surely last all day,
Sweet was thy welcome voice, when it did say
        The storm about his ears
        Should cease and die away.

How oft hast thou observ'd the hapless wight,
Who'd toil'd, and raked, and scraped, from morning light,
    Till nearly *three*;
And yet had not enough his Note to pay,
    Turn round to thee;
While throbbing brow, and nervous gait did say,
Hold — hold — Clock, another quarter stay —
    For if I cannot raise, or beg or borrow,
    My credit will have died before tomorrow,
For this I do assure you's, my "last day."
The Sun *stood still*, at Joshua's command,
Oh! be as kind, or I can never *stand*;
Ah! do — if you of pity have one drop,
If you "go on," by Heaven I'll have "to stop,"

How many dashing blades have gone to pot,
    Who sought on Folly's files the first to be;
But never one, of all the precious lot,
    Could live, old friend, so long "on tick" as thee.
The cunning fellows, too, thou put'st to shame,
    Who scheme, and plot, and plan from morn till eve;
Thy "wheels within wheels" always go the same,
    While they, some "screw loose" failing to perceive,
On ev'ry side their wreck'd machinery leave.

A good example
To all the idle chaps about town,
    Who trample
On precepts by economists set down,
    You always gave;
Your "hands" were going night and day;
From year to year you toil'd away
    Like any slave;
Your limbs from heavy weights no hour were free
And "Sunday dawned no holiday to thee."
You "the whole figure" went while others faltered,
And howsoe'er times changed, your time ne'er altered.

CHARLES DICKENS

*   *   *   *   *   *   *

Charles Dickens was born at Portsmouth in 1812 and was raised in London and Chatham. After receiving some schooling from his mother and a Chatham schoolmaster, he was forced, at the age of twelve, to work in a blacking factory while his father was imprisoned for debt in Marshalsea Prison. Dickens subsequently returned to school for three years before becoming a solicitor's clerk and later a court reporter. During the 1830s he graduated to parliamentary journalism and began contributing sketches to a number of journals, including The Monthly Magazine *and the* Evening Chronicle. *Not long after the appearance of his first book,* Sketches by Boz *(1836), he published* The Pickwick Papers *(1836-37), which made him famous. Active as an editor and a reformer, he emerged as the greatest English novelist of the nineteenth century. Among his major works are such classics as* A Christmas Carol *(1843),* David Copperfield *(1849-50),* Hard Times *(1854),* A Tale of Two Cities *(1859), and* Great Expectations *(1861). He was working on* The Mystery of Edwin Drood *at the time of his death in 1870.*

The following passage is from Chapter II of American Notes *(1842), Dickens' book about his 1842 visit to North America. Dickens' first port of call during his tour was Halifax, where, following an exceedingly rough crossing, he spent the day of January 21. His chief host during his stay was the Speaker of the House of Assembly, the writer Joseph Howe. Although* The Nova Scotia New Monthly Magazine *later complained in its February 1842 issue that the Halifax literati failed to organize a "plan whereby the inhabitants might welcome so worthy a guest," it is obvious that Dickens' impressions of the city were most favourable. It should be noted, however, that the novelist was somewhat less complimentary about Halifax and Howe in the comments that are found in his correspondence to his friend and biographer John Foster (see Louis Hamilton's article "Dickens in Canada" in the October 1950 issue of* The Dalhousie Review*).*

from **American Notes**

Divided between our rubber and such topics as these, we were running (as we thought) into Halifax Harbour, on the fifteenth night, with little wind and a bright moon — indeed, we had made the Light at its outer entrance, and put the pilot in charge — when suddenly the ship struck upon a bank of mud. An immediate rush on deck took place, of course; the sides were crowded in an instant; and for a few minutes we were in as lively a state of confusion as the greatest lover of disorder would desire to see. The passengers, and guns, and water casks, and other heavy matters, being all huddled together aft, however, to lighten her in the head, she was soon got off; and after some driving on towards an uncomfortable line of objects (whose vicinity had been announced very early in the disaster by a loud cry of "Breakers ahead!") and much backing of paddles, and heaving of the lead into a constantly decreasing depth of water, we dropped anchor in a strange outlandish-looking nook which nobody on board could recognise, although there was land all about us, and so close that we could plainly see the waving branches of the trees.

It was strange enough, in the silence of midnight, and the dead stillness that seemed to be created by the sudden and unexpected stoppage of the engine, which had been clanking and blasting in our ears incessantly for so many days, to watch the look of blank astonishment expressed in every face: beginning with the officers, tracing it through all the passengers, and descending to the very stokers and furnace-men, who emerged from below, one by one, and clustered together in a smoky group about the hatchway of the engine-room, comparing notes in whispers. After throwing up a few rockets and firing signal guns in the hope of being hailed from the land, or at least of seeing a light — but without any other sight or sound presenting itself — it was determined to send a boat on shore. It was amusing to observe how very kind some of the passengers were, in volunteering to go ashore in this same boat: for the general good, of course: not by any means because they thought the ship in an unsafe position, or contemplated the possibility of her heeling over in case the tide were running out. Nor was it less amusing to remark how desperately unpopular the poor pilot became in one short minute. He had had his passage out from Liverpool, and during the whole voyage had been quite a notorious character, as a teller of anecdotes and cracker of jokes. Yet here were the very men who had laughed the loudest at his jests, now flourishing their fists in his face, loading him with imprecations, and defying him to his teeth as a villain!

The boat soon shoved off, with a lantern and sundry blue lights on board; and in less than an hour returned; the officer in command bringing with him a tolerably tall young tree, which he had plucked up by the roots, to satisfy certain distrustful passengers whose minds misgave them that they were to be imposed upon and shipwrecked, and who would on no other terms believe that he had been ashore, or had done anything but fraudulently row a little way into the mist, specially to deceive them and compass their deaths. Our captain had foreseen from the first that we must be in a place called the Eastern passage; and so we were. It was about the last place in the world in which we had any business or reason to be, but a sudden fog, and some error on the pilot's part, were the cause. We were surrounded by banks, and rocks, and shoals of all kinds, but had happily drifted, it seemed, upon the only safe speck that was to be found thereabouts. Eased by this report, and by the assurance that the tide was past the ebb, we turned in at three o'clock in the morning.

I was dressing about half-past nine next day, when the noise above hurried me on deck. When I had left it overnight, it was dark, foggy, and damp, and there were bleak hills all around us. Now, we were gliding down a smooth, broad stream, at the rate of eleven miles an hour: our colours flying gaily; our crew rigged out in their smartest clothes; our officers in uniform again; the sun shining as on a brilliant April day in England; the land stretched out on either side, streaked with light patches of snow; white wooden houses; people at their doors; telegraphs working; flags hoisted; wharfs appearing; ships; quays crowded with people; distant noises; shouts; men and boys running down steep places towards the pier; all more bright and gay and fresh to our unused eyes than words can paint them. We came to a wharf, paved with uplifted faces; got alongside, and were made fast, after some shouting and straining of cables; darted, a score of us, along the gangway, almost as soon as it was thrust out to meet us, and before it had reached the ship — and leaped upon the firm glad earth again!

I suppose this Halifax would have appeared an Elysium, though it had been a curiosity of ugly dulness. But I carried away with me a most pleasant impression of the town and its inhabitants, and have preserved it to this hour. Nor was it without regret that I came home, without having found an opportunity of returning thither, and once more shaking hands with friends I made that day.

It happened to be the opening of the Legislative Council and General Assembly, at which ceremonial the forms observed on the commencement of a new Session of Parliament in England were so closely copied, and so gravely presented on a small scale, that it was like looking at Westminster through the wrong end of a telescope. The governor, as her Majesty's representative, delivered what may be called the Speech from the Throne. He said what he had to say manfully and well. The military band outside the building struck up "God save the Queen" with great vigour before his Excellency had quite finished; the people shouted; the ins rubbed their hands; the outs shook their heads; the Government party said there never was such a good speech; the opposition declared there never was such a bad one; the Speaker and members of the House of Assembly withdrew from the bar to say a great deal among themselves, and do a little; and, in short, everything went on, and promised to go on, just as it does at home upon the like occasions.

The town is built on the side of a hill, the highest point being commanded by a strong fortress, not yet quite finished. Several streets of good breadth and appearance extend from its summit to the water-side, and are intersected by cross-streets running parallel with the river. The houses are chiefly of wood. The market is abundantly supplied: and provisions are exceedingly cheap. The weather being unusually mild at that time for the season of the year, there was no sleighing: but there were plenty of those vehicles in yards and by-places, and some of them, from the gorgeous quality of their decorations, might have "gone on" without alteration as triumphal cars in a melodrama at Astley's. The day was uncommonly fine; the air bracing and healthful; the whole aspect of the town cheerful, thriving, and industrious.

We lay there seven hours, to deliver and exchange the mails. At length, having collected all our bags and all our passengers (including two or three choice spirits, who, having indulged too freely in oysters and champagne, were found lying insensible on their backs in unfrequented streets), the engines were again put in motion, and we stood off for Boston.

RICHARD HENRY DANA, JR.

$*$ $*$ $*$ $*$ $*$ $*$ $*$

Richard Henry Dana, Jr. was born in Cambridge, Massachusetts in 1815 and attended Harvard University. In 1834 his education was interrupted by a bout of measles, which weakened his eyesight and led to the prescription of a long sea voyage. After two years at sea, he returned to Cambridge and completed his studies, graduating at the head of his class. In 1840, the year he was admitted to the Bar, Dana published Two Years Before the Mast, *an account of his experiences as a merchant seaman. The book quickly became an international best seller and prompted calls for maritime reform. As a lawyer, Dana distinguished himself in the fields of maritime law and international law. He was also very active in the anti-slavery movement and was noted for his assistance to seamen. Dana died suddenly in 1882 and was buried, near the English poets Keats and Shelley, in the Protestant cemetery in Rome.*

The following account by Dana of his visit to Halifax in July 1842 is taken from The Journal of Richard Henry Dana, Jr.; Volume II *(1968) edited by Robert F. Lucid. Unexpectedly, Dana's journal entries, which represent one of the few American literary references to the city, include a remarkable description of the writer's foray into Victorian Halifax's underworld of rum, prostitution, and violence, where he had an unforgettable encounter with a young woman named Kitty Morricay. Dana's second trip to Halifax, nine years later, which is also detailed in his journal, was not nearly so eventful.*

$*$ $*$ $*$ $*$ $*$ $*$ $*$

from **The Journal of Richard Henry Dana, Jr.**

JULY 20, WEDNESDAY. Parade again at 10. About noon started off with Mr. Codman on horseback to Cole Harbour, about 6 miles distant. Delightful ride there & back. Country very green. Dined at six. In the evening put on my rough clothes again & strolled off towards the barracks to hear the tattoo. While there, saw two girls accosting men for bad purposes. I was struck with the manner of one of them. She looked very young, had rather an interesting face & could not muster the impudence necessary for her calling. The girl with her went [boldly] up to the men, but this one kept behind & seemed to be new in her calling. Observing that I was watching them, & mistaking me in the twilight for a sailor or some *rowdy* (from my dress) they came towards me, & the elder solicited me in a very forward manner. I turned her off, but looked full into the face of the other & her eye fell. I walked away & watching them from a distance, saw that their relative conduct was the same. I felt a sudden interest in the younger girl, & knowing that I was a stranger & was completely disguised for the light there then was, went up to the girls & beckoned the younger one to follow me. Thinking it to be in the way of her trade she followed me, & the other said nothing. I walked until I was hidden from view by the side of a fence in a lane & then called the girl to me. I told her at once that I did not want her in the way of her calling, but wished to say a word to her. I then in a careless manner opened my coat to show her that I had the dress of a gentleman, & she saw by my voice & man[ner] that I was different from what they supposed, & she answered me very respectfully. I told her plainly & at once that I knew what she was, what her life was & had been, & asked her if she knew what she was fast going to. She made no reply; but looked down. I then set before her in as kind & affectionate a manner as I could, the end which inevitably awaited her. I told her that she would fall from step to step, would become diseased & in time a burden upon the persons who kept [her] & then would be left to die a miserable death of neglect, suffering & remorse. She was a good deal affected, the tears stood in her eyes, & after a time she said she knew it all. I then asked her how she came into that situation. Finding, from something she said, that she supposed me to belong to Halifax, I let her go on in the error, thinking that she would be more careful to tell me no more than the true story. She told me her name, the name & occupation of her father & where he lived. She said her mother died when she was fourteen & left her father with herself & two younger brothers. The brothers were put into the almshouse & bound out to trades. She could not go to the almshouse & begged her father to take a room & she would keep it for him; but her father was rather intemperate & refused to do it, & she went out to service. A boy of about 16, the son of a baker, (whom she mentioned as a person I must know) attended to her & in time, being left without helps or advisors, he had his way with her. This was discovered before long, & the person she lived with turned her away, without any effort to save. She could not get another place as she had no certificate of character. In this difficulty she went to her father, who turned her away with contempt. One of her brothers had gone to sea, & the other was too small to help her. At this trying time she was invited to the house of a washer-woman & went there to work. This was a bad house, & she fell into a set of the lowest girls of the town, & was soon out in the streets in the manner I saw her: — Such was her story. I could not but believe it, partly because, taking me for a resident, she referred to so many sources from which I could easily learn its falsity, if it were false, & partly from its probability. Had she been seduced by a man of wealth or gentility she would have been passed about as a kept mistress, for she was very good looking, but having been turned loose upon the town where she was well known for an affair with a poor lad, she naturally fell thus early into the lowest walks of her calling.

I asked her if she ever went to church? She answered — "It would only be making a mock of it, Sir, to go to church & then go right away & do bad again." I found that her parents were

Richard Henry Dana, Jr.

Catholics & that she had been baptised by Father Laughlan, the priest who usually attended upon the poor. I then told her to go him, & tried to encourage her that he might get her a place & that she might in time regain her respectability, being young, & find herself in a decent situation in the world. I told [her] that girls in her situation, if taken away at once, had been reformed, had married respectable men & found themselves happy & comfortable, instead of dying in misery & despair. She said she had thought often of this, but that all were against her where she lived & would not permit her to leave & that no one had encouraged her. She promised me that she would see Father Laughlan the next day & would do all she could to get away. I gave her some money & told her to keep away from men, & asked her if she could not — "God knows," said she, seriously, & as though she was speaking her whole mind "I never saw any pleasure in it." She then told me what her life was, of the dreadful death of one of the girls in her house, & seemed completely stirred up to extricate herself from it.

I then told her that I was a stranger & married, & that I had spoken to her from what I observed of her with the other girl & from a desire to do her good. I said that I should be at the same place the next night, & that if she was sincere & went to the priest, & wished to tell me so, I should be glad to hear it; but that she might do as she chose, &, as I should go away the day after never to return, if she did not do as she promised, she need not meet me, & I should never know more of her. This left her perfectly at liberty to do as she chose.

I had left her but a few minutes & was going down a street near the South barracks when, I saw a crowd rushing up the street with cries of "down with him," "kill him," "knock him over" &c, & saw a soldier running for his life toward the barrack gate. One man brought him a blow by the side of the head which knocked him down, & two or three more struck him as he fell. Some money fell from his pocket, upon the stones of the gutter, & the men stopping to pick it up, the soldier got upon his feet, looked round a moment as though bewildered, & then ran for his life toward the gate, calling out "By the Holy Ghost" — "Oh, dear! Oh, dear!" as though half stunned & in pain. The mob was too near the barracks to pursue him. I followed & saw him go in, & in an instant there was cry of "Serjeant of the guard!" "Picket, fall in!" &c., & in a minute more a dosen soldiers of the picket for the night, dressed in their long grey coats & high cloth caps, with muskets in hand & bayonets fixed, headed by their serjeant, rushed from the gate in the direction from which the crowd came. They overtook another soldier who had been beaten & who went with them to point out the men. In five minutes the picket returned with three or four prisoners, rowdyish looking fellows, whom they put in the watch house. I went up to the scene of the row, & there saw about half a dosen houses, in each of which a fiddle, with tambourines or triangles, was playing, & a crowd of the lowest description, both males & females were going [in] & out. A decently dressed man standing near told me that this street, between the two barracks, on the hill, was the nest of the brothels & dance-houses, & that dancing went on here every night. Buttoning up my coat & pulling my cap over my face, I went into the larger of these houses. The door was open & people passed in & out as they chose. The entry terminated in an oblong room with low & black walls, sanded floor & closely barred shutters, used as a dancing hall. At one end was a platform holding two chairs upon which the fiddle & triangle player sat. At the other end was the bar, at which the bloated, red faced master of the house sold the glasses of rum, brandy & wine to the girls & their partners. In the middle of the room, in an arm chair, sat the old harradan, the "mother" of the house, with a keen wicked eye, looking sharp after the girls & seeing to it that they made all the men dance & pay the fiddler & treat them at the bar after each dance. There were about a dosen girls, nearly all of whom were dancing, & the average number of men in the room at a time was from 20 to 30. Having looked with sufficient disgust & horror at the old creatures who conducted the orgies & made gain out of this dreadful trade, I turned my attention to the girls, & after carefully watching them singly for some time, looking at their faces, for many of them came up & spoke to me as they did to others, & hearing them talk, I can sincerely say that there was not one of them would not, to my mind, excite only loathing & pity in the breast of any but a man as degraded as they. Indeed, I asked myself several times — Can any man be in such a state as to have intercourse with these creatures? There was almost a certainty of disease, for every one of them looked broken down by disease & strong drink. The chance of a man's becoming diseased by connexion with them would certainly be ten to one with each of them. Then, with the exception of two or three who seemed coarse & hardened, they were such pitiable objects. One of them came up & spoke to me, — the best looking at a distance. She had bright cheeks, though thin, good features, & black hair curling in ringlets from the top of her head. When she came close to me, the marks of degradation were plain upon her. The skin was tight to her bones, her chest was fallen in, her eyes were wild & sparkling partly from liquor, but with dark lines & cavities under them, every sign of health, natural animation & passion had left her, & with a wasted form, hectic & fallen check, glassy eyes, & a frisette fastened to her head, she looked like a painted galvinised corpse. Her breath too was strong of brandy, & she was partly stupefied with drink. With the exception of two or three thick set, clumsy, coarse featured, pug-nosed & pock-marked Irish wenches, who seemed in good keeping, this poor girl was a fair specimen of the company. She is an instance of the effect of such a life upon those who have been handsome & in better circumstances, while those who have been coarse & vulgar & but little better than harlots from earliest life, brought up in vice, often retain their robustness, even when diseased. Black & white, too, were mixed up together, & the girl I have described had been dancing with a sooty fellow in a sailor's hat & duck trowsers torn at the knees, probably the cook of some merchant vessel.

Having staid as long as I dared to without either dancing or going to the bar, or attracting notice, I slipped out & went into the next house. This was smaller & more filthy, & there were only two or three white girls of the lowest description among half a dosen black girls or women, for some of them seemed quite advanced. There was very vulgar & rough work here, two or three drunken sailors & a good deal of horse-play. One of the girls kicked a man in the back not much below the shoulders while they were dancing & there was a good deal of swearing & hard talking. I was glad to slip out soon after I came in; but as it was one of the girls saw me going out & sprang towards me & got me by the arm, but I pulled my arm away from her & jumped through the narrow entry into the street. Fearing some of [the] drunken men might follow, & having no weapon of defence, — not even a cane — I stood under the shadow of the opposite building until I saw there was no pursuit.

Determined to see the whole of this new chapter in the book of life, I went into a third & a fourth house, in which the scenes varied between the two first I had seen, neither quite so bad as the second, & neither superior to the first.

It being now 11 o'clock, having seen fair specimens of the life on Halifax Hill, & most other such places on the globe, I presume, & having got through in safety, I walked slowly home to my hotel. The two adventures I had met with so possessed my mind that I lay awake for hours. Poor Kitty Morricay! (for that is her name) are you coming to such a dreadful end as this? Will you end your days among the negroes & outcasts on the hill? What a dreadful fate has society ordered for a single fault in a woman! No pity! No repentance can help her! No return! Yet this must be God's order, & it is necessary. No lesser terrors would guard female virtue.

How unjust, too, the world is! Fanny Ellsler, or any other admired & successful strumpet, though her whoredoms are a part of the history of Europe, & notorious as the death or birth of a crowned head, — will be applauded & followed after & the world sees nothing but her grace & the "poetry of motion"; but if to vice is added poverty & misfortune, the virtue of the world is stern & has no eye for pity. What will probably be the eternal condition of the people I have seen tonight? — immortal souls, — made in God's image, living by his grace & power!

Prayed earnestly & I trust sincerely, that God would touch the heart of the poor girl & save her from such an end.

JULY 21ST. THURSDAY. Parade at ten, & went fishing immediately afterward. Before I went fishing, called at a tract & bible store to get a book that might be of use to poor Kitty, intending to give it to her that evening if she came to the place appointed. A short story, setting before her her life & its end, & try which would stir up her religious feelings might be of use to her. I found no one in attendance but a woman, & I could neither find such a book myself nor describe it to her, — so I left the shop.

The Bedford basin where I sailed is the most [remarkable] sea-bay I was ever in. The harbour passes Halifax town like a wide river, & then, about 2 miles above the town, after narrowing in a little, it spreads out into this large, deep, irregular basin, surrounded by well wooded shores, but little affected by the tide, without flats or rocks, & containing, I was told, *14 square miles of anchorage!* It is the most complete sailing ground for boats & small vessels that can be imagined, & is at the same time large & deep enough to hold the whole British navy. This great *head of water* above the town, flowing in & out with the tides, & itself supplied by springs, small rivers & creeks, keeps the harbour deep & prevents any danger of its filling up. It would be almost impossible for a hostile force to get up into this basin, as there is but one passage way into it. The ride around the basin is said to be quite beautiful.

After fishing at the narrows some time I sailed about the basin in all directions, having a fine breese. There were several other boats & small vessels there at the same time. Coming back, towards night, I sailed close under the lee of two sloops of war, just arrived from the West Indies, — the Race Horse & Volage, both with yellow fever on board. The old frigate Pyramis lay at her moorings, used as a receiving ship.

After dinner learned that Mr. Wm. Young had sent his servant with a horse for me to take a ride. Wrote a note to thank him.

Towards nine sauntered along in my boating dress towards the South Barracks. It began to rain & the tattoo was played within the gates. I went into the garrison by permission, & for a few minutes it rained quite heavily. When the music was over it had stopped raining but was cloudy. It was nearly half an hour later than the time I had agreed to meet the poor girl, & the rain would have kept her away, I was quite sure, or she would have gone away thinking I would not come, — even if she meant to come at all. I felt quite sure that she would not come unless she had been to her priest, for I had told her that I would call on the priest & speak to him about her, & thus she would suppose I would find her out. I passed along the parade & down the street, but saw no one. Returning I thought I saw some one at a distance, & walked back again slowly. Looking behind me I saw a figure coming toward me, & walking slowly on it overtook me, & it was she. I walked aside & she followed me. I asked her what she had to tell me, & she told me she had been to Father Laughlan that morning early, & he treated her kindly, remembering her family, & told her to come the next day & he would try to aid her. (This she told me, before knowing that I had not been to see the priest, as I told her I might). She said he asked her how she came to think of reforming, & she told him how it happened, & that a gentleman who was a stranger had spoken to her & sent her to him. I told her that I had tried to get a book for her, & she said she could read easily & wished to have it. I told her, too, that I expected to go away the next day or the day after, & that if it should not be until the day after, I would meet her in the same place the next night & give her the book. I made her promise to read it [&] to keep it, & said that if she reformed & became happy & comfortable, the book would be a remembrance, & if she did not — still to keep it, & it might some day be of use to her. All this she promised, & seemed very much affected. I told her I had a wife at home to whom I should tell her story, & who would feel for her. She asked when I should come back. I told her probably never; but added that I had friends here who would inform me, if her efforts succeeded. I did not think it safe to let her know my name. I told her that if I did not meet her the next night, she might be sure that it was because I had gone away. She promised to be there. I once more set before her the certainty of the fate that awaited her, & drew the best picture of the chances in case she changed, & left her.

JULIANA HORATIA EWING

*   *   *   *   *   *   *

Juliana Horatia Ewing was born at Ecclesfield, Yorkshire in 1841. The eldest daughter of the vicar of Ecclesfield and the writer Margaret Gatty, Juliana displayed talent at an early age as both a writer and an artist. In 1861 her writing career began with the publication of several stories in The Monthly Packet. *Her first book,* Melchior's Dream and Other Tales, *was published a year later and was followed by more than thirty volumes, making her one of the Victorian era's most popular children's authors. In 1867 she married Major Alexander Ewing and travelled with him to various postings, including a two-year stay in Fredericton, New Brunswick. Dogged by ill health for many years, she died at Bath, England in 1885.*

The following passage is from Canada Home: Juliana Horatia Ewing's Fredericton Letters, 1867-1869 *(1983), a collection of Ewing's letters from Canada that was edited by Margaret Howard Blom and Thomas E. Blom. Taken from the first letter in the book, a long epistle that Ewing wrote to her mother between June 14 and June 20, 1867, the excerpt describes Ewing's stopover in Halifax as she and her husband, "Rex," made their way from England to Fredericton, where he was to serve with the 1st Battalion of Her Majesty's 22d (Cheshire) Regiment. (Several deletions have been made to the letter and are indicated by ellipses.) Although Fredericton became Ewing's Canadian home, it is obvious that Halifax charmed her, prompting a sympathetic and somewhat painterly depiction of the city on the eve of Confederation. Some of the sketches that Ewing made while in Halifax can be seen in* Canada Home *and Donna McDonald's* Illustrated News: Juliana Horatia Ewing's Canadian Pictures, 1867-1869 *(1985).*

*   *   *   *   *   *   *

from **Canada Home**

Monday Evening [17 June 1867]. Halifax. Arrived — safe & well thank GOD. Sunday was a wretched foggy day, so I stayed in my berth. We ought to have been in on Sunday evening — but the fog put us on 1/2 speed & kept us back. Then towards dark the fog suddenly lifted — & we were told we might be "in" about midnight!!! I had just turned seedy again so poor Rex had to pack — & help me to dress. However the fog came down again — we slept in our clothes ready for a start — but did not get in till about 9.A.M. Happily there was no wind — so though we lay kicking about all night — we invalids were none the worse — & a little before 8.A.M. (after fog signals — & firing guns for a pilot — & no end of weary waiting) the fog lifted, & Rex got me on deck. I was too muddleheaded to enjoy it at first, but the air revived me, & I think the first sight of Halifax was one of the prettiest sights I ever saw. When I first came up, there was no horizon: we were in a sea of mist. Gradually the horizon line appeared — then a line of low coast — muddy looking at first — it soon became marked with lines of dark wood — then the shore dotted with grey huts — then the sun came out — the breeze got milder — & the air became *strongly* redolent of pine woods — Nearer, the coast became more defined, though still low, rather bare & dotted with brushwood & gray stones low down, & crowned always with "murmuring pines." As we came to habitations which are dotted — & sparkle along the shore — the effect was what we noticed in Belgium — as if a box of very bright new toys had been put out to play with — red roofs — even red houses — cardboard looking churches — little bright wooden houses — & stiffish trees mixed everywhere. It looks more like a quaint watering place than a city — though there are some fine buildings. It is built of wood — & I should imagine that once set alight 6 & 30 hours would about see the last of it!!! We took a great fancy to the old place — which was like a new child's picture book, & I was rather disappointed to learn it is not to be our home. But Fredericton (where we are going) has superior advantages in some respects — & will very likely be quite as pretty. It is not so liable to fogs — house rent is cheaper — Rex will have sole command there — & it is a nice quiet place. It entails miles of rail & 8 hours more steamer — but then we settle! — A commissariat officer met us — & was awfully civil — had got a carriage for us — & arranged what hotel we were to go to. (We get ^{S}10/- a day extra the 3 days we are detained here for accidental expenses.) My 1st effort was to have a good wash — & put on all the clean things I could find — & then the view from the window was one too many for me & with the spinning head & valour which Regie will remember at Antwerp — I began to sketch with Mrs. B.'s new block & paint box — (By the bye. Do let somebody tell her they are *charming* — the blocks take color so well — & the box so handy.) I felt very bad though — & rather down. It is all so strange — & I was so weak — when up came the sarvint — with a cup of tea & toast saying it was too long to wait till luncheon. It was so good — & the taste of *real* toast — & clean victuals & fresh butter — so jolly I fairly cried! It freshened me up no end — & I have really made a very fair sketch of the harbour — & Rex & I have had a long walk — & when we came back our glass was stuck over with cards of callers!! Rex's chief & wife & daughter — the one who met us ditto ditto — & another, who has called again since, & asked us to dine with him tomorrow on the other side of the harbour. We are to go about 3 & I shall take my sketching things. It is very hot & jolly, & the intense smell of pine ought to be a universal panacea!

... Monday Night [17 June].

Mr. Routh (R.'s Chief) & his daughter, & another officer have been in again. I like them all very much. Mr. R. is most kind & jolly, & has asked us to tea on Wednesday, for we are not to be moved now till Friday, & then are to go to S. John's for a few weeks to take another man's place, before going forward to Fredericton. Mr. R. says F. is very pretty. S. John's very nice too. I expect I shall sketch my head off! The one care on my mind

amid all these changes — is the Dixon's porcelain card-dish!!!!
Hitherto I have preserved it unbroken, & now we have so many
cards to put in it, it wld be 1000 pities if it fell a victim to the
changes of military life!!! Such a warm moonlight night, with
such a strong smell of pines! — I am very glad we stay till Friday
in some ways. I want to get 2 or 3 sketches of the place before we
leave it. But I pity poor old Rex & his baggage — & indeed am
not perfect in that line myself — living at present on my oldest
hat & one garter!) — We tried for some linen collars today, but
are far behind the Atlantic Wave of Civilisation — "We sell
nothing but *paper* now Sir!" — Good night dearest Mum. Yr
loving & very jolly — J.H.E.

... Wednesday. 19. June. Rex is out, so I write a bit more dear
Mum, before this goes. We are getting on capitally, & liking it
all better than at first — even. I think it does capitally for us. We
are in a private hotel, the best in the place — a small queer
looking wooden house, but very comfortable inside — & *capital*
grub. Mr. Routh says it is rather expensive, but we get our extra
$10/- till we leave — & I believe Mr. R. is going to try & continue
it till we leave S. John's. (We shall be there probably about a
fortnight or 3 weeks) Our room here was high up, but today
some people have cleared out, & we are down in a jolly one
looking out on trees, with some splendid arm chairs & awfully
comfy. Yesterday I had a grand *tidy* of all Rex's things whilst he
was out — & my own too! — Our dressing table looks very swell.
I put out all Mr. Hawthorn's bottles from the dressing case &c.
&c. & Rex's & my photo.s in their frames stand on each side. We
feed table d'hôte, & hitherto have had no sitting room, the house
being too full, & now this room is so very jolly, I think we shall
hardly need one. Breakfast at 8.30 when Miss Lovett (whom we
secretly call Todgers — she being a good specimen — & a
splendid "Bailey Junr" waiting at table under her orders.)
presides. Very good breakfasts — broiled salmon & hot rolls &c.
Lunch at one. Dinner at 6 — & then tea. Yesterday we drove in
a cab to call on the McKinstreys, & drove on over the Common
where reviews are held — & saw the rink where they skate in

winter — & I got Rex to stop the cab, & we got out to hunt on the boggy ground for flowers. I found two lovely ones I never saw, & having no means of preserving — I have made coloured drawings of them. Rex has given me his big note:book — & I am going to devote it to drawings of plants. I have made a successful beginning I think, & we are very proud of this new "collection." One flower is a pale blue 4 pointed star with yellow centre. The other a low growing dark leaved thing, the actual flower being like a single blossom of white hawthorn. Neither have scent. Also I found a pale pink lichen. As this is early summer I hope I shall pretty well see all the flowers through. I hear there is one like white wax & sweet — the "May Flower" — we are going to look for it. (Queen's accession [20 June].) I have discovered that there are daily prayers at S. Luke's at 9.15. So this morning Rex & I went to Church. Plain reading, but chanting, & a hymn — "Holy, Holy, Holy." No great "performance" — but *very* blessed & pleasant somehow to hear the familiar Lord's Song in a strange land! The last 2 Sundays were wretched enough — & I have not been to Church since All Saints in London. I *did* feel thankful dear old Mum, as you will understand, for all my happiness — to be here safe & sound, my Boy *so* good & kind — & such a hopeful lookout before us, & so many little pleasures by the way. I pray every day that we may all meet happily in old England after a while — & I believe we shall, & I even now look forward to all we shall have to show you. I think you will almost like my *new* sketchbook (the flowers) best of all — I do *the* flower in colours — & accessory bits of grass &c. in pencil. Rex says one *bud* is the loveliest thing I have ever done!!!! But he likes all I do — GOD bless him! Excuse promiscuous information, but washing is dear. $2/- a dozen. House rent *here* is awfully dear — but cheaper in Fredricton. Another happy fact is that the oldest of old clothes pass muster — & from all we hear — I think a young couple who want to live cheaply, & at the same time keep up the imperial dignity of an Alexander & a Juliana could not have a more fortunate destination. A *sole command* — in a quiet lovely place where you may wear anything, & I fancy living is cheap. We know 4 nice people there to start with. We are to succeed a man who was very fond of a *garden*, so if we get his house I shall have a bit to grub in in summer, & to crown all though *here* Church matters are dull looking enough they say the Cathedral at Fredricton is beautiful, & the service musical & good: so you will probably hear of Rex in connection with it — & we shall speak of practise nights as composedly as if we were in Ecclesfield. I have begun my little legend for A.J.M. but somehow my hands seem full — & we are going out for the afternoon to some jolly people — the Mannings. N.B. *She* came out as a bride, & was ill the whole way, & *they* were a fortnight coming!! *She* had a throat, & is now strong & well. So the Rouths tell me. We went there to tea last night, & they were awfully jolly & kind. Rex & the young Indian flirted at the piano, & I chatted to Mr. R. & his wife. Nothing could be kinder than they were. We walked home in the moonlight about 11. We are rather lucky in being here tomorrow, as it is *the* grand day of the year in Halifax. The birthday of the city. 100 salutes are to be fired at sunrise, & 100 at sunset, & all sorts of festivities through the day, which will be fun. My cursory judgement of shops here, is that everything is *dearer & inferior* — like a mushroom watering place. I see no prospect of engraving our plate, & wish we had left it — *I* believe it will be cheaper to send home for anything we want. By the bye tell Madge that unfortunately *her* old winter dress was sent instead of mine. It lasted the voyage, but will do no more. Tell her that *mine* is I know in much better condition, & that when we *do* have a parcel I had better have it. It will last me the winter for common, in this out of the way region — will probably not fit her well — & she had much better have a new one than I, as Ecclesfield requires much better dressing than Nova Scotia!!! Rex just came in — has been to the fish market he tells me to tell you — & it is a wonderful sight — awfully fine salmon, one — 24 lbs weight — & ^{d}6 a pound!! If we get very low in the world we must live on fish! — *Such* dear old black Dogs "go about the city"!! — Best love to all the doges — including dear Trotus. P.M. Rex & I went down to the fish market that I might see it.

Splendid fish certainly! Coming back we met an old N. American Indian woman — such a picturesque figure. We talked to her, & R. gave her something. I do not think it 1/2 so degraded looking a type as they say. A very broad — queer — but I think acute & pleasant looking face. Since I came in I have made 2 rather successful sketches of her. She wore an old common striped shawl, but curiously thrown round her so that it looked like a chief's blanket — a black cap embroidered with beads — black trousers stuffed into moccasins — a short black petticoat — & a large, gold colored cross on her breast, & a short jacket trimmed with scarlet, a stick & basket for broken victuals. She said she was going to catch the train! It sounded like hearing of Plato engaged for a polka!!... Am I not industrious? But I feel that though I have years before me in Fredricton we *may* never come here again. I think I must now say Goodbye dear old Mum. You will hear again in a fortnight — & it will take you nearly that time to read this.... My — *Our* dear love to all. We are very well and very very very happy.

ISRAEL ZANGWILL

*   *   *   *   *   *   *

*Israel Zangwill was born in London's Whitechapel Jewish ghetto in
1864 and grew up in Bristol and London. He attended the Jews' Free
School in London and eventually became a pupil-teacher before continu-
ing his studies at London University. During the 1890-1925 period
Zangwill emerged as an important British playwright and novelist,
creating a large body of work, most of which tended to reflect his
commitment to Zionism, pacifism, and radical social reform. Among his
best-known plays are* Merely Mary Ann *(1904) and* The Melting Pot
(1909). His many novels include The Bachelors' Club *(1891),* Children of
the Ghetto *(1892), and* The Mantle of Elijah *(1900). Zangwill died in
1926.*

*The following excerpt is from "A Wander-Year," Chapter VIII of
Book I of Zangwill's novel* The Master *(1895). Set largely in Nova Scotia
and England, the book explores the role of the artist in society, portraying
the career of a Nova Scotian painter, Matthew Strang. In this passage,
Matthew has a brief sojourn in Halifax before leaving his native province
for Boston. While Zangwill's description of the city contains much local
colour, it is apparent that it is not based on first-hand experience, which
is not to say that Zangwill was without a Halifax connection. Not long
after the appearance of* The Master, *he sent a letter of encouragement that
changed the life of a young Haligonian writer named Michael Williams
(see Williams' autobiography,* The Book of the High Romance, *which
was first published in 1918 and then reissued in a revised edition in 1924).*

*   *   *   *   *   *   *

from **The Master**

Halifax exceeded Matt's expectations, and gave him a higher opinion of his mother. For the first time his soul received the shock of a great town, or what was a great town to him. The picturesque bustle enchanted him. The harbour, with its immense basin and fiords, swarming with ships and boats, was an inexhaustible pageant, and sometimes across the green water came softened music from a giant iron-clad. High in the background of the steep city that sat throned between its waters rose forests of spruce and fir. From the citadel on the hill black cannon saluted the sunrise, and Sambro Head and Sherbrooke Tower shot rays of warning across the night. The streets throbbed with traffic, and were vivid with the blues and reds of artillery and infantry; and the nigger and the sailor contributed exotic romance. On the wharves of Water Street, which were lined with old shanties and dancing-houses, the black men sawed cord-wood, huge piles of which mounted skyward, surrounded by boxes of smoked herrings. On one of the wharves endless quintals of codfish lay a-drying in the sun. And when the great tide, receding, exposed the tall wooden posts, like the long legs of some many-legged marine monster, covered with black and white barnacles and slime of a beautiful arsenic green, the embryonic artist found fresh enchantment in this briny, fishy, muddy water-side. Then, too, the Government House was the biggest and most wonderful building Matt had ever seen, and the fish, fruit, and meat markets were a confusion of pleasant noises.

In the newly opened park on the "Point" the wives of the English officials and officers — grand dames, who set the tone of the city — strolled and rode in beautiful costumes. Matt thought that the detached villas in which they lived, with imposing knockers and circumscribing hedges instead of fences, were the characteristic features of great American cities. He loved to watch the young ladies riding into the cricket-ground on their well-groomed horses; beautiful, far-away princesses, whose exquisite figures, revealed by their riding-habits, fascinated rather than shocked his eye, accustomed though it was to the Puritan modesty of ill-fitting dresses, the bulky wrappings of a village where to go out "in your shape" was to betray impure instincts. He would peer into the enclosure with a strange, wistful longing, eager to catch stray music of their speech, silver ripples of their laughter. He wondered if he would ever talk to such celestial creatures, for whom life went so smooth and so fair. What charming pictures they made in the lovely summer days, when the officers played against the club, and they sat on the sward drinking tea under the shady trees, in white dresses, with white lace parasols held over their softly glinting hair to shield the shining purity of their complexions — a refreshing contrast of cool colour with the scarlet of the officers' uniforms. Sometimes the wistful eyes of the boy grew dim with sad, delicious tears. How inaccessible was all this beautiful life whose gracious harmonies, whose sweet refinements, some subtle instinct divined and responded to! At moments he felt he could almost barter his dreams of Art to move in these heavenly spheres, among these dainty creatures whose every gesture was grace, whose every tone was ravishment. There was one girl, the most bewitching of all, whom he only saw in the saddle, so that in his image of her, as in his sketches of her, she was always on a beautiful chestnut horse, which she sat with matchless ease and decision; a tall, slender girl, with yellow-brown hair that lay soft and fluffy about the forehead of her lovely English face. Her favourite canter was along the beach-road; and here, before he had found work, he would loiter in the hope of seeing her. How he longed — yet dreaded — that she might some day perceive his presence; sometimes so high flew his secret audacious dream that in imagination he patted her horse's glossy neck.

In such an exhilarating atmosphere the boy felt great impulses surge within him. But, alas! the seamy side of great cities was borne in on him also. He had a vile lodging in the central slums, near the roof of a tall tenement-house that tottered between two groggeries, and here drunken wharfingers and sailors and negro wenches and Irishmen reeled and swore. To a lad brought up in a godly Cobequid, where drunkenness was spoken of with bated breath, this unquestionable supremacy of Satan was both shocking and unsettling. Nevertheless, Matt spent the first days in a trance of delight, for — apart from and above all other wonders — there were picture-shops in the town; and the works of O'Donovan, the local celebrity, were marked at twenty, or thirty, and even fifty dollars apiece. They were sea-paintings of considerable merit, that excited Matt's admiration without quite overwhelming him. On the strength of O'Donovan's colossal prices, Matt invested some of his scanty stock of dollars in a kit of paint at a fairy shop, where shone collapsible tubes of oil-colour, such as he had never seen before, and delightful brushes and undreamed-of easels and canvases. He also bought two yellow-covered books, one entitled *Artistic Anatomy*, and the other *Practical House Decoration*, which combined to oppress him with his ignorance of the human form divine and the house beautiful, and became his bed-fellows, serving to raise his pillow. His conceit fell to zero when he saw a portrait by Sir Joshua Reynolds among the collection in the Session Hall.

After a depressing delay, mitigated only by the sight of his fair horsewoman, he found work in a furniture shop at the top of an old rambling warehouse that was congested with broken litter and old pianos. The proprietor not only dealt in débris, but bought new furniture and had it painted in the loft. Matt received six dollars a week, half of which he saved for his English campaign. At first he had the atelier to himself, but as the proprietor's business increased he was given a subordinate — a full-grown Frenchman, rather shorter than himself, who swore incomprehensibly and was restive under Matt's surveyorship. By this time Matt had learned something of the wisdom of the serpent, so he treated his man to liquor. After the Frenchman had got drunk several times at the expense of his sober superior, he discovered that Matt was his long-lost brother, and peace reigned in the paint-shop.

But Matt did not remain long in Halifax. The Frenchman's jabber of the mushroom millionaires of the States (though he failed to explain his own distance from these golden regions) fired Matt's imagination, and he resolved to go to Boston in accordance with his original programme. He considered he had sufficiently studied his mother's wishes, and her letters had become too incoherent for attention. It was a pain, not a pleasure, to receive them. He was not surprised to learn from Billy's letters that domestic broils were frequent, and that the deacon's proverbial wisdom did not avail to cope with Mrs. Strang's threats of suicide. It was only poor Ruth's girlish sweetness that could bring calm into these household cyclones.

And so one fine evening Matt set sail for the city of culture and "Crœsuses." Everything seemed of good augury. Though the expense of the trip had wellnigh eaten up his savings, his heart was as light as his pocket. He was going only to the States, but he felt that, in quitting his native soil, the voyage to London, the temple of Art, and to his uncle, its high-priest, had begun. The moon shone over the twinkling harbour like a great gold coin, and as the vessel spread its canvas wings and glided out of the confusion of shipping, Matt felt that its name was not the least happy omen in this auspicious moment. The ship was named *The Enterprise.*

RUDYARD KIPLING

*   *   *   *   *   *   *

Rudyard Kipling was born at Bombay in 1865 and was educated in England. In 1882 he returned to India, where he worked for several years as a journalist and launched a literary career that made him one of the world's most famous and influential writers, bringing him many honours, including a Nobel Prize (1907). After living for a time in the United States, he returned to England in 1896 and settled in East Sussex, where he remained until his death in 1936. Kipling, who came to be very closely identified with British Imperialism, was a prodigious short-story writer, poet, and novelist. Among his best-known works are The Light that Failed *(1890),* Barrack-Room Ballads *(1892),* The Jungle Book *(1894), and* Kim *(1901). One of the most significant collections of Kipling-related material — including editions of his works, memorabilia, and manuscripts — is located at Dalhousie University in Halifax.*

The following stanza from "Song of the Cities" was first published in Kipling's collection The Seven Seas *(1896). Part of a longer sequence entitled "A Song of the English," the poem actually appeared earlier, in the* English Illustrated News *(May 1893), but without the "Halifax" stanza. In this memorable quatrain, Kipling, who visited Halifax in the 1890s, immortalizes the city in its role as an imperial garrison and a naval station. Thomas H. Raddall, whose work was admired by Kipling, would later use a phrase from the third line of the poem for the title of his classic history* Halifax, Warden of the North. *For Raddall's updated version of the poem, reflecting the sad reality of Halifax following the departure of the imperial troops and the Royal Navy, see Chapter 30 of* Halifax.

*   *   *   *   *   *   *

from **Song of the Cities**

HALIFAX
Into the mist my guardian prows put forth,
    Behind the mist my virgin ramparts lie,
The Warden of the Honour of the North,
    Sleepless and veiled am I!

MARSHALL SAUNDERS

*   *   *   *   *   *   *

Marshall Saunders was born at Milton, Nova Scotia in 1861 and spent her childhood in the Annapolis Valley and Halifax. At the age of fifteen she went to school in Edinburgh and then continued her studies at Orleans. After returning to Halifax, she taught school for a time and began writing for magazines. Her first novel, My Spanish Sailor, *appeared in 1889. A few years later, she placed first in an American Humane Association literary contest and saw her prize-winning novel,* Beautiful Joe: An Autobiography *(1894), become an international best seller and eventually the first Canadian book to sell over a million copies. Her first two works were followed by many animal stories written for children and by a number of historical romances and contemporary novels. Among the latter was* The House of Armour *(1897), an ambitious work set in Halifax. In 1914, after living for several years in the US, Saunders settled in Toronto, where she devoted herself to writing and various humanitarian causes. Her last book was the semi-autobiographical* Esther de Warren; The Story of a Mid-Victorian Maiden *(1927). She died in Toronto in 1947.*

"Home Again" is Chapter III of Saunders' Halifax novel, The House of Armour. *Although the book is, at times, extremely earnest, reflecting the author's zeal for social reform, it does contain more than a modicum of humour and romantic melodrama, as evidenced by this account of the return of the novel's protagonist, Vivienne Delavigne, to Halifax from Europe.*

*   *   *   *   *   *   *

from **The House of Armour**

HOME AGAIN

One of the long wharves was sprinkled with people watching the "Acadian" come in from the sea. Custom-house officials were there, wharf laborers, sailors, loafers, and at the very end of the wharf was a group of fur-clad individuals who were laughing, joking, stamping their feet, or pacing briskly up and down while waiting to welcome the friends and relatives drawing so near to them.

With them, yet a little apart from them, stood a man who did not move from his place and who seemed indifferent to the extreme cold. He was wrapped in a black fur coat, and a cap of the same material — a fine and costly Persian lamb — was pulled down over his brows.

His pale, cold face was turned toward the "Acadian," and his blue eyes scanned without emotion the people hurrying to and fro on her decks.

When the steamer swung around toward the wharf, he watched the gangways being thrown out and the living tide pouring down them and overflowing in all directions. The air was full of greetings. Mothers and fathers, lovers and friends, were looking into each others' eyes, and embracing one another tenderly. Then the first gush of salutation over their thoughts reverted to business. In a mass the passengers precipitated themselves upon the custom officials and eagerly watched for and identified their luggage as it was rapidly hoisted from the hold of the steamer to the wharf.

The man in the fur coat pressed his way through the throng of people and gained the deck of the steamer. The Macartneys and Vivienne Delavigne stood together.

The girl saw him coming, went to meet him, and putting out her hand said, "How do you do, Mr. Armour?"

Composed as his face usually was she yet caught an almost instantly repressed look of repulsion. Unspeakably chilled by it and the brevity and stiffness of his greeting, yet too proud and philosophical to show the slightest sign of disappointment, she said steadily:

"This is Mrs. Macartney, who has been kind enough to chaperon me across the Atlantic."

Mr. Armour bowed politely, his cap in his hand. Captain Macartney she found to her surprise he already knew, though he spoke to him almost as formally as if they had never met before.

Patrick, after a searching glance at Mr. Armour, turned away muttering, "Iceberg!"

When Mr. Armour in a few brief sentences thanked Mrs. Macartney for her kindness to his ward, she said cheerfully: "She's one of the right sort is Miss Delavigne. She is the only girl I have ever seen that would have satisfied my old grandmother. I was the one that never could please her." Mr. Armour stared slightly at her as if he did not understand what she was saying, then turning to Vivienne he said shortly, "What luggage have you?"

"Four boxes," she replied; "black ones with V.D. on the covers."

"Will you come with me to find them?" he said, and after a brief leavetaking of the Macartneys he preceded her to the gangway.

Vivienne looked regretfully over her shoulders. Mrs. Macartney waved her hand good-naturedly, Captain Macartney smiled and lifted his cap, and Patrick blew a kiss from the tips of his fingers and exclaimed, "*Au revoir, mademoiselle.*"

However they met again. After a time, borne to and fro in the surgings of the crowd, they found themselves in the shed where the luggage had been taken to be examined. Vivienne was a short distance from Mrs. Macartney, who had seated herself on a box that she recognized as her own. Neither Captain Macartney nor Patrick was in sight and she was surveying in

huge amusement the scene of civilized confusion so different
from the picture of their arrival that her fancy had conjured up
— a few logs thrown out in the water, their descent thereupon,
and welcome by swarms of half-clad savages dancing around,
their tomahawks in hand.

With amiable interest in the affairs of every one with whom
she came in contact, the Irish lady gazed attentively at a
custom-house official near her with whom a Halifax maiden
was reasoning, vainly endeavoring to persuade him that there
was nothing dutiable in her half a dozen open trunks, which
looked suspiciously like containing a wedding trousseau.

Mrs. Macartney at intervals took a hand in the argument,
and looking sympathetically at a heap of new kid gloves that the
officer had just drawn from some hidden recess, she remarked
in a wheedling voice: "What's the good of being under the
English flag if one is so particular about bits of things like that.
Come now, officer, let them pass. I'm sure the duty on them is a
mere trifle."

"Thirty-five per cent," he said, throwing up his head to look
at her.

Her thoughts reverted to herself and she exclaimed: "Faith,
I'll be ruined! Have I got to pay you that for the privilege of
covering my hands in cold weather?"

"Yes'm," he said smartly, "that is if your gloves have not been
worn." Then fixing her with his appraising eye, as if he gathered
from her comfortable appearance that she might be one to
indulge in soft raiment and fine linen, he rattled off a list of
articles which she would have done well to have left behind her.

"We've got to protect our merchants, madam. If you've
brought any description of silk gloves, kid gloves, mitts, silk
plush, netting used for manufacture of gloves, we'll assess you.
If you've any silk cords, tassel girdles, silk velvets except church
vestments —"

"That's a very likely thing for me to have," she interrupted
indignantly.

"Silk manufactures," he said, "including gros grains, satins,
sarcenet, Persians, poplins, ribbons, shawls, ties, scarfs, bows,

handkerchiefs, mantillas, —" and he gabbled on till his breath failed him.

Mrs. Macartney was speechless for the first time in her life. She turned from him with a shudder, as if to say, you are a dangerous man, and hailed an agile young official who was pursuing a comet-like career over trunks and boxes and leaving a trail of white chalk marks behind him.

At her signal he bore down upon her box with bewildering rapidity, opened it, and with long cunning fingers extracted there from every dutiable article. The new gloves still stitched together, the silk and linen and dainty trifles still in the wrappers in which they had come from the Dublin shops, lay in a heap before him.

"Twenty dollars," he ejaculated, and she had with his assistance mechanically abstracted from her purse a sufficient amount of the foreign currency to pay him, and he had given her box the pass mark and was away before she realized the extent of the weakness which she had displayed in not uttering one word of protest.

With a sign of dismay she turned and met Vivienne's eye. They had had many jokes together and with a simultaneous impulse they began to laugh.

" 'Tis a country of surprises, me dear girl," said Mrs. Macartney wagging her head. "Ah, Geoffrey, hear a tale of distress," and looking at Captain Macartney, who suddenly appeared before them, she poured her troubles in his always sympathetic ear.

Vivienne was listening with interest when amid all the bustle and excitement she felt her guardian's cold eye upon her.

"Your boxes are marked," he said; "will you come now?"

With a hasty good-bye to her friends the girl followed him from the building.

A few sleighs and cabs were drawn up in the shadow of a square warehouse that stood at the head of the wharf. Before one of these sleighs Mr. Armour stopped. A coachman in an enormous fur cape and with his head half hidden in a heavy cap hurried from his seat and went to the horse's head.

Mr. Armour assisted Vivienne into the sleigh, then gathered up the reins in his hands and placed himself beside her. The coachman sprang to the back seat and they passed slowly under a black archway and emerged into long Water Street that follows closely the line of wharves running from one end of the old colonial town to the other.

Once upon the street the horse, a beautiful black creature, impatient from his long time of waiting and feeling lively in the keen frosty air, struck into a quicker pace. Smoothly and swiftly they slipped over the snowy streets, sometimes between rows of lighted shops whose windows sparkled with frost, and sometimes by dwelling houses whose partly closed curtains afforded tantalizing glimpses of light and good cheer within.

The girl's heart beat rapidly. Home — home — the magic word was ringing in her ears. Earnestly pouring out from her wraps to observe what changes had taken place during her absence, she scarcely noticed the silence of the man beside her, except when some eager question leaped to her lips and was instantly repressed by an upward glance at his frigid face.

Cold as a statue, dumb as a mummy, he sat. One might have thought him a dead man but for his handling of the whip and reins. He seemed to be plunged in a profound and painful reverie, and did not once break the silence from the time of their leaving the wharf until their arrival within sight of his own house.

They had passed beyond the city limits and on each side of them stretched wide snowy fields bounded by low stone walls. They were approaching the shores of the Arm, where many of the merchants of the town had erected substantial, comfortable houses for themselves.

When they stopped before a gate and the man jumped out to open it, Mr. Armour pulled himself together with an effort and looked down at Vivienne with a confused, "I beg your pardon."

"I did not speak," she said calmly.

"I thought you did," he replied; then touching his horse with the whip they again set out on their way, this time along a winding road bordered by evergreens.

"It was kind in you to come and meet me," said Vivienne when they drew up before a large, square white house with brilliantly lighted windows.

Mr. Armour murmured some unintelligible reply that convinced her he had not heard what she said.

"What curious behavior," she reflected. "He must be ill."

Mr. Armour was looking at the closed sleigh standing before the door.

"Who is going out to-night?" he asked of the man.

"Mrs. Colonibel and Colonel Armour, sir," said the coachman touching his cap. "There is a ball at Government House."

Mr. Armour turned to Vivienne and extended a helping hand, then drawing a latchkey from his pocket he threw open a large inner door.

Vivienne stepped in — stepped from the bitter cold of a Canadian winter night to the warmth and comfort of tropical weather. The large square hall was full of a reddish light. Heavy curtains, whose prevailing color was red, overhung each doorway. A group of tall palms stood in one corner and against them was placed the tinted statue of a lacrosse player. Pictures of Canadian scenery hung on the walls and over two of the doorways hung the heads and branching antlers of Nova Scotian moose.

Her quiet scrutiny of the hall over she found Mr. Armour was regarding her with a look of agitation on his usually impassive face.

"Will you be kind enough to take off your hat?" he said; "it shades your face."

The girl looked at him in surprise and removed the large felt hat that she wore. Somewhat to her amusement she discovered a huge mirror mounted on a marble bracket at her elbow. A passing glance at it showed that her smooth black hair was not dishevelled, but was coiled in the symmetrical rolls imperiously demanded by Dame Fashion as she reigned in Paris. Her face beneath was dark and glowing, her eyes composed as she would have them, and her resemblance to her dead father was extraordinary.

She looked expectantly at Mr. Armour. He bit his lip and without speaking drew aside a velvet *portière* with a hand shaking from some strong and overmastering emotion and signed to her to enter the drawing room.

L. M. MONTGOMERY

* * * * * * *

Lucy Maud Montgomery was born in 1874 at Clifton, Prince Edward Island and was educated at Prince of Wales College and Dalhousie University. After teaching for a few years she spent over a decade — with the exception of a brief stint in Halifax working as a proofreader and columnist for the newspaper the Echo — *keeping house for her grandmother. In 1911 she married the Rev. Ewan Macdonald and moved to Ontario, living in Leaksdale, Norval, and then Toronto, where she died in 1942. A prolific contributor to periodicals, she became world famous with the publication of her first novel,* Anne of Green Gables *(1908). In addition to seven Anne sequels, Montgomery published many more novels, several story collections, and other works. Since her death, she has been the subject of a number of biographies and critical studies. Many posthumous collections of her writings have also appeared, including selections from her correspondence and journals.*

The following journal entries are from The Selected Journals of L.M. Montgomery; Volume I: 1889-1910 *(1985) edited by Mario Rubio and Elizabeth Waterston. The entries date from the seven-month period in 1901-02 when Montgomery worked for the Halifax* Echo. *While Montgomery witnessed a number of interesting events during her second stay in Halifax, including a royal visit and the end of the Boer War, she was clearly not enamoured of the city and longed for her return to her beloved Cavendish.*

* * * * * * *

from **The Selected Journals of L.M. Montgomery**

Monday, Nov. 18, 1901
Echo Office
Halifax, N.S.

This has been one of the days when things reveal their naked, natural *cussedness*. I didn't sleep well last night and felt grumpy all day, and so did everyone else apparently. Then one of those wretched editorial jokes got off its trolley again this afternoon; and altogether life has seemed like a howling wilderness.

However, the cloud is lifting now. The paper has gone to press and somebody below in the business office has just sent me up a big molasses "kiss" in the copy box. This delicate attention has smoothed my ruffled plumage.

Well, "to resoom and to proceed": — after a week at the W.C.A. I removed to my present domicile at 23 Church St. I like it only fairly well....

I have had a hard time trying to arrange for enough spare minutes to do some writing. As my salary only suffices for board and bed and as it is against the law, not to mention the climate, to go about naked, I have to make enough money to clothe myself in other ways.

My first idea was to write in the evenings. Well, I tried it. I couldn't string two marketable ideas together. Besides, I had to keep my stockings darned and my buttons sewed on!

Then I determined to get up at six every morning to write before going to work! I did that twice — or maybe it was three times. Then I concluded that was impossible. I could not do good work in a chilly room on an empty stomach, especially if, as was often the case, I had been up late the night before. So I said to myself, very solemnly,

"Now, Maud, what are you going to do? Leaving the tenets of the Plymouth Brethren out of the question, you have to choose between two courses. You must either decamp back to the tight little Island or you must hit upon some plan to make possible the production of pot-boilers."

So Maud thought hard.

Now, it used to be at home, that I thought undisturbed solitude was necessary that the fire of genius might burn. I must be alone and the room must be quiet. It would have been the last thing to enter into my imagination to suppose that I could ever write anything at all, much less anything of value, in a newspaper office, with rolls of proof shooting down every few minutes, people coming and going and conversing, telephones ringing and machines thumping and dragging overhead. I would have laughed at the idea — yea , I would have laughed it to scorn. But the impossible has happened. I am of one opinion with the Irishman who said you could get used to anything, even to being hanged!

Every morning here I write and not bad stuff either. I have grown accustomed to stopping in the midst of a paragraph to interview a prowling caller and to pausing in full career after an elusive rhyme to read a batch of proof and snarled-up copy. It's all in the day's work — but I don't like it over and above. It's trying. However, it has to be done and I won't grumble, no, not one little bit!

I have got into some first-class magazines lately, so you may pat me on the back. Among others, the *Delineator, Smart Set* and *Ainslee's* have opened their fold to this poor wandering sheepkin of thorny literary ways.

Saturday, Nov. 23, 1901
Echo Office
Halifax

... I have just received a check for $25 from the Delineator for a story. *Watch me smile!*

Another week has come to an end. Tomorrow is Sunday, glory be! I have been indulging in a sort of religious dissipation ever since coming to Halifax — that is, I've been making the rounds of all the churches. Last Sunday evening I went up to the North End to the Universalist Church. I found it quite interesting but certainly would not care for it as a steady thing. It is much like a lecture and a concert combined. The pastor gave a very logical and painfully truthful talk on "What Do Men Really Believe concerning Immortality?" The music was charming and I enjoyed the whole service but couldn't exactly see where the religion came in. I couldn't help smiling as I imagined what some of the dear orthodox bodies in Cavendish would think of the whole performance. To be sure, they wouldn't understand half of it and the other half would probably fill them with horror.

The service was very simple. I was at the other extreme the Sunday I went to St. Luke's. It is very "high" and religious observance there has become positive mummery without pith or meaning. The kernel of Christianity is so shrouded in the husks of ritual that it is almost lost altogether.

I don't know what they are doing overhead in the composing room but they seem to be celebrating a very carnival of thumping and rolling and dragging. I expect every minute to see the ceiling come crashing in.

That composing room is a curious place. I ventured up one day and found myself in a big grimy room, with a lot of grimy figures bending over grimy galleys of type, and a grimy row of linotype machines along one side. It looked like a dingy workshop of gnomes. As for the linotype, I believe it is magic! It seems fairly to possess a brain of its own, so wonderful are the things it can do.

My next visit was to the basement — "Hell's Kitchen" as it is poetically termed here — where the big press takes a huge roll of white paper in at one end and drops it out of the other, cut and folded *Echoes*. Truly the epic of human genius in this century is its colossal mechanical contrivances. Two and three thousand years ago men wrote immortal poems. To-day they create marvellous inventions and bend the erstwhile undreamed-of forces of nature to their will. Which is the better, oh, ye gods of the Golden Age? After all, have we not lost as much as we have gained? The beautiful childhood of the world is gone forever.

I believe its happiest days were in the dead-and-gone centuries of its songsinging, love-making, war-waging youth!

Bless me, I have forgotten that I am in a newspaper office.

The great Haligonian event of the season was the Royal Visit in October. Halifax fairly stood on its head, tricked out in bunting which might be gay and gorgeous and patriotic enough but was certainly not beautiful. Our office was adorned with yellow-and-green and looked as if it had jaundice.

The Duke and Duchess arrived here on Saturday afternoon, October 19. Everybody had a holiday except us newspaper fags. However, we rushed things to get off by two o'clock. About eleven I slipped out and ran over to the Provincial building where I stood freezing for half an hour before the gates while some corner stone was being laid. At last I had my reward and when the carriage containing the Duke and Duchess left the gates I had a good, unhindered look at them.

Our future king is an insignificant man with a red nose. The duchess looks to be the best man of the two. She was a big, rather fine-looking woman dressed rather dowdily in black.

I got off at 2 o'clock but I did not go to the review on the common although I suppose everybody else in Halifax went. I had nobody to go with and I knew I wouldn't be able to see anything if I did go so I just stayed home and celebrated my quarter-holiday by reading a new magazine and eating candy.

In the evening I went out with Minnie MacDonald and her sister Kate to see the illuminations. They were all good and the warships were magnificent — "like one's childish dreams of fairyland," as Cynthia took good care to remark in her next "copy." There were twelve warships in port and all, hulls, spars and funnels, were picked out with electric lights. The effect against the inky blackness of the harbor was magical.

In due time it began to rain and as I did not have my umbrella with me, I got well drenched and went home in a very disgruntled mood, vowing that I had had enough of royal visits. I caught a fearful cold and my best hat has had a cowed, apologetic appearance ever since.

Well, I have at last brought this journal up to date and written, I doubt not, a vast deal of nonsense. But then, one must have a little nonsense somewhere to give zest to existence and there certainly isn't much elsewhere in my life. It is so deadly serious that it is no wonder my account of it is frivolous. So let it be!

Saturday, Dec. 8, 1901
Echo Office, Halifax

Have been busy of late — as if that were news indeedy! But I have been Busy with a capital B. 'Tending to office-work, writing pot-boilers, making Xmas presents — or buying them, which is just as harrowing — etc., etc., etc...

One of the "etcs" is a job I heartily detest. It makes my soul cringe. It is bad enough to have your flesh cringe but when it strikes into your soul it gets on your spiritual nerves terribly. We are giving all the firms who advertise with us a free "write up" of their holiday goods, and I have to visit all the stores, interview the proprietors, and crystallize my information into "two sticks" of copy. From three to five every afternoon I potter around the business blocks until my nose is purple with the cold and my fingers numb from scribbling down notes. So "no more until next time." Perhaps I shall have got back my self-respect by then. It has quite wilted under the haughty patronage of the Halifax clerks.

Wednesday, Dec. 12, 1901
Echo Office, Halifax

If I have not got back my self-respect I *have* got a new hat! It's an ill wind that blows no good and my disagreeable assignment has brought me some. The other evening I went in to write up the *Bon Marche*, which sets up to be *the* millinery establishment of Halifax. I found the proprietor very genial. He said he was delighted that the *Echo* had sent a lady and by way of encouraging it not to weary in well-doing he would send me up one of the new walking hats if I gave them a good write-up. I rather thought he was joking — but sure enough when the write-up came out yesterday up came the hat and a very pretty one it is, too. Thanks, *Bon Marche*.

Thursday, Dec. 20, 1901
Echo Office, Halifax

All the odd jobs that go a-begging in this establishment are handed over to the present scribe. The very queerest one up to date came yesterday.

The compositors were setting up a story called "A Royal Betrothal," taken from an English paper, and when about half through they lost the copy. Whereupon Mr. Taunton requested me to write an "end" for the story. I gasped, not seeing how I could. I had never seen the story and what was set up was not enough to give me any insight into the final development. Moreover, my knowledge of royal love affairs is limited and I have not been accustomed to write with flippant levity of kings and queens.

However, I went home last night and fell to work. I got it done somehow or other. So to-day out came "The Royal Betrothal" bravely and as yet nobody has guessed where the "seam" comes in. If the original author ever sees it I wonder what he — or she — will think.

PAULINE JOHNSON

*   *   *   *   *   *   *

Pauline Johnson was born on the Six Nations Indian Reserve near Brantford, Ontario in 1861. The daughter of a Mohawk chief and an English woman who was related to the American writer William Dean Howells, Johnson received very little formal education. In 1884 she began her literary career with a contribution to the New York magazine Gem of Poetry *and would eventually appear in major periodicals like* The Pall Mall Gazette, Harper's Weekly, *and* Saturday Night. *Her first book of poems,* White Wampum *(1895), was followed by a second poetry collection,* Canadian Born *(1903), and by a collection of tales,* Legends of Vancouver *(1911). Starting in 1892, Johnson became a popular performer, reciting her poetry on tours that took her not only throughout Canada, but also to the United States and England. In 1909 she retired to Vancouver, where she died in 1913. A third collection of her poetry,* Flint and Feather *(1913), and two collections of her short fiction,* The Shagannappi *(1913) and* The Moccasin Maker *(1913), appeared not long after her death.*

"The Guard of the Eastern Gate" was first published in Johnson's collection Canadian Born. Wilfred Campbell later included the poem in The Oxford Book of Canadian Verse *(1913). Johnson, who spent nearly two weeks bed-ridden in Halifax during her Boer War national tour of 1900, even surpasses her fellow Imperialist Kipling in the use of martial imagery to depict the city.*

*   *   *   *   *   *   *

The Guard of the Eastern Gate

Halifax sits on her hills by the sea
    In the might of her pride, —
Invincible, terrible, beautiful, she
    With a sword at her side.

To right and to left of her, battlements rear
    And fortresses frown;
While she sits on her throne without favour or fear,
    With her cannon as crown.

Coast-guard and sentinel, watch of the weal
    Of a nation she keeps;
But her hand is encased in a gauntlet of steel,
    And her thunder but sleeps.

ARCHIBALD MACMECHAN

*   *   *   *   *   *   *

Archibald MacMechan was born in 1862 at Berlin (Kitchener), Ontario and was educated at the University of Toronto and Johns Hopkins University. Not long after completing his Ph.D., he became professor of English at Dalhousie University in Halifax, where he would teach for over forty years. A prolific contributor to a wide variety of newspapers and periodicals, MacMechan also published more than a dozen books, including Sagas of the Sea *(1923),* Headwaters of Canadian Literature *(1924), and* There Go the Ships *(1928). As one of Canada's most accomplished local historians, he wrote numerous pieces about his adopted city and its landmarks. His two-part article "Halifax in Books" (*Acadiensis *April-July 1906) was the first study of Halifax's depiction in literature. Following the Halifax Explosion, he was appointed Director of the Halifax Disaster Record Office; however, his official history of the disaster wasn't published until 1978, when Graham Metson collected it in* The Halifax Explosion, December 6, 1917. *MacMechan died in Halifax in 1933.*

"A Day in Dolcefar" appeared in MacMechan's collection of essays on Nova Scotia, The Book of Ultima Thule *(1927). As a token of his affection for the province and its capital, MacMechan referred to Nova Scotia as Ultima Thule and to Halifax as Dolcefar (Italian for "pleasant doing"). In addition to reflecting MacMechan's love for the city, the essay typifies a lost era when, in the words of one of his students, Hugh MacLennan, Halifax had "her back to the continent and her face to the Old Country."*

*   *   *   *   *   *   *

A Day in Dolcefar

Dolcefar, is, of course, not the real name of this city; but, when I tell you that it is the capital of Ultima Thule, you will easily find it on the map. I gave it this name privately because it has given me almost everything I ever wanted in this world, and because one of the most agreeable of pastimes is inventing friendly nick-names for your friends. Moreover, if you will search into the title, you will perceive that it connotes qualities, whereof some critics would make a reproach. There be some who hold that our city lacketh energy, enterprise, all sorts of modern commercial virtues, — virtues which bring their own reward of fat balances at the bankers. In other words, Dolcefar is a quiet nook in a bustling, rushing continent; it has discovered the value of leisure; it is a haven for such as rate life above dollars.

Each city has a face, a body and a more or less imperfect soul, of its own. Some are after a set pattern, — know one, know all, — but Dolcefar is unlike any other that I know. The best time to get close to the heart of Dolcefar is on a Saturday in summer.

Saturn, the gloomy planet, has little influence over his day in the city of Dolcefar; the seventh is usually the brightest day of the week. If it should happen to dawn overcast, the unwonted bustle and stir of the population seems to dispel the sea-mist, or the cloud. Besides, in these latitudes, a dull morning is no bad sign of a fair afternoon; and with us, the afternoon is the better portion of the day. The half is greater than the whole.

Cities differ much in their customs. In a southern city I know well, the housewife, attended by her black cook, with ample basket on her arm, sallies forth on Saturday evening to do her marketing for Sunday. There are long processions of her, passing up and down those endless arcades of busy stalls that stretch from street to street; and there is reason in the custom. Here our thrifty Northerner performs this duty in the morning; for the market-folk bring their butter and eggs into the city at dawn, or earlier; and the first to come is first served. The market is held in picturesque, mediaeval fashion upon the open street. Their wares are disposed along the kerbstone, while the vendors stand behind them in the gutter. White Ultima-Thulians they are, for the most part, but at one end are black Africans, the descendants of slaves, while near them, red Indians squat against a wall, behind piles of cleanly baskets. On one side, a soldier with his lethal weapons, is on perpetual guard, standing in a little sentry-box, or pacing up and down his appointed beat. Hither repair the house-keepers of Dolcefar, before breakfast even, with bag and basket. All morning, they are coming and going, up and down the market; you will meet everyone you know down town on a Saturday morning. The men are busy too, in banks and offices, cramming a day's work into four hours. Many are concerned with English letters; for we have direct communication with the motherland; and the English mail bulks large in the mind of Dolcefar. Grocers' waggons and butchers' carts rush to and fro in fierce career, with materials for a thousand Sunday dinners. The Saturday forenoon is the active part of the week.

In the afternoon, the city makes holiday and devotes itself to various forms of athletic sport, either actively or vicariously. At two o'clock, there is much stir about the Royal Ultima Thulian Yacht Squadron. The club-house has the aspect of a dumpy man who has drawn his cloak close around him against the wind, and it stands on a high wharf by the water-side. The swift, new-fangled boats have their moorings directly opposite; they are hovering about, ready to start at the firing of the gun. At the signal, they dart off on long stretches to the harbour-mouth, past Thrum Cap, to the open sea, or, if need be, they can find ample courses within the great land-locked haven. Every Saturday there is a breeze; and every Saturday, there is a race. The blue water is alive with white skimming sails. An hour later, the ladies begin to arrive in gala dresses, to listen to the band, drink tea, talk to their friends and watch the races finish. It is entertaining, even to consider the water from a chair on the wide verandah of the second storey.

About the time that the yachts begin their race, the first arrivals appear at the tennis-grounds. They are young business men, who want to make the most of their one chance in the week to practise. The lady players, the enthusiasts, are not long behind them. By three o'clock, all the courts are busy, and the blackboard is covered with a waiting-list of those, who may console themselves with Milton's famous anticipation, "They also *serve*, who only stand and wait." From the little pavilion on the terrace, the five nets make one white line down the centre, and the twenty active combatants, advancing, receding so swiftly on the green, seem to be engaged in the figures of some strange dance. On Saturday, the "tea-members" visit the grounds, those who are past their dancing-days. To them and to the thirsty players, tea is dispensed from the pavilion at five o'clock, tea being almost as much a universal lubricant in Dolcefar as in China. If you do not play, you can sit on the benches at the side and look on. A great elm frames part of the blue harbour within the curve of its lower branches, and shows you the white sails passing and re-passing. Play will last far into the long northern twilight, as long in fact, as the ball can be seen or felt.

Not a pistol-shot away are the golf-links. They are not upon the sea-sand, nor are they famous for extent; but they are sufficient; they are just on the outskirts of the city, and can be easily reached from any quarter. There is a large attendance this afternoon of men golfers, in groups of two generally, with attendant caddies. The club-house was the lodge of an old estate at the end of some woods. Old stone walls, a grove of pines, the new road running through the grounds of an old privateersman delimit these links and afford the picturesque, if golfers care for the picturesque, or have an eye for anything but the small white sphere they so unceasingly pursue.

If you walk up the street for three minutes from the first hole of the links, you will come to an old-fashioned house standing back from the road. It bears the name of a family seat in England, and was built and christened by a graduate of Oxford more than a century ago. He was a judge and a classical scholar, whose fame is preserved in the *Dictionary of National Biography*. He left his mark on the history of Ultima Thule, and rather a black mark it is; but the local fame of the old mansion rests on different grounds. In a small enclosure, fenced in and not unlike a pound or a lot in a cemetery, the quoit club meets about three, every Saturday in the season, to hurl the discus, possibly "in the high Roman fashion," I cannot say. Two pitches are sufficient for the players, and there are always onlookers "in the shade of the whispering trees." Under this pleasant shelter, admirals and generals, viceroys and princes of the blood have been proud to sit, as guests of the club. Silver cups and wooden spoons are here contended for, not without dust and heat. As ladies are not eligible for membership, it follows that tea is not the club's diversion. A strange and famous refreshment called "hodge-podge" is served here once a year, on a gala day, when the members bring their friends to share their pleasures. Sometimes it is apparently as fatiguing to watch the play as to stand in the sun and hurl the massive quoit.

But Saturday afternoon is passing away and half our pastimes are unreviewed. Northward lie the spacious and beautiful grounds of the athletic club, we are all so proud of. As likely as not, a cricket-match is going on, watched from under the elms by a small assembly of the fashionable and the connoisseurs. Visiting clubs come from afar, and some are famous. There is room in the corners of the grounds for quoits, bowls and tennis. Some members in costume that is almost Greek, or Fiji, in its simplicity are practising for coming struggles on the track or in the football field. Across the way, the soldiers are at cricket at the foot of the glacis. On the common, the sons of the *commonalty* are busy with baseball, for the necessary apparatus is cheap, and neither uniform nor level ground is needed. If you push on farther north, till you reach the upper end of the harbour, you will find that many boats have been hired, and are rowing about among the wonderful war-ships, which are always at anchor there. The lean out-riggers of the local rowing-club are out for practice, as well as the gigs and cutters of the men-o'-war. From the floating bath comes a perpetual uproar of laughing, boyish shrieking, and splashing.

But you could not see all this in one day, with comfort. It would be wiser to turn south from the quoit-grounds, and walk to the pride of Dolcefar, the three-mile fiord we call the "Arm." It is quite near, and running up into the land makes the ground on which Dolcefar stands almost an island. From the landward end, you can look out to the harbour-mouth, where the squat little light-house made out of a razeed martello tower shows the way to hesitating ships on the dark nights. The shores are rather steep and wooded, and along the northern bank are stately houses of our well-to-do people. Each has its own name, as "Bircham," "Belmont," "Oaklands," "Maplewood," "Winwick"; for Dolcefar has rather a pretty knack in christening places. The "Arm" is as safe and pretty a place for boating as can be well imagined, and so it is a favourite haunt of those who affect the frail canoe. Many are the canoes and the boats of heavier build. Except where commercialism has stamped its infernal hoof, the "Arm" is a perpetual delight. Landscape becomes well-known in every feature, but the subtle way that water, and especially tide-water seems to change the face of the mere earth beside it creates a charm that never grows old. On the city-side, is a boat-house, empty this afternoon, and a bathing-house which is crowded. The floats about the swimming pool are rich in anatomical studies. On the country-side many picnic parties are making fires on the shingle, and boiling the kettle for tea. When night falls, there may be bon-fires along the bank, with merry youths and maidens carolling to the tinkling of a mandolin; and the boats on the water will draw near and listen.

Such is the city of Dolcefar, on a Saturday in the pleasant months of the year. It is the one city of its size on this continent which possesses a summer climate, that permits white people to work and play with comfort. Dolcefar in its wisdom chooses to play, and to make time for play. It sets store by leisure, and its citizens are sportsmen, devotees of the rod and gun, which they use in their season, or think of care-free days spent along the streams or in the woods. Chess, the leisurely king of games, is much cultivated. In short, Dolcefar is resolved to live in a rational way, and to secure a time for healthy recreation from the fleeting days.

This is not our city's only virtue. There is no hospitality like the hospitality of Dolcefar; there is no kindness like its kindness, when you are sick or in trouble. It is rather a pity that her sister-cities do not try to know better this castle of wise indolence, this town of pleasant doing.

HUGH MACLENNAN

*   *   *   *   *   *   *

Hugh MacLennan was born at Glace Bay, Nova Scotia in 1907 and grew up in Halifax. He was educated at Dalhousie University, Oxford, and Princeton. In 1935 he became a teacher at Lower Canada College in Montreal, a position which he occupied until the success of his classic novel about the Halifax Explosion, Barometer Rising *(1941), resulted in his spending a year in New York on a Guggenheim Fellowship. He later returned to teaching but left again in 1945 following the appearance of his second novel,* Two Solitudes *(1945), which won him the first of five Governor General's Awards that he would receive for his work. Although he eventually resumed his academic career, at McGill University, Mac-Lennan was active for several decades as one of Canada's leading novelists, essayists, and commentators. His distinguished career has been the subject of several critical works and a biography, Elspeth Cameron's* Hugh MacLennan: A Writer's Life *(1981).*

"An Orange from Portugal" first appeared in Chatelaine *(December 1948) and was then collected in MacLennan's* Cross-Country *(1949), which also reprinted his memorable essay celebrating Halifax, "Portrait of a City." Part memoir and part fiction, the story draws on MacLennan's vivid recollections of Halifax during the "war Christmases" of 1915 and 1916.*

*   *   *   *   *   *   *

An Orange From Portugal

I suppose all of us, when we think of Christmas, recall Charles Dickens and our own childhood. So today, from an apartment in Montreal, looking across the street to a new neon sign, I think back to Dickens and Halifax and the world suddenly becomes smaller, shabbier and more comfortable, and one more proof is registered that comfort is a state of mind, having little to do with the number of springs hidden inside your mattress or the upholstery in your car.

Charles Dickens should have lived in Halifax. If he had, that brown old town would have acquired a better reputation in Canada than it now enjoys, for all over the world people would have known what it was like. Halifax, especially a generation or two ago, was a town Dickens could have used.

There were dingy basement kitchens all over the town where rats were caught every day. The streets were full of teamsters, hard-looking men with lean jaws, most of them, and at the entrance to the old North Street Station cab drivers in long coats would mass behind a heavy anchor chain and terrify travellers with bloodcurdling howls as they bid for fares. Whenever there was a southeast wind, harbour bells moaned behind the wall of fog that cut the town off from the rest of the world. Queer faces peered at you suddenly from doorways set flush with the streets. When a regiment held a smoker in the old Masonic Hall you could see a line beginning to form in the early morning, waiting for the big moment at midnight when the doors would be thrown open to the town and any man could get a free drink who could reach the hogsheads.

For all these things Dickens would have loved Halifax, even for the pompous importers who stalked to church on Sunday mornings, swinging their canes and complaining that they never had a chance to hear a decent sermon. He would have loved it for the waifs and strays and beachcombers and discharged soldiers and sailors whom the respectable never seemed to notice, for all the numerous aspects of the town that made Halifax deplorable and marvellous.

If Dickens had been given a choice of a Canadian town in which to spend Christmas, that's where I think he would have gone, for his most obvious attitude toward Christmas was that it was necessary. Dickens was no scientist or organizer. Instead of liking The People, he simply liked people. And so, inevitably, he liked places where accidents were apt to happen. In Halifax accidents were happening all the time. Think of the way he writes about Christmas — a perfect Christmas for him was always a chapter of preposterous accidents. No, I don't think he would have chosen to spend his Christmas in Westmount or Toronto, for he'd be fairly sure that neither of those places needed it.

Today we know too much. Having become democratic by ideology, we are divided into groups which eye each other like dull strangers at a dull party, polite in public and nasty when each others' backs are turned. Today we are informed by those who know that if we tell children about Santa Claus we will probably turn them into neurotics. Today we believe in universal justice and in universal war to effect it, and because Santa Claus gives the rich more than he gives the poor, lots of us think it better that there should be no Santa Claus at all. Today we are technicians, and the more progressive among us see no reason why love and hope should not be organized in a department of the government, planned by a politician and administered by trained specialists. Today we have a super-colossal Santa Claus for The Customer: he sits in the window of a department store in a cheap red suit, stringy whiskers and a mask which is a caricature of a face, and for a month before every Christmas he laughs continually with a vulgar roar. The sounds of his laughter come from a record played over and over, and the machine in his belly that produces the bodily contortions has a number in the patent office in Washington.

In the old days in Halifax we never thought about the meaning of the word democracy; we were all mixed up together in a general deplorability. So the only service any picture of those days can render is to help prove how far we have advanced since then. The first story I have to tell has no importance and not even much of a point. It is simply the record of how one boy felt during a Christmas that now seems remote enough to belong to the era of Tom Cratchit. The second story is about the same. The war Christmases I remember in Halifax were not jolly ones. In a way they were half-tragic, but there may be some significance in the fact that they are literally the only ones I can still remember. It was a war nobody down there understood. We were simply a part of it, swept into it from the mid-Victorian age in which we were all living until 1914.

On Christmas Eve in 1915 a cold northeaster was blowing through the town with the smell of coming snow on the wind. All day our house was hushed for a reason I didn't understand, and I remember being sent out to play with some other boys in the middle of the afternoon. Supper was a silent meal. And then, immediately after we had finished, my father put on the great-coat of his new uniform and went to the door and I saw the long tails of the coat blowing out behind him in the flicker of a faulty arc light as he half-ran up to the corner. We heard bagpipes, and almost immediately a company of soldiers appeared swinging down Spring Garden Road from old Dalhousie. It was very cold as we struggled up to the corner after my father, and he affected not to notice us. Then the pipes went by playing "The Blue Bonnets," the lines of khaki men went past in the darkness and my father fell in behind the last rank and faded off down the half-lit street, holding his head low against the wind to keep his flat military cap from blowing off, and my mother tried to hide her feelings by saying what a shame the cap didn't fit him properly. She told my sister and me how nice it was of the pipers to have turned out on such a cold day to see the men off, for pipe music was the only kind my father liked. It was all very informal. The men of that unit — almost entirely a local one — simply left their homes the way my father had done and joined the column and the column marched down Spring Garden Road to the ship along the familiar route most of them had taken to church all their lives. An hour later we heard tugboat whistles and then the foghorn of the transport and we knew he was on his way. As my sister and I hung up our stockings on the mantelpiece I wondered whether the vessel was no farther out than Thrum Cap or whether it had already reached Sambro.

It was a bleak night for children to hang up their stockings and wait for Santa Claus, but next morning we found gifts in them as usual, including a golden orange in each toe. It was strange to think that the very night my father had left the house, a strange old man, remembering my sister and me, had come into it. We thought it was a sign of good luck.

That was 1915, and some time during the following year a boy at school told me there was no Santa Claus and put his case so convincingly that I believed him.

Strictly speaking, this should have been the moment of my first step toward becoming a neurotic. Maybe it was, but there were so many other circumstances to compete with it, I don't know whether Santa Claus was responsible for what I'm like now or not. For about a week after discovering the great deception I wondered how I could develop a line of conduct which would prevent my mother from finding out that I knew who filled our stockings on Christmas Eve. I hated to disappoint her in what I knew was a great pleasure. After a while I forgot all about it. Then, shortly before Christmas, a cable arrived saying that my father was on his way home. He hadn't been killed like the fathers of other boys at school; he was being invalided home as a result of excessive work as a surgeon in the hospital.

We had been living with my grandmother in Cape Breton, so my mother rented a house in Halifax sight unseen, we got down there in time to meet his ship when it came in, and then we all went to the new house. This is the part of my story which reminds me of Charles Dickens again. Five minutes after we entered the house it blew up. This was not the famous Halifax explosion; we had to wait another year for that. This was our own private explosion. It smashed half the windows in the other houses along the block, it shook the ground like an earthquake and it was heard for a mile.

I have seen many queer accidents in Halifax, but none which gave the reporters more satisfaction than ours did. For a house to blow up suddenly in our district was unusual, so the press felt some explanation was due the public. Besides, it was nearly Christmas and local news was hard to find. The moment the first telephone call reached the newspaper offices to report the accident, they knew the cause. Gas had been leaking in our district for years and a few people had even complained about it. In our house, gas had apparently backed in from the city mains, filling partitions between the walls and lying stagnant in the basement. But this was the first time anyone could prove that gas had been leaking. The afternoon paper gave the story.

DOCTOR HUNTS GAS LEAK WITH BURNING MATCH — FINDS IT!

When my father was able to talk, which he couldn't do for several days because the skin had been burned off his hands and face, he denied the story about the match. According to modern theory this denial should have precipitated my second plunge toward neurosis, for I had distinctly seen him with the match in his hand, going down to the basement to look for the gas and complaining about how careless people were. However, those were ignorant times and I didn't realize I might get a neurosis. Instead of brooding and deciding to close my mind to reality from then on in order to preserve my belief in the veracity and faultlessness of my father, I wished to God he had been able to tell his story sooner and stick to it. After all, he was a first-class doctor, but what would prospective patients think if every time they heard his name they saw a picture of an absent-minded veteran looking for a gas leak in a dark basement with a lighted match?

It took two whole days for the newspaper account of our accident to settle. In the meantime the house was temporarily ruined, school children had denuded the chandelier in the living-room of its prisms, and it was almost Christmas. My sister was still away at school, so my mother, my father and I found ourselves in a single room in an old residential hotel on Barrington Street. I slept on a cot and they nursed their burns in a huge bed which opened out of the wall. The bed had a mirror on the bottom of it, and it was equipped with such a strong spring that it crashed into place in the wall whenever they got out of it. I still remember my father sitting up in it with one arm in a sling from the war, and his face and head in white bandages. He was philosophical about the situation, including the vagaries of the bed, for it was his Calvinistic way to permit himself to be comfortable only when things were going badly.

The hotel was crowded and our meals were brought to us by a boy called Chester, who lived in the basement near the kitchen. That was all I knew about Chester at first; he brought our meals, he went to school only occasionally, and his mother was ill in the basement. But as long as my memory lasts, that Christmas of 1916 will be Chester's Christmas.

He was a waif of a boy. I never knew his last name, and wherever he is now, I'm certain he doesn't remember me. But for a time I can say without being sentimental that I loved him.

He was white-faced and thin, with lank hair on top of a head that broke back at right angles from a high narrow forehead. There were always holes in his black stockings, his handed-down pants were so badly cut that one leg was several inches longer than the other and there was a patch on the right seat of a different colour from the rest of the cloth. But he was proud of his clothes; prouder than anyone I've ever seen over a pair of pants. He explained that they were his father's and his father had worn them at sea.

For Chester, nobody was worth considering seriously unless he was a seaman. Instead of feeling envious of the people who lived upstairs in the hotel, he seemed to feel sorry for them because they never went to sea. He would look at the old ladies with the kind of eyes that Dickens discovered in children's faces in London: huge eyes as trusting as a bird-dog's, but old, as though they had forgotten how to cry long ago.

I wondered a lot about Chester — what kind of a room they had in the basement, where they ate, what his mother was like. But I was never allowed in the basement. Once I walked behind the hotel to see if I could look through the windows, but they were only six or eight inches above the ground and they were covered with snow. I gathered that Chester liked it down there because it was warm, and once he was down, nobody ever bothered him.

The days went past, heavy and grey and cold. Soon it was the day before Christmas again, and I was still supposed to believe in Santa Claus. I found myself confronted by a double crisis.

I would have to hang up my stocking as usual, but how could my parents, who were still in bed, manage to fill it? And how would they feel when the next morning came and my stocking was still empty? This worry was overshadowed only by my concern for Chester.

On the afternoon of Christmas Eve he informed me that this year, for the first time in his life, Santa Claus was really going to remember him. "I never ett a real orange and you never did neether because you only get real oranges in Portugal. My old man says so. But Santy Claus is going to bring me one this year. That means the old man's still alive."

"Honest, Chester? How do you know?" Everyone in the hotel knew that his father, who was a quartermaster, was on a slow convoy to England.

"Mrs. Urquhart says so."

Everyone in the hotel also knew Mrs. Urquhart. She was a tiny old lady with a harsh voice who lived in the room opposite ours on the ground floor with her unmarried sister. Mrs. Urquhart wore a white lace cap and carried a cane. Both old ladies wore mourning, Mrs. Urquhart for two dead husbands, her sister for Queen Victoria. They were a trial to Chester because he had to carry hot tea upstairs for them every morning at seven.

"Mrs. Urquhart says if Santy Claus brings me real oranges it means he was talkin' to the old man and the old man told him

I wanted one. And if Santy Claus was talkin' to the old man, it means the old man's alive, don't it?"

Much of this was beyond me until Chester explained further.

"Last time the old man was home I seed some oranges in a store window, but he wouldn't get me one because if he buys stuff in stores he can't go on being a seaman. To be a seaman you got to wash out your insides with rum every day and rum costs lots of money. Anyhow, store oranges ain't real."

"How do you know they aren't?"

"My old man says so. He's been in Portugal and he picks real ones off trees. That's where they come from. Not from stores. Only my old man and the people who live in Portugal has ever ett real oranges."

Someone called and Chester disappeared into the basement. An hour or so later, after we had eaten the supper he brought to us on a tray, my father told me to bring the wallet from the pocket of his uniform which was hanging in the cupboard. He gave me some small change and sent me to buy grapes from my mother at a corner fruit store. When I came back with the grapes I met Chester in the outer hall. His face was beaming and he was carrying a parcel wrapped in brown paper.

"Your old man give me a two-dollar bill," he said. "I got my old lady a Christmas present."

I asked him if it was medicine.

"She don't like medicine," he said. "When she's feelin' bad she wants rum."

When I got back to our room I didn't tell my father what Chester had done with his two dollars. I hung up my stocking on the old-fashioned mantelpiece, the lights were put out and I was told to go to sleep.

An old flickering arc light hung in the street almost directly in front of the hotel, and as I lay in the dark pretending to be asleep the ceiling seemed to be quivering, for the shutters fitted badly and the room could never be completely darkened. After a time I heard movement in the room, then saw a shadowy figure near the mantelpiece. I closed my eyes tight, heard the swish of tissue paper, then the sounds of someone getting back into bed.

A fog horn, blowing in the harbour and heralding bad weather, was also audible.

After what seemed to me a long time I heard heavy breathing from the bed. I got up, crossed the room carefully and felt the stocking in the dark. My fingers closed on a round object in its toe. Well, I thought, one orange would be better than none.

In those days hardly any children wore pyjamas, at least not in Nova Scotia. And so a minute later, when I was sneaking down the dimly lit hall of the hotel in a white nightgown, heading for the basement stairs with the orange in my hand, I was a fairly conspicuous object. Just as I was putting my hand to the knob of the basement door I heard a tapping sound and ducked under the main stairs that led to the second floor of the hotel. The tapping came near, stopped, and I knew somebody was standing still, listening, only a few feet away.

A crisp voice said, "You naughty boy, come out of there."

I waited a moment and then moved into the hall. Mrs. Urquhart was standing before me in her black dress and white cap, one hand on the handle of her cane.

"You ought to be ashamed of yourself, at this hour of the night. Go back to your room at once!"

As I went back up the hall I was afraid the noise had wakened my father. The big door creaked as I opened it and looked up at the quivering maze of shadows on the ceiling. Somebody on the bed was snoring and it seemed to be all right. I slipped into my cot and waited for several minutes, than got up again and replaced the orange in the toe of the stocking and carefully put the other gifts on top of it. As soon as I reached my cot again I fell asleep with the sudden fatigue of children.

The room was full of light when I woke up; not sunlight but the grey luminosity of filtered light reflected off snow. My parents were sitting up in bed and Chester was standing inside the door with our breakfast. My father was trying to smile under his bandages and Chester had a grin so big it showed the gap in his front teeth. The moment I had been worrying about was finally here.

The first thing I must do was display enthusiasm for my parents' sake. I went to my stocking and emptied it on my cot while Chester watched me out of the corner of his eye. Last of all the orange rolled out.

"I bet it ain't real," Chester said.

My parents said nothing as he reached over and held it up to the light.

"No," he said. "It ain't real," and dropped it on the cot again. Then he put his hand into his pocket and with an effort managed to extract a medium-sized orange. "Look at mine," he said. "Look what it says right here."

On the skin of the orange, printed daintily with someone's pen, were the words PRODUCE OF PORTUGAL.

"So my old man's been talkin' to Santy Claus, just like Mrs. Urquhart said."

There was never any further discussion in our family about whether Santa Claus was or was not real. Perhaps Mrs. Urquhart was the actual cause of my neurosis. I'm not a scientist, so I don't know.

THOMAS H. RADDALL

*   *   *   *   *   *   *

Thomas H. Raddall was born at Hythe (Kent), England in 1903 and moved to Halifax in 1913. After graduating from the Halifax Academy he worked as a wireless operator from 1919 to 1922. In 1923 he became an accountant for the McLeod Pulp and Paper Co. in Queens County, Nova Scotia. Six years later, he joined the staff of Mersey Paper in Liverpool. During the late twenties and early thirties he began his writing career with contributions to such periodicals as Sea Stories, Excitement, *and* Blackwood's. *In 1938 he left his job to write full time. The author of close to thirty books, Raddall has received many honours and awards, including three Governor General's Awards. Although he spent less than ten years of his life in Halifax, his attachment to the city remained very strong. In addition to writing the classic history* Halifax, Warden of the North *(1948), he utilized Halifax as a setting in five novels:* His Majesty's Yankees *(1942),* Roger Sudden *(1944),* The Nymph and the Lamp *(1950),* The Governor's Lady *(1960), and* Hangman's Beach *(1966). He has also written numerous articles about the city.*

"Winter's Tale" was first published in the January 1936 issue of Blackwood's. *The story was later reprinted in the US magazine* Fiction Parade and Gold Book Magazine *(March 1936) and was then collected in Raddall's first short story collection,* The Pied Piper of Dipper Creek *(1939). One of Raddall's most powerful and most-anthologized stories, it describes a fourteen-year-old boy's harrowing experiences in the aftermath of the Halifax Explosion of December 6, 1917. As Raddall's memoir,* In My Time *(1976), testifies, the story is largely autobiographical.*

*   *   *   *   *   *   *

Winter's Tale

The air in the classroom was warm and rather stuffy because it had snowed a little the night before, and Stevens the janitor had stoked up his great furnace fiercely. Grade Nine, coming in rosy-cheeked from the snow outside, found it oppressive, but nobody dared to open a window. Old Mr. Burtle, who conducted the educational fortunes of Grade Nine, was Principal of the school and a martyr to asthma.

The rest of the big brick school was empty and silent. The lower grades were not required to answer roll-call until half-past nine. It was just one minute past nine by the clock on the classroom wall when James hung his school-bag on the back of his seat and flung an arithmetic manual on the desk. He also produced two pencils and sharpened them with his jack-knife, dropping the shavings on the floor and keeping a wary eye on Old Gander Burtle, who disapproved of that procedure. All about him was a bustle of preparation. Fifty boys and girls were busy with books, pencils, and erasers.

"Attention!" demanded Old Gander, with his asthmatic cough. Everyone sat up very straight. "We shall sing the morning hymn." The class arose with a clatter, shuffled a little, and then burst raucously into "Awake my soul and with the sun" as Old Gander raised his bony forefinger. James had a point of vantage when they stood up to sing; for his desk was near the windows and he could look down into the street, two storeys below. It was certainly too nice a morning to spend indoors. The sky was blue, without a speck of cloud anywhere, sun very bright on the snow, and wisps of smoke rising straight into the air from a forest of chimneys that stretched away southward. The snow was not deep enough for sleighing. There were a few wheel-tracks in the street, and the sidewalks were a mess of brown slush already, and when the several hundred kids of the lower grades had scampered in, there would be nothing but thin black puddles. Grade Nine intoned a long "Ahhh-men!" and sat down. It was five minutes past nine by the clock on the wall.

The act of sitting down in unison always produced a clatter, but this morning the effect was astounding. The hardwood floor began to move up and down very rapidly, like a gigantic piston of some sort; the walls swayed drunkenly to and fro, so that the blackboards came down and were followed by plaster, crumbling away from the walls in lumps and whole sheets. The great clock dropped from its fastening high on the wall, missed Old Gander's head by an inch, and spewed a tangle of springs and cogs over the heaving floor. The opaque glass in the door of the boys' coat-room sprang across the classroom, sailing over James' head, and went to pieces in a mighty splatter on the wall in front of him. The windows vanished, sashes and all. Not only the inner everyday windows, but the big storm-windows that were screwed on outside every Fall and taken off in the spring. The room, the big echoing school, the whole world, were filled with tremendous sound that came in waves, each visible in breakers of plaster dust.

Then the sound was gone, as suddenly as it had come, and in its place there was a strange and awful hush that was emphasized, somehow, by distant noises of falling plaster and tinkling glass. Grade Nine was on its feet, staring at Old Gander through a fog of plaster dust, and Old Gander stared back at them, with his scanty grey hair all on end, and his long seamed face the colour of snow when rain is turning to slush. A waft of cold air came in from the street, where the windows should have been, and the fog cleared before it. A girl broke the silence, screaming shrilly. James perceived that her cheek was laid open from ear to mouth, with a great red river pouring down her chin, and that others were putting fingers to cut faces and heads, and staring strangely at the stains. Grade Nine was covered with plaster dust, and looked like a company of startled ghosts, and when James saw the thin red trickles running out of those white masks he knew he was dreaming, because things like that did not really happen. The girl with the red mask screamed again, and there was a chorus of screams, and then with one impulse the class turned and fled, as if it were Friday afternoon fire practice. James heard them clattering down the stairs into the street, with glass grinding and tinkling under their shoes. For a moment James was poised for similar flight, but in that moment he remembered the time he was frightened by a signboard groaning in the wind at night, and Dad's deep steady voice saying, "Never run from anything son, till you've had a good look at it. Most times it's not worth running from."

Old Gander was standing beside his desk like a statue, staring at the lone survivor of his class. His watery blue eyes seemed awfully large. They looked like Mum's breakfast saucers. James moved jerkily towards him, licking plaster-dust from his lips. "What is it, Mister Burtle?" His own voice seemed queer and very far away, the way it sounded when you talked in your sleep and woke yourself up. Old Gander gazed at James in enormous surprise, as though he had never seen James before, as if James were speaking some foreign language not authorized by the School Board. Then he said in his old asthmatic voice, "James! Is that you, James?" and without waiting for a reply he added, as though it were the most ordinary thing in the world, "Some of the little boys have been playing with dynamite in the basement." James nodded slowly. Old Gander knew everything. The kids in the lower grades said he had eyes in the back of his head. He was a very wise old man.

They stood, silent, in the wrecked classroom for a space of minutes. Another gust of chill air stirred the thin hairs that stood out like a halo from the schoolmaster's head.

"You are a good boy, James," murmured Old Gander in a dazed voice. James squared his shoulders instinctively. After all, he was a sergeant in the school cadet corps. It was all right for the others to go if they wanted to. Old Gander passed a shaking hand back over his head, smoothing down the straggled hairs. Bits of plaster fell upon his dusty shoulders in a small shower, like a brittle sort of dandruff. "I think," he said vaguely, "we'd better see if there is any fire."

"Yes, sir," James said. It occurred to him that Mr. Burtle ought to look in the basement where the little boys had played with the dynamite. "I'll go through the upstairs classrooms, sir."

"Very good," murmured Old Gander, as if James were a superior officer. "I will search the lower floor and then the basement," And he added, "Don't stay up here very long, James." They separated.

James passed from room to room on the second floor. Each was like the one he had left, with blackboards tumbled off walls, heaps of plaster, doors hanging splintered in the jambs. Along the south side of the school the windows had disappeared into the street, but on the north side the shattered sashes were festooned over desks, and shards of glass in the tumbled plaster gave it the glitter of snow. The big assembly hall occupied most of the north side. Miraculously, the doors were still in place but they refused to open. One was split badly in the panel, and James peeped through at a tangle of wood, piled against the doors on the inside. He thrust an arm through the hole and pushed some of the rubbish aside. The hall was a strange sight. The tall windows which occupied almost the entire north wall had come inwards, had swept across the hall, carrying chairs with them, and the shattered sashes had wedged against the south wall and the side doors in a complete barricade. There was no trace of fire.

James walked down the stairs, along the lower hall, and out through the main entrance into the snow. The stained glass that formerly cast a prism of colours from the transom over the great main door had gone outwards, and was littered over the snow in a jig-saw puzzle of many hues. Old Gander stood there in the snow amid the coloured fragments, staring up at the mute ruins of his school. James gave him a glance, no more. Something else had caught his eye. To the north-east, over the roofs of silent houses, a mighty mushroom was growing in the sky. The stalk of the mushroom was pure white, and it extended an enormous distance upward from invisible roots in the harbour; and at the top it was unfolding, spreading out rapidly in greasy curls, brown and black, that caught the December sun and gleamed with a strange effect of varnish. An evil mushroom that writhed slightly on its stalk, and spread its eddying top until it over-shadowed the whole North End, strange and terrible and beautiful. James could not take his eyes from it.

Behind him a voice was speaking, a woman's voice that penetrated the mighty singing in his ears from a great distance. Miss M'Clintock, the Grade Seven teacher, arriving early for the day's work. She was a tall woman, masterful to the point of severity. There was a wild look on her face that astonished James; for he had spent a term under her much-libelled rule and had never seen her anything but calm and dignified. "... all along the street. I can't tell you what I've seen this morning. Are you listening to me, Mr. Burtle?" Old Gander removed his wide gaze from the ravaged building. "My first really modern school," he murmured in that quaint asthmatic falsetto. "Dear, dear. What will the School Board say?"

James was watching that poisonous fungus in the sky again, but something Miss M'Clintock was saying made him look towards the houses about the school. They were like the school, void of window-glass, and in some cases of doors as well. There was a great silence everywhere, a dead quiet in which nothing moved except Old Gander and Miss M'Clintock and James and the mysterious mushroom that grew in the sky. But now over the whole city there came a great sigh, an odd breathless sound that was like a gasp and like a moan, and yet was neither. James saluted Old Gander awkwardly. "I — I guess I'd better go home now, sir." If Mr. Burtle heard him, he gave no sign. Miss M'Clintock said, "What a blessing the lower grades don't go in till half-past nine. All those big windows. Your hand is bleeding, James." James nodded and left them, walking through the school gate and into the street.

Now there was a flurry of movement and a chorus of wild human sounds about the shattered houses. An oil wagon stood at the kerb, with a pair of great Percheron horses lying inert under the broken shaft. The teamster squatted beside them in the slush with his hands on their heads, addressing blood-stained people who scurried past without attention. "Dead!" he said to James in a queer surprised voice. "An' not a mark on 'em. Would you think a man could stand a Thing that killed a horse?" James began to run.

Home was not far up the street. The old brown house stood two hundred yards from the school. (Dad had said, "It'll be handy for the kids going to school. When I get back we'll look for something better.") Just now it was silent, without doors or windows. Ragged wisps of curtain dangled in the gaping window-frames fluttering with every stir of the December breeze like signals of distress. James went up the front steps shouting, "Mum! Mum!" The house was cold and still. Like a tomb. James ran, frantic, through that ominous quiet. Margery's room was empty, the bed littered with broken glass. Mum's room. His own room. Broken glass, crumbled plaster, shattered doors. Slivers of glass thrust like arrows through the panels of Margery's door. Bare laths where the plaster should have been, like the naked ribs of a skeleton. In the lower hall the long stove-pipe from the big anthracite heater lay in crumpled lengths, with soot mingled in the littered plaster, and the painting of Fujiyama that Dad brought home from a trip to the East was half-buried in the rubble, broken and forlorn. Confusion reigned, too, in the living-room; a window-sash, void of glass, was wedged against the piano, and the dusty mahogany was scored deep by invisible claws. In the wrecked kitchen he heard voices at last. Mum's voice, outside, in the garden. The rear door and the storm porch were lying, splintered, in the tiny scullery, amid a welter of broken chinaware and tumbled pots.

Mum's voice again, "James! Is that you, James?" James scrambled through the wreckage of the back door and ran into her arms, and they stood in the snow for several minutes. Mum and Margery and James, holding each other in silence. There was a bloody handkerchief about Mum's forehead, and little rivulets of blackish-red drying on her cheeks. Margery wore a coat over her nightdress.

Mum said, "I was looking out of the kitchen window, and suddenly across the way all the windows glowed red, as if they'd caught a gleam of sunset. Then our windows seemed to jump inwards." James said quickly, "Are you hurt, Mum?" but she shook her head. "Just cut a little about the forehead, I think, James. The window in Margery's room came right in on her bed, and she walked downstairs in her bare feet without a scratch. Over all that broken glass! It's a miracle, really."

"Why are you standing out here?" James demanded. It was cold, there in the snow without a coat. Mum waved her hand vaguely towards the street. "Somebody shouted, 'They're shelling the city — get behind your house!' So we came out here."

"I don't see how that could be," James considered gravely. "All the houses along the street are just like ours — doors and windows blown to pieces, and all the plaster down. The school, too. They couldn't do that. Not all at once, I mean."

There were sounds from next door. Old Mrs. Cameron appeared, embracing her husband in a strange hysterical way. He was breathing very heavily, for he was a fleshy man. Sweat made little clean streaks in the grime on his face. Mr. Cameron was something in the railway.

"Station roof came down!" he shouted across to them. "All that steel and glass! Crawled out somehow! Ran all the way!" They came slowly to the garden fence, arms about each other, and Mum walked to meet them flanked by Margery and James.

"You hurt, Mrs. Gordon?" Mum shook her bandaged head again. "Nothing serious, Mr. Cameron, what does it all mean?" Mr. Cameron took an arm from his wife's waist and wiped his streaming face with a sleeve. "There was a terrible explosion in the harbour, down by the Richmond wharves. A munitions boat, they say. A French boat with two thousand tons of T.N.T. on board. She came up the harbour flying the red flag — the powder flag — and ran into another ship in the Narrows. She caught fire and blew up. It was like an earthquake. The whole North End of the city is smashed flat. Houses like bundles of toothpicks. And the boat went to pieces about the size of a plum — that big ship! When I ran up North Street the sky was raining bits of iron. I don't think many got out of the station alive."

Mum shivered. "No use standing here," James said. They went into the house and tramped silently through the shattered rooms. A motor-truck went past, soldiers leaning from the cab, shouting something urgent and incoherent. The street emerged from its dream-like silence for a second time that morning. Feet were suddenly splattering in the slush along the sidewalks, voices calling, shouting, screaming. Another truck went by, one of the olive-green army ambulances, going slowly. Soldiers hung from the doors, from the rear step, shouting up at the yawning windows. "What are they saying?" Mum said.

James said, "Sounds like, 'Get out of your houses.' " Mr. Cameron appeared on the sidewalk outside, shouting in to them through cupped hands. "... out! Magazine's on fire! Big magazine at the Dockyard! On fire!"

"Put on your coats and overshoes first," Mum said, her mouth in a thin white line. "Where's your coat, James?"

"In school," he mumbled, embarrassed. It was hanging in the coat-room, covered with plaster dust, like all the others, and he had run away forgetting everything, like the other kids after all. "Put on your old one," Mum said. Margery went upstairs, and after a few minutes came down again, dressed in a woollen suit. They went down the street steps together, and beheld a strange and tragic procession approaching from the direction of the city. Men, women, and children in all sorts of attire, pouring along the sidewalks, choking the street itself. Some carried suitcases and bundles. Others trundled hand-carts and perambulators laden with household treasures. Two out of three were bandaged and bloody, and all were daubed with soot and plaster. Their eyes glistened with an odd quality of fear and excitement, and they cried out to Mum as they stumbled past, "Get out! Out in the fields! There's another one coming! Dockyard's afire!"

Margery said, awed, "It's like pictures of the Belgian refugees." James looked at Mum's firm mouth and held his own chin high. They joined the exodus without words or cries. The human stream flowed westward. Every sidestreet was a tributary pouring its quota into the sad river. Open spaces began to appear between the houses, with little signboards offering "Lots for Sale." Then the open fields. The nearest fields were black with people already, standing in the snow with rapt white faces turned to the north-east, as in some exotic worship. The vanguard of the rabble halted uncertainly, like sheep confronted by a fence, and under the increasing pressure of those behind a great confusion arose. Their backs were to the stricken city. Before them lay the little valley of the Dutch Village Road, and beyond it the timbered ridges that cupped the city's water supply. Cries arose. "Here! Stop here!" And counter cries, "Too near! Move on!" At last someone shouted, "The woods! Take to the woods!" It was taken up, passed back from lip to lip. The stream moved on with a new pace, but Mum turned off the road into a field. They halted in a group of those strange expectant faces.

At the roadside was a pile of lumber. James went to the pile and pulled down some boards, made a small platform for Mum and Margery. Some of the people turned from their fearful gazing and said, "That's good. Better than standing in the snow." The lumber pile disappeared in a space of minutes. The great retreat poured past the field towards the Dutch Village Road for half an hour. Then it thinned, disintegrated into scattered groups, and was gone. The street was empty. The field was a human mass. Many of the women were in flimsy house-dresses, hatless and coatless. Two were clutching brooms in blue fingers. A blonde girl, with rouge-spots flaming like red lamps in her white cheeks, said, "Standing room only," with a catch in her voice. Nobody laughed. Most of the men were old. North-eastward rose fountains of smoke, black, white, and brown, merging in a great pall over the North End. The weird mushroom of those first tremendous minutes had shrivelled and disappeared in the new cloud. People watched the biggest of the black fountains. "That's the Dockyard," they said.

Two hours went by; long hours, cold hours. Still, the people faced that black pillar of doom, braced for a mighty upheaval that did not come. There were more smoke fountains now, gaining in volume, creeping to right and left. A tall old man joined the crowd breathlessly, cried in a cracked voice. "The fire engines are smashed. The city is doomed." A murmur arose over

153

the field, a long bitter sigh, like the stir of wind among trees. Someone said, "Nineteen days to Christmas," and laughed harshly. Three hours, and no blast from the burning Dockyard. Only the smoke poured up into the December sky. Old Mrs. Cameron came to them. She had become separated from her husband in the crowd and was weeping. "Joey! Joey!" she moaned, very softly. James thought this very strange. Joe Cameron had been killed at the Somme last year, and her other son's name was George. He was in France, too, in another regiment. But Mrs. Cameron kept moaning "Joey! Joey!" and wiping her eyes. She had no coat.

James said, "Looks as if we might be here a long time. I'll go back to the house and get some blankets, and something to eat." Mum caught him to her swiftly. "No," she said, through her teeth. Surprisingly, old Mrs. Cameron said, "That's right, James. I'll go with you. Mrs. Gordon, you stay here with Margery." Margery was not well. James looked at Mum. "Anywhere outdoors we'll be just as safe as here. I won't be in the house very long." Mum stared at him queerly. "You sound like your father, James." They set off at a brisk pace, old Mrs. Cameron clutching his arm. The snow in the field had been packed to a hard crust under a thousand feet. Farther on, where the houses stood silent rows, it was like a city of the dead. Blinds and curtains flapped lazily in gaping window-frames. Clothing, silverware, all sorts of odds and ends were littered over hallways and doorsteps, dropped in the sudden flight. There were bloody hand-prints on splintered doors, red splashes on floors and entries. The slush on the sidewalks was tinged a dirty pink in many places, where the hegira had passed.

Home at last. Smoke curled, a thin wisp, from the kitchen chimney. It was absurd, that faithful flicker in the stove, when all the doors and windows were gone and the winter breeze wandered at will through the empty rooms. They paused outside for a moment. Old Mrs. Cameron said, "We must rush in and snatch up what we want. Don't stay longer than it takes to count a hundred. Remember, James." She moved towards her doorstep, drawing a deep breath. James nodded dumbly. He clattered up the steps, making a noise that seemed tremendous in the stark silence, then along the lower hall and upstairs, where his steps were muffled in fallen plaster. All the way he counted aloud. Numbers had a sudden and enormous significance. Margery's bed was full of broken glass, cumbered with wreckage of the window-sash. He stripped a blanket from his own bed and passed into Mum's room. Mum's big eiderdown was there on the bed. Her room faced south, and the window-glass had all blown out into the street. A gust of chill air came through the empty frame, and the bedroom door slammed shockingly. The interior doors had been open at the time of the great blast, and had suffered little injury. The slam gave James a sudden feeling of suffocation and made his heart beat terribly. He went to the door quickly and twisted the handle. It came away in his hand, and the handle on the other side fell with a sharp thud, taking the shaft with it. "Hundred-'n'ten, hundred-'n-'leven." James dropped his burden and tried to force back the catch with bits of wood. They splintered and broke, without accomplishment. Outside, old Mrs. Cameron was calling, "James! James!" her voice very loud in the awful silence. Fear came to James in a rush. He fancied that sidelong earthquake again, and the big brown house tumbling into the street, a bundle of toothpicks, as Mr. Cameron had said about the houses up Richmond way. He went to the window, and debated throwing the blankets into the street and jumping after them. It looked a terrible distance down there. Mrs. Cameron caught sight of him staring down at her, and waved her arms awkwardly and shouted. She had a blanket under each arm, a loaf of bread in one hand and a pot of jam in the other. Inspiration came to James at last. Dad's rifle kit. In the bottom drawer in Mum's big chiffonier. He snatched out the drawer, brought forth a tiny screwdriver, prised back the catch with it. Freedom! He came down the stairs in four leaps, dragging blanket and eiderdown, and was out in the street, sucking in an enormous breath. Old Mrs. Cameron scolded. "I thought you were never coming, James. You should have counted."

"I couldn't get out," James said. The breeze felt very cold on his brow. He put up a hand and wiped big drops of perspiration. "I forgot to get something to eat." He was very close to tears. Old Mrs. Cameron pulled at his arm. "I have bread and jam," she said. Mum and Margery were standing on the little wooden raft in the snow. Mum clutched James against her, and held him there a long time. It was two o'clock in the afternoon.

At half-past three an olive-green truck appeared from the city, stopped in the road by the field. Soldiers came. "Any badly injured here?" There were none. All the people in the field had walked there unaided. Most of them were bandaged roughly, but nobody wanted to go to the hospital. The hospital was in the city, too near that ominous pillar of smoke. Somebody said so. A soldier said, "It's all right now. You'd better go back to your homes. You'll freeze here. The magazine's all right. Some sailors went in and turned the cocks and flooded it." The truck roared away towards the city again. People stood looking at each other, with many side-glances at the smoke over burning Richmond. The old white-haired man wandered among them, shaking his bony fists at the smoke, a fierce exultation in his long face. "Woe unto ye, Sodom and Gomorrah! Alas, alas for Babylon, that mighty city! she shall be a heap." Old Mrs. Cameron muttered, "God have mercy." The girl with the rouge spots said, "You're getting your cities mixed, old man." A man cried, "Better to burn than freeze," and shouldering his bundle, walked off in the direction of the city, whistling "Tipperary." A few bold ones followed him. Then people began to move out of the field into the road in groups, walking slowly, cautiously, towards the city. The old man went with them, crying out in his wild voice. Nobody paid any attention.

Mum, James, and Margery got home at half-past four in the afternoon. Mr. Cameron was standing outside his house, staring at the sky. The sunshine had vanished. The sky had turned grey, like steel. "It's going to snow," he said.

Mum said, "We'll have to spend the night in the kitchen." James looked at the kitchen stove-pipe. It was all right. He put coal on the faithful fire, and got the coal shovel out of the cellar and began to scoop plaster and broken glass from the kitchen floor, throwing it out into the snow. He counted the shovelfuls. There were seventy-five. "There's an awful lot of plaster in a room," Margery observed. Mum took a broom and swept up the fine stuff that escaped James' big shovel. They looked at the yawning window-frames. "That old storm-window," James said suddenly. "It's still in the cellar." They carried it up to the kitchen, and Mum and Margery steadied it while James mounted a table and drove nails to hold it in place of the vanished west window. It was meant to go on outside, of course, but there was no ladder, and it was terribly heavy. "We must have something to cover the other window," Mum said. They stared at each other. The people in the field had said you could not get glass or tarpaper in the city for love or money. James said, "The lumber — back in the field." Mum thought for a moment. "That lumber's gone by now, James. Besides, you couldn't carry a board all that way." They gathered up the living-room carpet, tugging it from under the tumbled furniture and shaking it clean of plaster. They folded it double and nailed it over the north window-frame on the inside, and James stuffed the gaps between nails with dish cloths and towels. There were two doors to the kitchen. The one opening into the lower hall had been open at the time of the explosion, and was unhurt. The other, opening into the shattered scullery, had been blown bodily off its lock and hinges. Mum and James pushed it back into place and wedged it there tightly with pieces of wood. "The snow will drift into the house everywhere," Mum said. "But we can't help that." James nodded soberly. "The water-pipes are going to freeze and burst." They debated nailing a carpet over the bathroom window. Finally Mum said, "The hall stove is out and the stove-pipe is down. The pipes will freeze whether we cover the windows or not. We must let the taps run and hope for the best. We can get help in the morning, I hope. To-night it's everyone for himself."

Through the makeshift storm-window they could see snow falling rapidly in the winter dusk. Mum made tea, and they ate bread and butter hungrily by the light of a candle. The stove created a halo of warmth about itself, but the rising wind began to whistle through the impromptu window coverings. Margery said, "Couldn't we go somewhere for the night?" Mum shook her head. "Everybody's in the same mess," James said, "Lots of the houses looked worse than ours." Mum looked at the fingers of fine snow that were growing along the kitchen floor under the windows. "We must keep the stove going, James." James carried chairs from the living-room, grouped them close about the stove, and stuffed a towel into the crack under the hall door. The candle on the kitchen table guttered blue in the cross draught from the windows. "Thirteen hours before we see daylight again," Mum whispered, as if to herself.

There was a knocking. James opened the hall door carefully, and saw the dim figure of a soldier framed in the front doorway, rapping knuckles against the splintered jamb. "Does James Gordon live here?" Mum stepped into the hall, shielding the candle with her hand. "Colonel James Gordon lives here. But he's — away, just now." The dim figure lifted a hand in a perfunctory salute. "I mean young James Gordon that goes to the big brick school down the street." James stepped forward, but Mum caught his shoulder firmly. "What do you want with James?" The soldier made as if to salute again, but took off his fur hat and ducked his head instead. He was a young man with a uniform far too big for him, and a long solemn face, rather sheep-like in the candle-light. "We — the sergeant, I mean — has been sent up to this here school for a — well, a special kinda job, ma'am. The awf'cer telephoned to the head schoolmaster's house. He lives 'way down in the city somewheres, but he said there was a boy named James Gordon lived handy the school an' would show us how to get in the basement, an' all like that."

James moved quickly, and Mum's hand slipped from his shoulder and fell to her side. "I won't be long, Mum." The soldier mumbled, "It's only a coupla hundred yards." Mum said, "Put on your coat and overshoes, James."

It was pitch dark, and the night was thick with snow. James led the way. The soldier plodded silently behind him. It was strange to be going to school at night, and the great silent building seemed very grim and awful with its long rows of black window-holes. A dark blur in the main doorway disintegrated, came towards them. Four men in fur hats and long flapping overcoats. Soldiers. "You find the kid, Mac?" James' soldier said, "Yeah. This is him. Where's the sergeant?" One man waved a vague arm at the dim bulk of the school. "Scoutin' around in there somewheres, lightin' matches. Tryin' to find the basement door." James said, "Which door do you want? You can get in the basement from the street if you like."

"Ah," grunted the second soldier; "that's the ticket, son."

A tiny point of light appeared within the school flickered down the stairs. James wondered why the sergeant looked upstairs for a basement door. A stout figure, muffled in a khaki greatcoat, was revealed behind the feeble flame of the match. The sergeant came out into the snow, swearing into a turned-up collar. With the shapeless fur hat on his head he looked strangely like a bear roused out of a winter den. "Here's the kid, Sarge." The sergeant regarded him. "Hello, son." James pointed. "The basement door is around there." He showed them. The door had been blown off its hinges and wedged, a bundle of twisted wood, in the frame. They pulled at the splintered wood stoutly, and the doorway was clear. On the basement steps the sergeant lit another match. Their voices echoed strangely in that murky cavern.

James knew them now for soldiers of the Composite Battalion, made up of detachments from various home-guard units. They wore the clumsy brown fur hats and hideous red rubber galoshes that were issued to the home guard for winter wear. Some people called them "The Safety First"; and it was common for cheeky boys to hurl snowballs after their patrols from the shadow of alleyways, chanting —

"Com-Po-Zite!

They won't fight!"

Mum had cautioned James against such pleasantry. Somebody had to stay at home, and these men were mostly physical unfits, rejected by the overseas regiments.

"Big as all Hell," declared the sergeant, after a tour of the echoing basement. "Hold a thousand, easy." The soldiers said, "Yeah." The sergeant fumbled in the big pockets of his greatcoat and brought forth a dark bottle. He took a long swig, wiped his moustache with a sweep of mittened hand, and passed the bottle around. "Gonna be a cold job," he rumbled. "All the windows gone, an' snow blowin' in everywheres. Concrete floor, too." The sheep-faced soldier said, "What-say we tear up some floorboards upstairs an' cover some of these cellar winders?" The sergeant spat, with noise. "They gotta send up a workin' party from the Engineers if they want that done. We got dirty work enough." The soldiers nodded their hats again, and said "Yeah" and "Betcha life."

Wind swirled through the gloomy basement in icy gusts. The men leaned against the wall, huddled in their greatcoats, cigarettes glowing in the darkness. James walked up the concrete steps to street level and stood inside the doorway, staring into the snowy dark. He wondered how long he was supposed to stay. A glow-worm appeared down the street, a feeble thing that swam slowly through the whirl of snow towards the school. James experienced a sudden twinge of fright. There was a great white shape behind it. Then a voice from the darkness above that ghostly shape: "Hulloa!" James cleared this throat. "Hulloa!" A man rode up to the doorway on a white horse. A lantern dangled from the horse's neck, like a luminous bell. The rider leaned over, and a face became visible in the pale glow. He was a detective of the city police, and James recognized his mount as one of the pair that used to pull the Black Maria in the days before the war. He was riding bare-back, feet hanging down, and the big policeman looked very odd, perched up there. "Anyone else around, son?" James jerked his head towards the black hole of the basement entrance. "Some soldiers. Down there, sir. Do you want them?" The policeman turned his horse awkwardly. "Just tell 'em the first wagon will be right along." He kicked the glistening side of his mount and disappeared as silently as he had come, lantern a-swing. James shouted the message down into the darkness. "Okay!" There was a lull in the wind, and the bottle gurgled in the sudden stillness.

Another glow-worm came, as silent as the first. But as it turned in towards the school James caught a faint rattle of wheels, and a hoarse voice bellowed, "Whoa-hoa!" The soldiers came stumbling up the steps in the darkness, and James went with them towards the light. It was a wagon, one of the low drays that clattered along Walter Street from morn to night. A man climbed stiffly from the seat. He was crusted with snow, even to his moustache and eyebrows. "Let's have the lantern, fella," demanded the sergeant. They walked to the back of the wagon, and the sheep-faced soldier held the lantern high while the sergeant whipped a long tarpaulin from the mysterious freight.

"Black men!" rumbled the sergeant loudly. James, peering between the soldiers in astonishment, beheld six figures lying side by side on the dray: three men, two women, and a young girl. They were stiff and impassive, like the dummies you saw in shop windows. The women had dirty rags of cotton dress. One of the men wore a pair of trousers. The rest were naked. Ebony flesh gleamed in the lantern light. The snowflakes drifted lightly on the calm up-turned faces. Their eyes were closed, hands lay easily at their sides, as if they were content to sleep there, naked to the storm. "Looka!" called the sheep-faced soldier. "They bin hit, Sarge. But there's no blood!" The sergeant stooped over for a better look. Two of the dark faces were scored deeply, as if some vandal had gouged wax from the dummies with a chisel. "Concussion," announced the sergeant with immense assurance. "That's what. Drives the blood inwards. They was dead before they got hit. That boat went to pieces like shrapnel." He called it "sharpnel."

The teamster was complaining. "... get a move on, you guys. This snow gets much deeper I gotta go back to the barn an' shift to sleds. There's work to do." Two of the soldiers picked up a dummy by head and feet, carried it awkwardly down the basement steps, and dropped it. There was a dull 'flap' when it struck the concrete. They came up the steps quickly. "Froze?"

asked Sarge. "Stiff as a board," they said. The wagon was cleared of its silent passengers and went away into the night. The sergeant struck matches while the men arranged the bodies in a neat row. "Once," a soldier said, "I worked in a meat packin' plant. In T'ronta, that was."

"Well," Sarge rumbled, "you're keeping your hand in."

Another lantern swam up the street. Another dray. More silent figures under the tarpaulin. White people this time. A man and four young women, nude, flesh gleaming like marble in the lantern light. There was blood, a lot of it, dried black like old paint. "Musta bin farther away," observed the sergeant. "Them black men was from Africville, right by the place she went off." T'ronta said curiously, "Funny, them bein' stripped this way. Was their clo'es blowed off, would you say?" The teamster shook his head. "Nuh. These was all pulled outa the wreckage by the troops this afternoon. Clo'es caught an' tore off, I guess. Besides, lotsa people sleeps late winter mornin's. Prob'ly didn't have much on, anyway." More wagons. The intervals diminished. The sheep-faced soldier said, "The awf'cer's forgot us. We oughta bin relieved by now." "Quit beefin'," said Sarge. "All the troops is up Richmond way, pullin' stiffs outa the wreckage, huntin' for livin' ones. If it's okay for them it's okay for us." A teamster gave them a spare lantern which they stood on the basement floor, and in the fitful glow of that lonely thing the dummies lay in orderly rows, toes up, faces towards the dim ceiling. The shadows of the soldiers performed a grotesque dance on the walls as they went about their work. Sarge pulled something from his greatcoat pocket, and James give it a sidewise glance, expecting to see the bottle. Sarge thrust it back into the pocket again, but James had seen the silver figure of a baseball pitcher, and knew it had been wrenched from the big cup his school had won last summer. He said nothing. Sarge said, "You still here, son? We don't need you no more. Better go home."

Mum greeted James anxiously in the candle-lit kitchen. "How pale you are, James! What did they want? You've been gone three hours." James looked at the stove. "Nothing. Nothing much, Mum. I guess they —just wanted to fix up the school a bit." They sat in the cushioned chairs, huddling over the stove. Margery had her feet in the oven. James went upstairs and brought down blankets, and they muffled themselves up in the chairs. Mum said, "Don't you want something to eat, James? There's tea on the stove, and there's bread and butter." "Not hungry," James said in a low voice.

It was a long night. James had never known a night could be so long. Sometimes you would doze a little, and you would see the faces of the dead people on the drays as plain as anything. Then you would wake up with a start and find yourself sliding off the chair, and feeling terribly cold. Several times he took the hod and the candle down into the cellar and brought up more coal. When the candles burned down to the table he lit new ones and stuck them in the hot grease. After a while there was a pool of grease on the table, hard and wrinkled and dirty-white, like frozen slush in the street. Draughts came through the window-covers and under both doors, like invisible fingers of ice, and you had to keep your feet hooked in the rung of your chair, off the floor. The candles gave a thin blue light and made a continual fluttering sound, like the wings of a caged bird. Sometimes the house shook in the gusts, and twice James had to climb on the table and hammer more nails to keep the carpet in place. Snow drifted in between the carpet and the window-frame, and formed thin white dunes along the floor next the wall. The heat thrown off by the kitchen stove was lost between the bare laths of the walls and ceiling.

"There must be a lot of dead, poor souls," Mum said.

"Yes," James said.

"In the morning, James, you must go to the telegraph office and send a cable to your father. He'll be frantic."

"Yes," James said.

Mum had washed the blood from her face and tied a clean rag of bedsheet over the cuts on her forehead. James thought she looked very white and hollow, somehow. But when he looked in her eyes there was something warm and strong in them that made him feel better. When you looked in Mum's eyes you felt that everything was all right. Margery had drawn a blanket over her head, like a hood, and her head was bent, hidden in the shadow. Mum said, "Are you awake, Margery?"

"Yes," Margery said quickly.

"Are you all right?"

"Yes."

"It will be morning soon," Mum said.

But it was a long time. They sat, stiff and cramped, over the stove, and listened to the snow sweeping into the rooms upstairs, and the flap-flap of broken laths, and blinds blowing to rags in the empty window-frames; and the night seemed to go on for ever, as though the world had come to a dark end and the sun would never come back again. James thought of Sarge, and the sheep-faced man, and T'ronta, carrying frozen dummies into the school basement, and wondered if the owner had remembered them. Daylight crept through the storm-window at last, a poor grey thing that gave a bleak look to everything in the kitchen. Stove, blankets — nothing could ward off the cold then. The grey light seemed to freeze everything it touched. Outside, the snow still swept fiercely against the carpet and the glass. James found potatoes in the cellar, and rescued bacon and eggs from the wreck of the pantry. Mum brushed the snow and bits of plaster from the bacon and put it in a frying-pan. It smelt good.

The telegraph office was full of people waving bits of scribbled paper. The ruins of plate-glass windows had been shovelled out into the street, and the frames boarded up. Outside, a newsboy was selling papers turned out by some miracle on battered presses in the night. They consisted of a single sheet, with "HALIFAX IN RUINS" in four-inch letters at the top. Within the telegraph office, lamps cast a yellow glow. There was a great buzz of voices and the busy clack-clack of instruments. James had to wait a long time in the line that shuffled past the counter. A broad cheerful face greeted him at last.

"What's yours, son?"

"I want to send a cable to Colonel James Gordon, in France."

The man leaned over the counter and took a better look at him. "Hello! Are you Jim Gordon's son? So you are. I'd know that chin anywhere. How old are you, son?"

"Four —going on fifteen," James said.

"Soon be old enough to fight, eh? What's your Dad's regiment?"

James paused. "That'll cost extra, won't it?" he suggested shrewdly. "Everybody in the army knows my father."

The man smiled. "Sure," he agreed reasonably. "But France is a big place, son. It's their misfortune, of course, but there's probably a lot of people in France don't know your Dad."

James said, "It's the Ninetieth."

"Ah, of course. Jim Gordon of the Ninetieth. There's an outfit will keep old Hindenburg awake nights, son, and don't you forget it. What d'you want to say?"

James placed both hands on the counter. "Just this: 'All's well. James Gordon.' That's all."

The man wrote it down, and looked up quickly. "All's well? That counts three words, son, at twenty-five cents a word. Why not just, 'All well'?"

James put his chin up. "No, 'All's well.' Send it like that."

WILL R. BIRD

* * * * * * *

Will R. Bird was born at East Mapleton, Nova Scotia in 1891. He was educated at the Amherst Academy and then homesteaded in Alberta before serving overseas in World War I with the 42nd Royal Highlanders. Following the war he became a freelance writer, contributing to dozens of Canadian, American, and British periodicals. He also worked as an information officer for the Nova Scotia government and wrote close to thirty books, including Here Stays Good Yorkshire *(1945),* This is Nova Scotia *(1950), and* An Earl Must Have a Wife *(1969). The editor of the important regional anthology* Atlantic Anthology *(1956), Bird died in Halifax in 1984.*

The following excerpt is from the final chapter of Bird's memoir of World War I, And We Go On *(1930). While many writers have described their arrival in Halifax harbour, no one has done it with the emotional intensity that Bird displays here as he recounts his return to the city on a troopship in the fall of 1919.*

* * * * * * *

from **And We Go On**

On the evening of the last night out our emotions ruled us, turned us to a riot of horseplay. We scuffled and wrestled and dragged each other about and made mock speeches. Then, gradually, we quieted, each with his own thoughts. And when all was still I went on deck and stared over the dark waters ahead.

Darkness. The rush of the ship. I felt my way again into a stifling dugout, into an atmosphere rancid with stale sweat and breathing, earth mould, and the hot grease of candles ... I saw faces, cheeks resting on tunics, mud-streaked, unshaven, dirty faces, some with teeth clenched in sudden hate, some livid with pulse-stopping fear ... I saw men turning on their wire bunks, quivering as if on some red-hot grill ... I heard them gasp and sob and cry out in agony, and mutter as they tossed again. Then, a machine gun's note, louder, higher, sharper, crack-crack-crack as it sweeps over you in a shell hole where you hug earth ... the growl of guttural voices, heavy steps, in an unseen trench just the other side of the black mass of tangled, barbed barricade beside which you cower ... the long-drawn whine of a shell ... its heart-gripping explosion ... the terrible oppressive silence that follows, then the first low wail of the man who is down with a gaping, blood-spurting wound...

I moved about, shook myself, sniffed the salt air, tried to rid myself of my dreams, and as I stood there came a sudden chill. I grew cold as if I had entered a clammy cavern. I could not understand but went and got my greatcoat. A dim figure passed me as I returned to the deck and a voice said, "We're getting nearer home. I can feel the change."

Ah — I knew. We had left the warm current and were into the icy waters — nearer home. We had left behind the comradeship of long hours on trench post and patrols, long days under blazing suns and cruel marches on cobbled roads — the brotherhood of the line; and we were entering a cold sea, facing the dark, the unknown we could not escape.

Dark figures came and stood beside me. I had not thought that anyone save myself would come on deck, and here they were, ten, a dozen, still more, all hunched in greatcoats, silent, staring. I looked at my watch. It was three o'clock in the morning. These men could not sleep; they were come to see the first lights of Halifax. I moved quietly among them, scanning each blurred face. It was as I thought. They were all "oldtimers," the men of the trenches. We went on and on and on, and no one spoke though we touched shoulders. I tried to think of a comparison.

Ah — we were like prisoners. I had seen them standing like that, without speaking, staring, thinking.

Prisoners! We were prisoners, prisoners who could never escape. I had been trying to imagine how I would express my feelings when I got home, and now I knew I never could, none of us could. We could no more make ourselves articulate than could those who would not return; we were in a world apart, prisoners, in chains that would never loosen till death freed us.

And I knew that those at home would never understand. They would be impatient, wondering why we were so dumb, unable to put our experiences into words; and there would be many of the boys who would be surly, taciturn, moody, resenting good intentions, perhaps taking to hard liquor and aimless drifting. We, of the brotherhood, could understand the soldier, but never explain him. All of us would remain a separate, definite people, as if branded by a monstrous despotism.

But I warmed as I thought of all that the brotherhood had meant, the sharing of blankets and bread and hardships, the binding of each other's wounds, the talks we had had of intimate things, of the dogged simple faith that men had shown, flashes of their inner selves that strengthened one's own soul. Perhaps when my bitterness had passed, when I had got back to normal self, to loved ones tried by hard years of waiting, I would find that despite that horror which I could never forget I had equalizing treasure in memories I could use, like Jacob's ladder, to get high enough to see that even war itself could never be the whole of life.

The watchers stirred. I tingled. My throat tightened. Waves of emotions seized me, held me. I grew hot and cold, had queer sensations. Every man had tensed, craned forward, yet no one spoke. It was the moment for which we had lived, which we had dreamed, visioned, pictured a thousand times. It held us now so enthralled, so full of feeling that we could not find utterance. A million thrills ran through me.

Far ahead, faint, but growing brighter, we had glimpsed the first lights of *Home*.

CHARLES BRUCE

*   *   *   *   *   *   *

Charles Bruce was born at Port Shoreham, Nova Scotia in 1906. After graduating from Mount Allison University in 1927, he moved to Halifax and eventually joined the Canadian Press, a career which took him to New York and then Toronto, where, in 1945, he became the CP General Superintendent. While in Halifax during the late twenties and early thirties he was an active member of the poetry group the Song Fishermen and emerged as a major Maritime writer. The author of several books of poetry, he won the Governor General's Award for his 1951 collection, The Mulgrave Road. *In 1954 he published his only novel,* The Channel Shore, *a classic exploration of a Nova Scotia rural community during the 1919-46 period. Bruce died in Toronto in 1971. An excellent biography of the writer,* World Enough and Time: Charles Bruce; A Literary Biography, *by the Halifax poet Andy Wainwright, appeared in 1988.*

"Tide" was first published in the Halifax Harbour Commissioners' magazine, The Open Gateway *(August 1931). Bruce published another sonnet about Halifax, "Halifax Harbour," in* The Open Gateway *(March 1931), but "Tide" is a more lyrical celebration of the city. It is also more indicative of his considerable strengths as a poet.*

*   *   *   *   *   *   *

Tide

The pride of life is in this city's heart;
(No trull with head forever bowed is she)
Sharing the sway of queens a world apart,
Sired of empire, mothered by the sea.

Beyond MacNab's the white flotillas pass;
By Richmond flies the sign of tempered spears,
That iron scaled with rust, and shining brass,
May lie untroubled at a hundred piers.

From what deep well the endless strength, and whence
The will to raise the towers her dream attains —
Playground and busy warehouse, grim defense?

One current are the vision and the force,
This the compelling virtue and the source:
The pulse of tide along her granite veins.

KENNETH LESLIE

* * * * * * *

Kenneth Leslie was born in Pictou, Nova Scotia in 1892 and grew up in Halifax. He attended Dalhousie University, the Colgate Theological Seminary, Nebraska University, and Harvard. A member of the Halifax literary group the Song Fishermen, he won the 1938 Governor General's Award for his fourth collection of poetry, By Stubborn Stars and Other Poems. *In 1938, while living in New York, Lesiie launched an influential left-wing journal,* The Protestant Digest, *which he published in the United States until 1949, when he was driven from the country by McCarthyism. Returning to Halifax, he continued espousing his Christian socialist views and writing poetry. His last collection,* O'Malley to the Reds and Other Poems, *appeared in 1972. Leslie died at Halifax in 1974.*

"Halifax" first appeared in Leslie's collection By Stubborn Stars. *While the diction and imagery of the poem recall the imperial vision of Halifax exemplified by Kipling and Johnson, Leslie underscores the city's defiant Maritime character, an attribute which he clearly admired and shared.*

* * * * * * *

Halifax

Robed in my emerald citadel,
    throned above the tide,
marking the tangle of the winds,
    my destiny I bide.

Peering out of the shadows
    that bruised the sunset bars,
over my clambering housetops
    I speak back to the stars:

More than a key in a mighty gate
    for a strong first to turn,
more than a lonely road to walk
    and a bitter book to learn,

more than a Roman guard am I
    to watch by the Roman way;
I have a pledge of my own to keep
    and a word of my own to say.

IRVING LAYTON

*   *   *   *   *   *   *

Irving Layton was born in Romania in 1912 but emigrated to Montreal with his family at the age of one. He graduated from Macdonald College in 1939 and served in the Canadian Army during the war before receiving a M.A. from McGill University in 1946. After several years of high-school teaching and part-time lecturing at Sir George Williams University, he was appointed writer-in-residence at Sir George Williams and then at the University of Guelph. From 1969 to 1978 he taught at York University. A member of Montreal's First Statement poetry group, which was founded in 1942 by the Nova Scotian John Sutherland, Layton became an editor of Northern Review *and, in 1952, a co-founder of Contact Press. His first poetry collection,* Here and Now, *was published in 1945. Among the more than forty books he has published since that time are* A Red Carpet for the Sun *(1959), which won a Governor General's Award,* The Collected Poems of Irving Layton *(1971), and* A Wild Peculiar Joy, 1945-1982 *(1982). A book of his selected letters,* Wild Gooseberries, *appeared in 1989.*

The following passage from Layton's autobiography, Waiting for the Messiah *(1985), focusses on his experiences in Halifax during the fall and winter of 1939-40 — just after his marriage to a Nova Scotian, Faye Lynch — when he worked as a salesman for the Fuller Brush Company (which, incidentally, was founded by a native of Welsford, Nova Scotia, Alfred C. Fuller). Like fellow poet Thomas Moore, Layton obviously didn't regret his departure from the city.*

*   *   *   *   *   *   *

from **Waiting for the Messiah**

The following autumn, we moved to Halifax where I thought there would be better job opportunities. My first job was selling insurance for Confederation Life. The war had broken out, and in Montreal I'd tried to enlist in the Medical Corps. However, at the interview, the pink-cheeked, clean-shaven major eyed me suspiciously when I said in all innocence that I wished to join the Medical Corps because I wanted to be with the men. Over and over I kept urging, "I want to be with the men, I want to be with the men!" I shall never forget the perplexed look faintly tinged with disgust in the major's eyes. My request to join the Medical Corps was turned down, for reasons that totally escaped me at the time.

I lacked the needed ingredients to make a good insurance salesman. My confident know-it-all air had fooled the manager, just as it had fooled Mac's students and the characters with whom I'd verbally jousted at Horn's. But it was not really aggressiveness at all, it was insecurity that made me eager to give battle, to contradict, and argue. After all, if someone disputed with me, it obviously meant I was being taken seriously. It did not take the manager of the company long to see that I was ill-suited for the job since I barely averaged the sale of one small policy per week.

I then became a Fuller Brush salesman. I was now like any other married man with responsibilities and a wife. I even found myself a part of the Jewish community, and because Halifax was both smaller and less diversified than Montreal, it was also more philistine, more narrow-minded, more conventional. Not a single Heinrich Heine among them. Spinoza? Not even his wan ghost. The main things the Jews of Halifax had on their minds were money-making and bar mitzvahs, and the rabbi's orotund platitudes that asked to be taken for profundities. The picture I had of myself was that of a trussed-up eagle on a poultry farm, moreover an eagle that was expected to take seriously the pecking order paraded before his eyes.

For several months we lived on what I earned as a Fuller Brush salesman. My territory was Dartmouth and the only interesting person I met during that whole time was a mad theosophist who claimed she had powers of divination. Her husband had died some time ago but he still remembered her fondly, bringing her affectionate messages from the beyond that, since he had had a scatological mind, were written on pink bum paper.

The end of my stay in Halifax was brought about when I was summoned by Sam Jacobson, brother of the same Hyman Jacobson who had proposed to Faye. He asked me to meet him at their warehouse in Dartmouth and said he wanted to talk to me on a matter of grave importance. But apparently the warehouse wasn't private enough for the discussion he had in mind, for, when I got there, he had to find a particular place, one that was isolated and seemingly sealed off. Wondering what he'd got on his mind, I followed him dutifully from storeroom to storeroom. He strode ahead of me with the stolid assurance that money, good digestion, and a total disinterest in ideas confer upon the middle-class Jew.

Reaching the centre of the room, and thinking it private and secure enough, he suddenly wheeled around to wag a thick forefinger at me and he said, "You know you're disgracing the Jewish community here." When I asked him why, he told me: "I've got a report that you're a member of the Communist party and we can't tolerate this. We're a good Jewish community. We've never been in trouble with the law. We want to keep our good name. We don't want the likes of you coming from Montreal and spoiling it."

I said: "Look, I'm not a Communist. I never have been. In Halifax I did go to one meeting of a Communist cell and when I heard the organizer say there was no difference between British imperialism and German fascism, I told him to get lost, that he was talking bull." All my contempt for mediocrity was in the articulation of that expletive, for the Sam Jacobsons of this world and the Communist organizers with their packet of lies and dogmas.

However, Sam wouldn't listen. He just stood there indignant, self-righteous, and I saw before me an irate turkey shaking his red wattles. Well, this was the best thing that could have happened. I needed the nudge. God had indeed moved in a mysterious way.

One afternoon, about a week later, I was on the Dalhousie campus. I was lying on the grass looking up at the trees and the blue sky, my Fuller Brush valise beside me. Suddenly I thought, What the hell am I doing here, selling Fuller Brushes, and truckling to fat, sly, middle-class Pharisees, even trying to interest them in poetry? I laughed aloud at the comedy of my efforts. I could see students enjoying the mild April day, walking gaily arm in arm across the campus. And there I was in my double-breasted suit, with a valise of Fuller Brushes to sell to dull, shapeless housewives. Seized by an acute feeling of nausea, and without any further thought, I picked myself up, grabbed my thick black valise, and made for the house.

It was my good fortune that Faye's mother had come to take her to shop for a stationery store for me to purchase and run. I could sell notepads and pencils and pens and erasers, New Year's and bar mitzvah cards for the rest of my life while taking care of Faye. I had less than three dollars in my pocket, but I dropped off the valise and ran all the way down to the train station as if ten devils were pursuing me. I asked the ticket agent how far two dollars would take me. It was something like fifteen or twenty miles, but at least it was out of Halifax. From there, I would hitch rides all the way back to Montreal.

EARLE BIRNEY

*   *   *   *   *   *   *

Earle Birney was born in Calgary, Alberta and was raised in Alberta and British Columbia. After working at a variety of jobs, he attended the University of British Columbia, the University of Toronto, and the University of California at Berkley. In 1938 he joined the faculty of the University of Toronto and became the literary editor of The Canadian Forum. *Following service overseas in World War II, he worked for the CBC and then became a professor at the University of British Columbia, where he remained until 1965. One of Canada's most distinguished writers, he has published over two dozen books, including many volumes of poetry, two novels, and a collection of short fiction and sketches. His first poetry collection,* David *(1942), won a Governor General's Award.*

"Halifax" was first published in the US literary magazine New *(December 1968) and was then collected in Birney's* Rag & Bone Shop *(1971). For Birney, who spent time in the city during World War II, Halifax only comes to life during times of war, a historical pattern that elicits a warning from the poet. Appropriately, Birney begins the poem with an epigraph from Hugh MacLennan's* Barometer Rising *(1941).*

*   *   *   *   *   *   *

Halifax

"periodically sleeps between wars"

(Hugh MacLennan)

Today you can see his dozing bones
under the mange of his fur
Poke him and he scarcely stirs
curled in the big den

177

the glaciers rooted out for him
rum secretly fuming in his old brain
belly with a memory of molasses and fish
He is coiled in dreams of Covenanters
and clowndances to the redcoats of Cornwallis

Foghorns never wake him nor bells of buoys
nor the sly tides that pluck his toes
not even the steel wool of the seawind
rubbing away at his haunches

It takes each generation's crack
of doom and then he stumbles out
young again and getting educated
chucking his sailor's cap
rolling the girls on the park grass
running a new jack up the citadel
totting up the lost convoys

Bear Halifax
surly in your matted pelt
bear that once tore your own entrails
with a great wound — and licked it whole
and ugly as ever —
bear with your paws at the end of rails
and your ass a port shitting for the world's wars
      sleep well
         the next one will wake you dead

DOUGLAS LOCHHEAD

*   *   *   *   *   *   *

Douglas Lochhead was born in Guelph, Ontario in 1922 and grew up in Fredericton, New Brunswick and Ottawa, Ontario. He studied at McGill and the University of Toronto before serving overseas in World War II. Since the war, he has had a distinguished career as a professor of English and a librarian. He has also emerged as a major poet, publishing over a dozen works of poetry, including The Full Furnace: Collected Poems *(1975),* Tiger in the Skull: New and Selected Poems, 1959-1985 *(1986), and* Upper Cape Poems *(1989). Lochhead is presently writer-in-residence at Mount Allison University. His paper "Halifax in Canadian Literature," which he delivered to a Royal Society symposium on Halifax, was published in* Transactions of the Royal Society of Canada; Series IV; Volume XIX; 1981 *(1982).*

"Winter Landscape — Halifax" first appeared in the Halifax-based journal The Dalhousie Review *(Winter 1956). It was later reprinted in Lochhead's* It Is All Around *(1960) and has since appeared in other collections by the poet. Written during the period when Lochhead was the Head Librarian at Dalhousie University, the poem captures the reality of a blustery December day on the edge of the North Atlantic. For an interesting discussion of the poem, relating it to earlier literary portrayals of Halifax, see Larry McCann's article "Of Sleighs, Trams, and Jeeps: Three Landscapes in the Evolution of Halifax" in* The Red Jeep and Other Landscapes: A Collection in Honour of Douglas Lochhead *(1987) edited by Peter Thomas.*

*   *   *   *   *   *   *

Winter Landscape — Halifax

A bright hard day over harbour where sea
in chips of white and blue speaks and toys, while
flurries of gulls spinning in wide deploys swoon
in sleigh-rides giddy and cold off government wharf.

At Devil's the sea spanks a winter's drum,
a hollow ballad and boom for sailors' throats
courting their winter mermaids battened down
somewhere off Scatari and heading home.

Now in December the wind leans rude and hard,
snow heaps and hides in the cormorant rocks,
and at the Citadel commissionaires
clap hands, stamp feet, turn backs against the cold.

BILL BISSETT

*   *   *   *   *   *   *

bill bissett was born at Halifax in 1939. At the age of nineteen he moved to Vancouver, where in the late 1960s and early 1970s he became active as a writer and as the publisher of blewointmentpress. Among his more than fifty books of experimental poetry are nobody owns th earth *(1971),* living with the vishyun *(1974), and* Selected Poems: Beyond Even Faithful Legends *(1980). A prolific visual artist, bissett has had art shows in a number of galleries in British Columbia and Ontario. He has also performed his sound poetry at various festivals in Canada and abroad.*

"halifax   nova scotia" was first published in bissett's canada gees mate for life *(1985) and was later reprinted in* Poetry Canada Review *(Winter 1985-86). Like all of bissett's work, the poem obliges readers to adjust to the idiosyncrasies of his spelling, but it is an effort well worth making, for the poem is one of the most memorable ever written about Halifax. An extended meditation on death and remembrance, it is at once macabre, visionary, and extremely poignant.*

*   *   *   *   *   *   *

halifax nova scotia

all th brave sailors what they had dun brave hous wives what they had
dun th ded n gone blunose sailing vessel daze whn halifax was lustee n
brawling rich th ghosts uv th sailor n th sea maidn lovrs rising
above th tides haunting th melodee uv all th resting bones at th bottom
shoal sea bed wher th othr tresurs lay goldn next to th mor ivoree ribs
uv th beechd n drownd peopul lament for th haunting as th brkrs roaring
onto th shore wher by a thin breth we can b separatid from our safetees
n join th deth romance uv th sailors embracing each othr hugging seeming
to stare back at th curious eyez uv th purpul spottid grey fish wer goin
down my boy th giant spray gushing into theyr lungs ther ar rubees undr
th eyelids emeralds in th fingr bones arms around each other n th sunkn
tresur uv th heart until we ride agen

on partikularlee stormee nites whn we ar all inside by th fire th long n
recentlee ded sail agen ovr th main n above th giant billows greet each
othr across th great tormentid sky we ar inside n that close to drowning
if th waves so whim it highr n loudr we heer th voices cry n laff hi n
stern jaggid tormentid n victorious dashing rocks to farthr obliviyun
hundrid metr waves tees th holographee uv th jumping so hi n deft wivvering
ghosts spirits uv th departid from ths place erth borne can we dance
agen can we fix it celebrate holograph images ducking n escaping agen
from th leviathan waves laffing th sounds uv echo in our freezing clap
bord houses th winds saw eezilee thru n into our skin fishing vessels
around th wharves down by th harbor wun wharf namd aftr my grandfathr from
inverness scotland his ships saild to portugal but we live on universitee
avenue in halifax a bit inland n safer from th immediate changes tho th
ocean powr is inside us at our window waiting n biting th glass

wher victor hugos dottr went mad trying to win ovr a spurning lovr wher
sum uv th ded from th titanik ship wreck ar burreed in th graveyard on
barrington street whn yu heer th wind blow it duz that nites uv fiers
winds yu dont go yu stay n listn to th howling n th screen lullabyes th
astors ar bureed ther peopul always going down to th harbor staring out to
sea for hours my dad wud sit in his car at th brek watr his eyez going far
out beyond th atlantik horizon aftr a long enuff time did land apeer or
atlantis surfacing from th trench meditaysyuns on th disapeering horizon
fish smell sea gull shrieks always announsing fresh storms at sea n detail
ing th kind uv bones bleechd on rocks what meet left on them n howevr bleed
id skraping against th bottom th sea takes evreething back th winds sum
times sounding like wraith creaturs suffocating for oxygen breeth into us
feed us life agen

near wher into th big park my mothr n i wud go hunting flowrs to take
home   she oftn wud look for laydeez slipprs   that was her favorit   th
flowrs wer a wondr for her   whn she was veree close to what we heer
considr th last veil   i remembr she went down th sevn blocks uv th
avenue to th altr to place flowrs thru a blinding snow storm   walking
gainst winds cumming home   remember a pictur uv my mothr n fathr whn
they wer veree young   both theyr hair strong theyr bodeez clasping in
embrace th winds raging with theyr hair   my mothrs hair black bfor th
cobalt treetments turnd it grey   full uv life they both wer   passyun
a gladness   smell th beautee   sand beech   so much to remember   so
much to forget   let go   th love is   reel   still burning   th flame
thru th sky   thru th fog   thru all th veils we pass thru   changing
n anothr wun to pass thru   change n let go   til thers th seering singing
care   offring   sharing th vanishing time   until we ride agen   my mothr

gone two yeers from th cancer settling into th lungs   last stage   heering
fathr aftr a long muffuld silens sing out uv his closd door bedroom   IUM
OKAAAAAAAAY   a great street lamp sign yell into th void   kay was my mothrs
name   his fred   mor silens   n sobbing   thn running watr n kleening his
teeth   sumthing abt memorees   an appul n spruce treez   thirtee mile view

uv th lake   a hot plate on fire that wasint plugged in   was my fathr out
looking at th huge ocean   its moods   deciphering   praying for th sea
maidn n th sailor   my parents   themselvs   all th lanterns blown out   no
witnesses for th miracul   themselvs riding th brekrs   soaring lullabyes
th masts n th wreckage   carnal spirit   lifting theyr great arms up above
th spray   aura beem   mor than sufficient lite   crooning to th whales   th
sea birds   th sun rising n setting   dansing above th waves   wings opn
n lifting theyr hopes n daring   th prayd for futur   a chorus uv drowning

sailors accompaneeing them   escaping th undrtow   into th moon change

until they ride agen   n th wethr was fair

BILL HOWELL

*   *   *   *   *   *   *

Bill Howell was born in Liverpool, England in 1946 and grew up in Halifax. A graduate of Dalhousie University, he worked as a freelance writer for a number of years before joining CBC Radio in the mid-1970s. Howell has lived in Toronto since 1977 and is presently the Executive Producer of CBC Radio Drama/Features. To date, he has published two collections of poetry, The Red Fox *(1971) and* In a White Shirt *(1982).*

"Seventeen Forty-Nine" initially appeared in Howell's first poetry collection and was later collected in the Nova Scotia anthology Nearly an Island *(1979) and in* The Atlantic Anthology, Volume 2/Poetry *(1985). One of a number of poems that he has written about Halifax, "Seventeen Forty-Nine" is a witty exploration of the city's past and of the Maritime identity.*

*   *   *   *   *   *   *

Seventeen Forty-Nine

Who cares who we've been? Those without roots
will never forgive those of us with them. ...

Weren't we the first Free Enterprisers here,
the ones who first helped haul the bells up
into old St. Paul's? Merchants from Bristol,
Portsmouth, and Liverpool, who came back
to the Banks with Cabot, and stayed
where "the fish slowed the progress
of our ships." The guys who laughed
at Humphrey Gilbert's plumes at St. John's
harbour, who made *money* while Hudson and Frobisher
were busy busting their asses for us. The guys
who were pressed into the Royal Navy, who turned
back the Armada. The guys who finally had enough
of England when England gave Louisbourg back, but
who went on anyway, because we've never run
from a fight we couldn't win, to take Quebec,
the Great Rock, the Key to All. ...Pity
the poor WASP, who has to sting himself first. ...

For don't we all make up our own histories
as we go, those of us who are "doing well"?

My father, bred and buttered in Portsmouth,
took me and my brother across the Great Sea
to this New World at ten months of age
from Abercrombie Hospital in Liverpool, and
we giggled and bawled the whole way over.
If that isn't formative, what is? My mother,
a Loyalist from St. John, lost her grandmother's
brooch playing Madame La Tour in high school,
and still loves to holiday in New England,
searching for distant, lost, Yankee relations.
And we all have cousins who hid the Explulsion out

in the Gaspereaux Hills. And cousins who gave
diesel oil to Nazi u-boats outside Lunenburg
just before I was born. ...Pity the poor WASP,
who has to sting himself last. ...
But how long have we been sleeping here,
beside our secret memory, the sea?

Too soon we seem old inside our trusty dream. ...
("Ah yes, bye, and we'd do it all again, by God!")
Most important of the things that don't work
in this city are the guns on Citadel Hill. ...
("And ah, she's a fine side, that one!")
And the noonday gun is just a vain attempt
to kill the rest of the afternoon. ...
("And there's always some pretty lively
steppers in the distance. ...")
There's a Zumburger stand in Scotia Square,
and nobody knows what *that* means. ...
("And you can always tell a man from his hands.")
And all the old electric Beltline trolley buses,
outdated with so many other dates around,
have been sold for a *fine* price to Toronto. ...
("And inland, bye, the continent starts from *here*!")
And here, bellbottoms will always be fashionable. ...

So shall we sell them Tidal Power
or tell them seabirds rule the world?

MARK GORDON

*   *   *   *   *   *   *

Mark Gordon was born at Halifax in 1942 and lived in the city until 1958, when he moved to Montreal. He attended McGill University, where he began writing, before spending three years in Israel. In 1964 he returned to Halifax and completed his B.A. at Dalhousie University. He later moved to Ontario, living for several years near Brantford before taking up residence in Toronto. Gordon has published two novels, The Kanner Aliyah *(1979) and* Head of the Harbour *(1983). Hugh Mac-Lennan, commenting on the former book, praised Gordon's "marvellous narrative gift."*

The following passage comprises Chapter Sixteen of Head of the Harbour, *which is set in Halifax during the mid-1960s. A powerful exploration of the roots of prejudice, the excerpt shifts back and forth between the experiences of the novel's protagonist, Martin Kanner, in the sixties and his memories of his childhood in Halifax during the 1950s.*

*   *   *   *   *   *   *

from **Head of the Harbour**

That same evening he was sitting in his room alone. It was getting dark outside. He hadn't bothered to turn on the light. He sat in the frayed armchair beside the radiator. He touched the radiator with the back of his hand. It was gradually getting warmer. She must have turned the heat up. It wasn't tremendously hot, but he could sit there now without his overcoat on. The sweater he was wearing was heavy, and corrugated with thick ribs of wool. Aunt Ida had given it to him. It was from her store on Barrington Street.

David's sarcastic gleam burned inside his head. His words echoed through his mind. Look. Look at that. Look at that, will you? He's totally crushed. If, he thought, David had not touched a nerve-ending, he wouldn't have felt so depressed by his cold remarks. But David had pointed to the truth. Yes, he had to admit to himself, when his friends hadn't noticed he was about to depart, hadn't acknowledged his good-bye, he had felt crushed.

It was a shock, though, to have someone like David Steeles point it out, and show it to his other friends, Yuri included. Why, Martin wondered, did his feelings hang so vividly on his face? Why did they sit there for everyone to see? It made him feel vulnerable, awfully vulnerable, in front of someone like David Steeles. And what was he supposed to do? Was he supposed to continually suppress his inner feelings? Was he supposed to wear a mask, to be on guard, to be forever on guard? Was he supposed to walk around with an icy shield over his eyes, a visor like the knights of old used to wear? Was that the solution to his problem?

He remembered the Capitol Theatre on Barrington Street. He would go there quite often as a child, when he was ten, eleven, twelve years old. He hopped the bus on Saturdays around noon hour. Yes, the bus at twenty after twelve that stopped at a corner near his house on Robie Street. Almost every

Saturday he dashed out of his house, ran the half block to South Street, crossed to the opposite corner, stood alone waiting for the bus, his old faithful friend that always arrived at twenty minutes after twelve. It was rarely late, rarely a minute either side of its scheduled arrival.

Down he'd travel into the heart of the city, the downtown area, to Barrington Street where his father had an office in the Roy Building, and Uncle Stan had his clothing store a few blocks away. Barrington Street — it was a huge-sounding name in his young boy's head. It was almost as if Halifax and Barrington Street were synonymous. What was one without the other? It was like the old song — Love and Marriage ... horse and carriage. Barrington Street. The words rolled inside his young head. No, no other street could vie for his affection, his awe, and sometimes his fear. After all, everyone came to Barrington Street when he was a kid. They came from the four distant corners of the city. They came from the slums, Water Street and Argyle, where his father grew up. They came from the new suburbs, like the one he was living in. They came to Barrington Street to work, to shop, to go to the movies. And there the sailors on leave could be seen. On Barrington Street everyone mingled — whoever they were — the colored people, the sailors, the ladies in feathered hats, the businessmen in suits, and kids like himself down there to haunt the movie houses.

His heart took a leap each Saturday afternoon as he got off the bus. Suddenly, he could see the rush of people. He was walking among them. They were walking so near to him that he could smell their odors: perfume and sweat, whiskey and fur. They were all around him, much taller than he was. They were brushing against him, against his shoulders, and sometimes a fabric — wool or cotton or silk — would brush against his cheek.

There on that street with the huge-sounding name — Barrington — he had his choice of movie houses. The Capitol. The Paramount. The Family. He could, if he wanted to, if he really rushed, go to all three theatres in one afternoon. (It cost him only a dime at each one.) He could get into the Capitol at one o'clock, dash to the Paramount at three, then tear over to the Family, and still get back home by seven-thirty.

He had done this a few times. But only a few. It was a marathon that tired him out, that left his mind jam-packed with images. Often he was satisfied, quite satisfied, by going to the Capitol and finishing off the afternoon at the Paramount. Then at five o'clock, he would go to the Roy Building, and catch his father before he left work.

He sat in the room on Preston Street thinking of David Steeles' cold remarks. And he sat there dreaming of those Saturday afternoons long ago. What a blessed relief those movies were from the weekdays at Pinebrook School. How he hated sitting in the classroom with the fluorescent lights buzzing. He'd look out the window at Robie Street as the teacher scraped notes on the blackboard. It looked drab out on the boulevard. It looked dark outside, and the fluorescent lighting made the wintry afternoon scene appear even drabber. The wind tunnelled down the boulevard, bending the newly-planted saplings. He used to sympathize with those tiny, young trees tied with burlap to pieces of two-by-four for support. Would they survive? — his young mind often wondered. Would they really grow into huge oaks and maples some day? Would he be able to come back, when he had grown up, and see how they had made out? Or would the wind go crazy, mount up in its fury, twist them and snap them beyond repair? Poor trees, he used to think, so thin and young and alone out there on the boulevard this wintry afternoon.

He gazed around the classroom. There was John O'Reilly, the "maestro," as everyone called him, John O'Reilly sitting in his seat at the back of the class rocking, forever rocking. What was wrong with him? Why did he have to continually rock like that? John, the "maestro," his queer schoolmate, looked bald. His head looked like a coconut barely covered with fuzzy strands that were supposed to be his hair. He was overweight, roly-poly, and he never stopped his rocking. Some kids found out that his mother took him to violin lessons twice a week. She was overheard one day, as she opened her car door to let him in.

"Hello, maestro," she said, "how are you this afternoon?" That was the end for John being called simply John. "Maestro!" the kids shrieked day after day. "How are you, dear maestro?"

They were yelling at John, poor John O'Reilly, but he could feel their icy shrieks travel up and down his spine. He was afraid. Why wouldn't they turn their gibes suddenly from John to him, Martin? No, his mind reasoned, they wouldn't do that. He didn't rock in his chair. He wasn't called the maestro. He didn't have a head that looked like a coconut. But...yes, but. Weren't there things about him, about him, Martin Kanner, that could suddenly catch their attention? Would they abruptly turn against him — notice the birth-scar on his cheek, remember that he was Jewish, and turn this into a mocking rhyme? He hoped that the weeks inside the classroom would pass, and no such horrible event would ever take place. His palms sweated when he thought about being made the object of their taunts. A lump caught in his throat, stuck there like a bone halfway down.

Yes, what a relief to go to the movies, to go down to Barrington Street on Saturday afternoons. The Capitol Theatre was built like a castle inside. It always surprised him, again and again, when he entered that strange-smelling place. Yes, like a castle. There was a moat with water, a drawbridge, castle doors with spikes of steel. And knights in full armour stood guard in front of the doors that led from the foyer to the thousand chairs of the auditorium. The Capitol Theatre had a smell of its very own. It comforted him. It was not just the scent of chocolate bars and orangeade. It was a distinct odor. The Paramount didn't have it, nor the Family. Somehow — and it amazed him — the Capitol smelled like he always imagined a real, honest-to-goodness castle would smell. It had the smell of old cushions, centuries and centuries old. It hit him in waves as soon as he walked inside from the street. It was like meeting a very good friend, someone he had known for a long, long time. Someone who would never think of hurting him. Someone whose arms were always open, always willing to wrap their warmth around him, take him in, and press him close. A music danced inside him whenever he entered the Capitol once again.

It was a strange feeling inside him as he walked through the foyer, crossed the drawbridge, gazed at the knights in armour. He felt small, small as a thread in the lush carpets on the floor. And, at the very same instant, he felt huge, tall, high as the huge crossbeams of wood on the ceiling. What a mixture of feeling! It rippled through his young body. Wasn't he, he thought, as great as this castle? He was no longer little Martin Kanner who lived on Robie Street and went to Pinebrook School. He was no longer the chubby boy who was afraid to take off his clothes after gym class, and take a shower with his schoolmates. No, it was as if that strange odor of the Capitol Theatre had the power to transform him, to make him taller and stronger and braver than any little boy could ever hope to be.

Slowly, he walked down the aisle to his seat. The carpets were soft under his feet. The lights were still dim, the curtains drawn, and he was sitting in that pit of soft darkness again. The kids had stopped their yelling. They were no longer throwing popcorn and jelly beans. They were waiting with Martin for the curtains to part. Now there was nothing to be seen. Nothing but the vague soft heads of kids. Aisles and aisles of heads turned up expectantly towards the screen in front of them.

Martin gazed around. Everything looked dark except for two white masks on either side of the theatre, high up on the walls. One mask was laughing, the other crying. One mouth was upturned, grinning; the other stretched downwards, sad and pathetic. How white those two masks were! Ghostly white. White as bone. What did they mean? — he wondered. Was it a message placed there for kids like himself to decipher?

John, the maestro, entered his head. He was rocking, rocking, scraping his desk along the linoleum floor. The noise was getting louder. The wooden desk was creaking under his weight. John was in a fury of rocking. Louder and louder, much louder than the fluorescents' buzzing, more insistent than the teacher's voice. Miss Tyrone turned quickly from the blackboard.

"John! Please! I can't stand it! Just stop for a minute."

The kids in the classroom giggled under their breaths. A few of them started to rock, imitating the maestro.

"No! Stop it!" Miss Tyrone shrieked. "I'll have none of this, do you here? So help me, every one of you will stay after school. Except John!"

John looked up, his blue eyes twinkling, and he slowed the pace of his rocking.

"Thank you, John," Miss Tyrone whispered, out of breath. "Thank you, dear."

"Thank you, maestro," his classmates mimicked in unison.

"Enough! Do you hear?" Miss Tyrone shouted. Her blackboard pointer swished through the air, and cracked loudly on her desk.

For a few minutes, the class was quiet. Miss Tyrone's fury was echoing inside their heads.

"Do you know how rude it is," Miss Tyrone sighed, "to make fun of your classmate that way? Just think of it. How it adds to his burden. Do you think God looks on that kindly?"

The children in the class hung down their heads. The word "God" had floated from Miss Tyrone's mouth like an enormous balloon.

Martin's gaze travelled from Miss Tyrone to John to the kids in the class with their eyes turned down. What, he wondered, was that burden that John, the maestro, carried around? Had Miss Tyrone noticed that he, Martin, had not joined in on their gibes?

"Now, let's get back to our work," Miss Tyrone smiled faintly. "Now, who can tell me how many counties there are on Cape Breton Island?"

Hands shot up around the classroom. It was an easy question. Even the maestro's hand was flailing around for attention. "Me, me, me, me," the classroom echoed.

Martin hunched down deep into the cushioned chair at the Capitol Theatre. The curtains started to part very slowly. His mind was blank now, waiting, blank as the huge screen before the movie began.

Martin got up from the tattered armchair in his room on Preston Street. He was thinking of Yuri Raglin and Moira. He was dreaming about Joan in her house on Dunbarton Road. He was thinking of Norrie, how his black eyes popped, how his jaws widened and snapped.

David Steeles' cool words were still nagging inside his mind. "Look at that! He's totally crushed, just because we didn't say good-bye."

Martin stood in the middle of his room. Could he learn, he wondered, to suppress his feelings? Could he learn to keep his face as cold and unrevealing as a steel mask?

He walked across the room to the small window. It was nearly dark outside, but there was nothing to be seen anyway from that window except the house across the alley. It was a wooden house also, like Miss Riley's, a white wooden house, two storeys high.

He gazed at the house. A light came on in a room in the upper storey. The venetian blinds were open. He stood there watching. A young girl of about fourteen came into the room. She tossed herself down on the bed and lay there on her stomach, one hand propped under her chin, and a book open in front of her on a pillow. She was wearing a short, plaid skirt. As she read, she bent her legs at the knees, and kicked them behind her rhythmically. They scissored the air. The movement made her skirt ride up on her thighs. He stood in the darkness and his heart began to pound. How young she looked, and fresh! How white and smooth her skin appeared! His head started to spin. His groin was burning with desire. Who was she? — he wondered. Perhaps a professor from Dalhousie lived in that white house across the alley and this was his daughter. She probably went to school nearby. Maybe she attended the same school he had gone to when he was fourteen. Stadacona Junior High. It was only a block away.

It seemed centuries ago, he thought, when he was her age. And much longer, aeons past, when he attended Pinebrook School on the other side of town.

He stood by the window, mesmerized. What young skin, he was thinking. What beautiful young skin! She wasn't too fat or too skinny. His thoughts were whirling around. What if he could go back, he dreamed, be her age again? What if he could start over? Perhaps he'd gotten off on a wrong track. Perhaps, long ago, he'd taken a route he should never have taken, which led only to madness.

But when? And where? When did he suddenly veer off on a wild careening trail that led him eventually to Jerusalem, to the stone cottage, to dreams about fighting off his father with can openers? Had he ever been as smooth and innocent as he imagined this young girl to be? Had he ever been as fresh and optimistic?

He looked across at her room again. She was still lying on her stomach, kicking her legs behind her. Someone came into her room. Martin couldn't make out who it was. The person was outside his range of vision. All he could make out was a shadow. The girl looked up from her reading, and was talking to the shadow. A few minutes later, she got up from her bed slowly, walked to the window, looked out quickly, and shut tight the venetian blinds.

Martin let out a sigh. It was a heavy, mournful sound. He walked back to the armchair, and let himself fall into its awaiting arms. He slumped down and closed his eyes. He was dreaming again of the Capitol Theatre. On that screen, he saw so many people long ago. Burt Lancaster. Victor Mature. Robert Mitchum. Grace Kelly. Donald O'Connor. Debbie Reynolds. Ma and Pa Kettle. The Bowery Boys. How he would laugh at the Bowery Boys until his stomach ached, until he couldn't laugh any more. And what brave men crossed that screen! What amazing things they did! There was Marlon Brando in *On The Waterfront*. What guts they all had! When he used to watch Humphrey Bogart fight alligators and malaria, Martin couldn't help but think of his father. His young boy's head was filled with awe. Didn't his father have eyes as black and daring as Humphrey Bogart's? Wasn't his father's chin as strong and defiant as Robert Mitchum's? And when his father stood in the bathroom in the morning with only his boxer shorts on, wasn't his chest every bit as powerful and muscled as Burt Lancaster's? He sat in the theatre and wondered — couldn't his own father play in one of those movies? Wasn't his father's life as exciting?

And always an agonizing doubt gnawed away at him. What would he, Martin, do if he were caught between the badmen and the alligators? Would he just break down? Would he crumble? Would he melt into a pool of tears? Or would he be able to gather from somewhere inside him the guts and courage that his father always talked about, the qualities his father admired? His mind wobbled on the edge of those questions. Yes, he could do it. Yes. Yes. But was he sure? Was he absolutely sure? Wasn't there a chance that he might not have the nerve? Wasn't there the chance that he might simply run away, run in the opposite direction and hide?

He never tired of listening to his father's stories of courage. They were always fresh, vigorous, and frightening when they poured from his father's mouth in that house on Robie Street. They carved their way into his mind. They rested in a dark cavity of his heart. It was like watching a movie when his father spoke. Except the movie was much closer now, just across the dining-room table. His father was the hero now, his own father with his jet-black hair, his long broken nose, his eyes that could turn from fierce black to warm pools of understanding in just a few seconds.

"Your mother and I were at the Med-O-Club one night near the end of the war. I was drinking, not too heavily, mind you, but I wasn't feeling too much pain. We got out on the dance floor, your mother and I. At first I thought I was imagining it. There was a tall guy in uniform. Jesus, he was tall! Must've been well over six feet. Anyway, he kept dancing closer to us and kind of knocking my elbow. I said to myself — 'Jake, just ignore it. Don't make an issue. Maybe he's drunk and doesn't know where he's going.' So, we take our seats, have a few more drinks. We get up for another dance. And by Jesus, don't you think this same oaf starts knocking my elbow again?" His father paused, tapped the ashes from his cigarette into an ashtray on the dining-room table. "Then he whispers under his breath to me — 'Hey, Jewboy, why aren't you in uniform?' The painted whore he was dancing with, as if on cue, leaves the dance floor and goes to her seat. 'Dahlia,' I whispered to your mother, 'go sit down, please.' And just as your mother starts for our table, don't you think this drunken lout takes a swing at me? I duck and he misses by a country mile. Now I start doing the swinging. But the fuckin' bastard's too tall. I can't reach his chin. 'Come on, Jewboy, fight like a man,' he keeps hissing."

His father started to chuckle. He was coughing over his cigarette and laughing.

"I was boiling by then, ready to tear him apart. Everything had gone quiet, deathly still. Everyone was gaping at us. 'Come on, kike, where are your balls?' he kept yelling. I took another swing. Same results — not even close! I almost fell on my ass. I was burning with embarrassment and rage. I walked back towards the tables. He followed. I spotted an empty chair. He reached out for me. You know what I did, Martin? I jumped on that bloody chair and hit him in the mouth so hard, I don't think he knew what hit him! Down he went — out cold on the floor!"

His father's eyes burned across the dining-room table in Martin's direction. He gazed into the blackness of his father's eyes. In the darkness and glow of his eyes, Martin could see the tall soldier stretched out on the floor, his jaw broken. He could see his father's story going backwards from end to beginning. He was reliving it in his mind. The Med-O-Club. The dance floor. The band. And the ugly words hissed at his father.

"I'll tell you, Martin," his father slowly began, "the only good Nazi is a smashed Nazi. The only good fascist is a dead one. I want you to remember that. Six million Jews went to the gas chambers in Germany without saying a word. They went like sheep with their heads bowed. Maybe they couldn't have done anything about it. Who knows? But if I had been in their shoes, I would have taken a few of those Nazi bastards with me. I would have died on my feet like a man. Not kneeling!"

His father's eyes were burning fiercely across the edge of the dining-room table at Martin. Martin bowed his young head. He looked down at the shiny mahogany surface of the table. He could see his own face staring back at him.

"But why, Dad? Why did the Nazis hate the Jews so much?"

His father drew on his cigarette and narrowed his eyes.

"First, they were led by that maniac, Hitler. And they followed him as if he were the messiah ...." His father paused. "You must understand, Martin, that the Jews were easy targets. They were rich, educated, leaders of German society before Hitler took over. Some of the finest minds in the world came out of that country — Freud, Einstein, Karl Marx. And yet they had no army to defend themselves with. They didn't even own personal weapons. So when Germany fell on hard times, what better scapegoat could Hitler use? The Jews were right there."

Martin hung down his head. Some of the words that flowed from his father's mouth had a strange sound to them. He was only twelve years old. He couldn't be expected to understand every single word. Yet he had an idea, a feeling about what his father was trying to tell him. A doubt lingered inside him, however. Had his father told him all the reasons for the Nazi hatred? For their murders and slaughter? Had his father left something out by mistake? Was there something, a tiny straw of truth, that his father perhaps didn't know about?

Memories were burning inside Martin's head as he sat in the armchair in the darkness on Preston Street. Memories were licking at him, tongues of fire in his mind, in the pit of his stomach. Pinebrook School. His father's face. His father's words. His father's deeds. The Capitol Theatre on Barrington Street. His father's broken nose. His father's fierce black eyes. And the same question that had been gnawing at him more and more as each day passed, attached him again. Who are you, Martin Kanner? What did it mean, he asked himself, to be Martin Kanner? What was he composed of? What was his deepest root? Was that such a crazy thing to ask? How could he go on with his courses in Classical Literature and Elizabethan Drama without that question forcing itself on his mind? A few weeks earlier, a chill had run up his spine. He had heard a voice in his room. He was sure it had been a dark, evil voice, the voice of the devil perhaps. It had whispered in his ear. Only one word came out of the ghastly mouth — sucker! He looked around the room. Was there someone there in the flesh? Had that word been formed by a real tongue?

He had been jarred by that encounter with the disembodied voice. No, I can't let that happen again, he warned himself. I can't allow this devil, or whatever it is, to speak to me. He was shocked by how well-formed, clear and distinct that single word came out. Sucker. There was no mistaking it for any other word or message. No, I can't let that happen again. I must not. He was afraid. Where would it end if he began listening for messages in the dark air? What horrible things would tumble out at him? He would end up crazier than his cousin Harvey.

After that voice had spoken to him, he attacked his books with new vigor. He used Shakespeare, Homer, and Hegel to cling to when his mind wandered into dark regions. He began writing an analysis of *King Lear*. The essay was supposed to be twenty thousand words long. But the essay he was writing kept growing. He analyzed the play scene by scene. He had forty thousand words on paper and it was still growing, not three-quarters finished.

Should he be sitting there now, he wondered, in the darkness, allowing those memories to flow through him? What if the voice, the ghastly disembodied voice, came back, and what if "sucker" was just the beginning of a huge river of madness and abuse it would hurl at him? Should he turn on the light? Should he act sensibly? Should he get back to the real, present world and his essay on *King Lear*, and his textbooks for introductory psychology?

But he didn't move from his armchair. He kept sitting there in the darkness between the arms of that battered chair.

In the Capitol Theatre he remembered watching *King Kong*. The huge furry beast had brought tears to his eyes. Why did the explorers wrap him in bands of steel? He gazed at the young woman who was the beast's only friend. Did she really love him?

— his young boy's mind wondered. Yes, it seemed as if she did. She was risking her life for that huge, hairy beast. And why not? — he sat in the movie house and reasoned. Didn't King Kong show more feeling than his tormentors — the hunters with pistols at their sides, the circus managers with whips, the photographers flashing painful bursts of light into his vast dark eyes?

Good. Good, King Kong, he thought, as the towering gorilla escaped from his cage. Run, King Kong, run. Martin's young heart was pounding with excitement. Good, he thought — the Empire State Building. Oh good. Yes, climb it, King Kong. Hurry. The police are coming. Please, King Kong, climb it. No one will get you up there. Martin watched, hypnotized, as the huge ape began its climb, with his friend, the young woman, held tenderly and delicately between his furry fingers. Go, King Kong, go to the top. No one can touch you up there. And there he was, Martin sighed, on top of the tallest building in the world. Would the young woman speak on King Kong's behalf? Would she tell the people to stop tormenting her friend? Would she explain to them that he meant no one any harm? Would she ask them in her soft, warm voice to let King Kong come down, to let him go back to the jungles where he belonged, back to his home?

But no ... the people weren't listening any more. They sent out planes to buzz around Kong's head. Good, King Kong, crush them, crush them into powder. Before he lost his balance, King Kong looked at his young friend one last time. There were tears in both their eyes. Tenderly, he slipped her through an open window into an office where she'd be safe. Martin was already crying. He cried even harder when the huge, feeling gorilla fell to its death.

He sat stunned in the Capitol Theatre when the curtain finally closed across the screen. He didn't want to move from his seat. Everyone was getting on their coats, moving towards the exits. But he sat there, his cheeks wet and warm with tears. Was this the world, he wondered, was the world composed like the movie he had just watched? Why? Why did something so noble and good as King Kong and his love for his young friend have to be destroyed, stamped out, obliterated? Why did those people have to build cages, stronger and stronger cages, thicker and harder bars of steel? Why had they come to the cage and thrown insults at the beast? Why did they have to taunt him, ridicule him, torment him? Couldn't they see that he had feelings, strong feelings like everyone else? And maybe his feelings were even deeper, larger, more easily hurt. Was the movie, young Martin wondered, a picture of the real world? And was that the world he had to go back to in a few minutes, the world on Barrington Street, the world at Pinebrook School?

Martin lit a cigarette. He blew a stream of smoke into the darkness of his room. He remembered Kurt Steiner, a German boy who was in his class at Pinebrook School. His hair was black, his eyes blue. In the winter his cheeks turned red easily in the cold weather. The skin around his cold-weather blush seemed very white, not pale exactly, but unusually white, like a sheet of paper, or the snow when it was fresh on the ground. Kurt, like Martin, was tall for his age. He was hefty, muscled, and overweight. In the showers after gym, some of the boys would shriek — "Hey, look at that, Steiner's got tits!" One of the boys would get brave and run up to him quickly, grabbing at his chest. "Hey, Steiner, how 'bout a feel?" Kurt swivelled, his fists cut the air, and just missed slamming into his tormentor's shoulder. "What's wrong, Steiner? Got a bean up your kraut ass?" someone would yell. And then the chorus would begin, the chorus of voices that was starting to get louder and more frequent that year. "Steiner is a German. Kurt is a kraut. Steiner loves Hitler. Of this we have no doubt!"

Anger arose in Kurt's blue eyes. His eyes started to blaze and pierce the air like the points of daggers. He got up from the wood bench, ran at one of the smaller boys, cornered him, hit him in the stomach. But revenge never lasted long. Five boys charged Kurt, pinned him against the stone wall of the shower room. "You do that again," Billy Eaton hissed, "and we'll cook your kraut ass in oil!"

Martin looked at what was happening out of the corner of his eye. He undressed quickly, wrapped himself in a towel, ran into the shower and out again as fast as he could, just barely dried himself, and got back into his clothes. What a relief when he was finally back in his corduroy trousers and his thick plaid shirt. He dreaded this one day of the week more than any other. He hated gym class, and he was terrified of the shower room. The odors of sweat from underarms and socks. His mind clanged with fear. What if the boys in his class suddenly turned their mockery from Kurt Steiner to him? He was almost as fat as Kurt. It could happen. And what if they suddenly noticed that he, Martin, never joined in on their mocking chorus? What if they noticed that? Wouldn't they find it strange? He asked himself one question, over and over again, day in and day out — how come they never noticed it? Had they noticed, and just never bothered to mention it? And if they noticed, why hadn't they thrown it up in his face?

"Dad," he whispered to his father late at night, as they sat alone together at the dining-room table, "Dad, why do they all gang up on Kurt?"

His father looked out the dining-room window. Martin gazed at his father's face. His father's eyes were narrowed and wrinkled, as if he were thinking deeply about the question. His father turned from the window. He seemed to be trying to get the answer from deep inside himself.

"Martin, I wish I could tell you. Do you realize that people have been killing each other for centuries? Do you know how much blood has been spilled? You've heard of the crusaders, haven't you?"

Martin nodded. Yes, he had read about them at school.

His father continued. "They slaughtered Jews and Moslems by the thousands. And what for? Do you know what for? For Christianity. For Christ. For love."

His father shook his head. "It sickens me, Martin, when I think about what has gone on in the world in the last two thousand years. We've advanced so much in medicine, science, education, but morally, we are still ants. In understanding and human kindness we haven't advanced one iota. Not one!"

His father's words reverberated in the quiet darkness of the dining room. Martin could almost feel them vibrating and echoing inside his own chest.

"I wish they would leave Kurt alone," Martin whispered.

"Yes," his father sighed. "I know how you feel."

His father raised his hand to his face and pinched his lips together. His father was thinking again. The room seemed to become even quieter.

"Do they ever bother you, Martin? Please tell me the truth."

"No," Martin shook his head.

"Good. That's good. It was different when I was a boy. Jewish kids were fair game back then."

His father looked directly into his eyes.

"Are you sure, Martin? They never say anything to you? Because believe me, if they ever do, I'll be in that principal's office so fast it'll make their heads spin." His father paused and lit a cigarette. "You see, Martin, those young boys, your friends at school, are not to blame. They're too young to understand. The truth of the matter is that they get that hatred from their parents, and nowhere else. Somehow they've picked up the idea that it's not wrong to torment this German boy. And there's only one place where an idea like that would come from. Do you understand what I'm saying?"

Martin nodded. His chest felt heavy, as if a boulder were sitting on it.

A few days later, he was standing outside Pinebrook School at recess. Flies were swirling around the huge garbage cans near the concrete steps. He stood there watching. Inside those cans, huge as empty oil cylinders, kids tossed their apple cores and half-eaten sandwiches. He was mesmerized by the swarm of flies. They rushed in, dived down into the bins, came back out in a dark cloud. They looked like an army attacking. Strange thoughts roamed through his mind. What was it like to be a hungry fly? Would it be better somehow than going to school? Would it be easier to have nothing on his mind but hunger for a rotten apple or a bit of peanut butter?

Often he stood alone at recess — away from the screaming crowd of kids. They were down on the playground tackling each other or crawling through the bars of the jungle gym. He didn't care for their games of tackle — when hard bodies crunched into each other. He preferred baseball, or flying kites, or trying to get a model plane to rise into the air powered by an elastic band. He stood there bundled in a sweater his Aunt Ida had knitted for him. It was made from very thick wool. It was warm enough to wear until the snows came. On the back she had designed a fish. Not a man casting into a stream, but just a huge fish with watery eyes. He was a little embarrassed by this fish on his back. It just sat there on his back. It wasn't swimming or leaping from the waves. No, it just hung there. Shouldn't it be moving? — he wondered. The other kids had deer on their sweaters, deer leaping through the woods. Why had Aunt Ida made it this way? Why was the fish so still?

Many recesses he had stood there alone crunching an apple, trying to make it last until the bell rang for classes again. He didn't want to be dragged into a game of tackle. The kids were screaming down below on the playing field. Why did they have to shout so loud? — he wondered. Why all the screaming? It rose up from the field in waves.

He stood there dreaming that day. The flies were extra active, swarms of them dancing around the huge, rusted garbage pails. Maybe they knew that the snows were coming and they had to get one last bellyful before the ice came in and froze them. They flew together in dark knots, dove into the darkness of the steel cans, disappeared for seconds, then came roaring out.

He stood there dreaming, his mind floating. He had almost forgotten where he was, or who he was. Even the screams in the playground had died down. They were duller now inside his head. Then suddenly, once again, he became aware of the shouts. They were much closer than before. He took his eyes off the flies. Down below him, not too far away, the kids had formed a circle. Somebody was in the middle. They were chanting together. The person in the middle was rushing at the circle, trying to get out. But the kids kept bunching together and flinging him back. Martin walked down the hill to get a closer look. Now he could see it. It was Kurt Steiner trapped in the middle of the circle. What startled him even more, however, was that there were just as many girls in the circle as guys. They were all yelling together. "Kurt is a kraut! Steiner's a dirty German!" Kurt ran towards them, trying to force his way out. But they knotted together and flung him back into the middle. Martin remembered his father's words — about kids learning their hatred from their parents. And what was the difference? — he wondered. If Kurt was in that circle, couldn't it must as easily have happened to him, Martin? Wasn't it possible that they might turn their hatred the following week against him, and he's find himself where Kurt was now? Wasn't that what he feared more than anything — being taunted by his schoolmates, being called a dirty Jew?

A feeling began to build inside him. It was a ridiculous thought, but he was starting to feel that he had no other choice. He had to break into the circle and be with Kurt. Once the thought and feeling entered him, it grew at a terrific pace. It seemed as if his legs were being moved by a force beyond his control. He ran towards the circle. He heaved himself against two joined hands and broke inside. Everyone's face looked shocked, even Kurt's. The screams suddenly stopped. Then words came tumbling out of his mouth. It seemed that they were not his words, that somebody else was speaking them, and he was listening to them along with the others. "Leave him alone!" he shouted. "He didn't do anything to you! How would you like to be in here?" No one spoke back. Everyone seemed to drop their heads at once, and the circle broke up. "Thank you," Kurt whispered. "But why did you do that? I'm not afraid of them. I could've gotten out." Now Martin dropped his head, embarrassed by Kurt's words. "Never mind," Kurt continued. "Thank you anyway." He slapped Martin on the shoulder. Then he grabbed Martin's hand and shook it.

He sat in the armchair on Preston Street, thinking of that event that had taken place so very long ago. How long ago it seemed — that recess, that circle, those voices yelling. Was it all covered now with the leaves which had fallen during the intervening years? Had time erased its meaning? Yet it was there in his mind, and in his feeling. He could hear the screams as if they had hit the air only hours ago. He could feel Kurt's hand squeezing his — a hard, determined handshake. And the flies, and the garbage cans, they were so real he could almost touch them, and smell the rotting apples.

Kurt Steiner, he mused. They became friends. He went up to Kurt's house. He was surprised at how dark it looked inside, compared to his own house or Aunt Ida's. The curtains were drawn. They were long, dark curtains that fell to the floor. The furniture was large and shadowy-looking. The floor was bare except for a few scatter-mats that looked thin and threadbare. He remembered meeting Kurt's mother. She was a tall, lean lady with hollowed-out, dark, tired-looking eyes. He remembered how bony she appeared — much skinnier than his nervous Aunt Ida. He remembered her voice. It vibrated and echoed in the living room with a German accent.

"Oh, I am so happy for Kurt. He needs a freund, a good freund like you. You are velcome to this house. You come anytime. Understand?"

Martin nodded. He could feel a rush of warm blood up his neck. When she left, Kurt snickered.

"Guess the old lady likes you."

Then he slapped Martin on the back, harder than necessary, burning the skin under Martin's shirt.

And how did it happen, Martin wondered as he sat in the darkness of his room on Preston Street, how did it slowly begin to happen — Kurt's gradual swing towards belligerence? And why didn't he fight back? Why did he let Kurt hit him with rubber boots, and chase him through the house, and jump on top of him, and pin him to the floor? It was more than a game, much rougher. Was he really afraid of Kurt? And it was Kurt who taunted him with the words "dirty Jew." "Spoken like a Jew," Kurt would sneer.

"Why does he say those things?" Martin asked his father.

"Somebody's told him it's okay," his father answered. "Have you ever met Kurt's father?"

Yes, he had met him. He remembered the big, beefy man with tattoos on his upper arms. He would swing into the house carrying boxes of beer. Kurt introduced him to Martin, but Mr. Steiner hardly said a word. He grumbled something out of the corner of his mouth, looking sideways at Martin, and walked out into the kitchen.

"Does he have any scars on his face?" Martin's father asked.

"I don't remember, Dad. Yes. Maybe."

"The Nazis love that kind of thing. Fencing duels, and cutting each other up."

The word "Nazi" hung in the air.

"You can never tell, Martin," his father continued. "Maybe old man Steiner was a true-blue stormtrooper during the war. That's where Kurt gets that crap. It's not really his fault. It's his old man."

Could it be, Martin wondered as a child, could Mr. Steiner be a Nazi? Had he gassed Jews in Germany during the war? The thought made Martin shiver. At night in bed, he dreamed of Mr. Steiner walking into the house wielding a sword. An ugly scar ran down the length of his face. And he dreamed of Kurt hitting him with rubber boots — how he didn't fight back.

And now on Preston Street, during his final years of B.A. studies, the memory was there as strong as ever, and the old questions unanswered. Had he done something, said something to make Kurt turn on him? He thought back, way back to Robie Street, to Pinebrook School, trying to come up with an answer. But the past looked almost as dark as it had been back then, when the flies swirled around rotten apples in the schoolyard and kids yelled and screamed at recess. It was all there to remember — inside him. Kurt and his mother. Kurt and his black rubber boots. Mrs. Steiner with her tall bony body and dark eyes that looked hollowed out down to the sockets. And the showers at school with kids snapping towels at each other. And old John O'Reilly, rocking, singing a song to himself, an endless song in his mind. The poor maestro with the coconut head. And the movie houses filled with kids on Saturday afternoons, aisles of kids looking up expectantly towards the tall white screen.

He sat in the battered armchair, in the room Miss Riley kept much too cold. He shook his head and rubbed his eyes, as if trying to wake himself up, as if he wanted to shake off those memories, to forget about them, and to begin again as if he had no past, no Robie Street, no Pinebrook School. No dark memories in his head. No Kurt Steiner with evil words in his mouth.

And David Steeles' cold remark — couldn't he forget that too? Forget that cold gleam in his eyes. Pretend it never happened a few short hours ago. Maybe David had been in a particularly bad mood. At least David had not jumped on his chest and held a knife to his throat. He remembered David's story — the boy he had almost killed a few days before Christmas when they were listening to Beethoven together.

Martin got up from the armchair. He turned on the light in the room. He had a few more pages to write about *King Lear*. He would have to get down and do it. And it wouldn't be long before he had to meet David Steeles again, and Yuri. Before he began studying that evening, he went out in the hall and called Joan up on the phone. Her voice sounded dreamy and far away.

"What have you been doing?" she asked. "I haven't heard from you in days."

"Studying," he replied.

"Do you want to get together on the weekend?" Her voice was soft and caressing.

"How about all three of us? You, Hugh, and me."

"That's not funny, Martin."

"I'm sorry. Sure. I'll see you this weekend."

He went back to his room feeling a bit warmer inside. He was glad that she'd suggested getting together. It warmed him to feel that she wanted to move towards him on her own, that he didn't always have to make the first move. He had missed her, missed being close to her, talking with her about her work, and the lonely scared people she dealt with day in and day out. He went back to his room with a faint smile on his face.

ELIZABETH JONES

*   *   *   *   *   *   *

Elizabeth Jones was born in Eshowe, South Africa in 1934. After completing her studies in Scotland and France, she taught at universities in South Africa and Canada. In the early seventies she settled in the Annapolis Valley, where she lived for fourteen years before moving to Halifax. A contributor to The Canadian Forum, The Dalhousie Review, The Antigonish Review, *and many other magazines, she has also published three books of poetry:* Castings *(1972),* Flux *(1977), and* Nude on the Dartmouth Ferry *(1980). Her historical study* Gentlemen and Jesuits: Quests for Glory and Adventure in the Early Days of New France *appeared in 1986.*

"Nude on the Dartmouth Ferry" was first published in the premier issue of The Pottersfield Portfolio, *in 1979. The following year it was collected in, and lent its title to, Jones' third poetry collection. The serigraph by Nova Scotia artist Roger Savage that inspired the poem was featured on the cover of the book. Jones, who is clearly fascinated by the incongruity of Savage's vision of a naked woman passenger on a Halifax-Dartmouth ferry, published an article on Savage's work in the Spring 1981 issue of* Arts Atlantic.

*   *   *   *   *   *   *

Nude on the Dartmouth Ferry
(after a print by Roger Savage)

White-collar worker
with neatly-cuffed wrists
nurse secretary
anonymous pillar of hospitals banks
a prefabricated unit
to be shunted
between city and city

dismantled
you uphold nothing
but your column of flesh
the tall trunk of your legs
swelling to hips
your spine a taut pull
against tilt of railings and planks

owning nothing
you rise from the waves
(those wrinkled vulvae)
your head topping the horizon

clear of the city's flanks
its grey erections
you stand poised
for this moment
in the pale light

your own caryatid
between sea and sky.

LESLEY CHOYCE

*   *   *   *   *   *   *

Lesley Choyce was born in Riverside, New Jersey in 1951 and studied at City University of New York. He moved to Lawrencetown, Nova Scotia in 1978. Since his arrival in the province, he has emerged as a prominent member of the Atlantic region's literary community. A professor of English at Dalhousie University and the publisher of Pottersfield Press, he is also an active editor, poet, short-story writer, novelist, and television host. Among his more than a dozen books are The Dream Auditor *(1986),* An Avalanche of Ocean *(1987), and* December Six/The Halifax Solution *(1988). His recent novel* The Second Season of Jonas MacPherson *(1989) includes one of the few literary depictions of Halifax's V.E. Day riots.*

"Fog" was first published in Choyce's poetry collection The End of Ice *(1985). Although the poem is a paean to the fog that not infrequently enshrouds Halifax, "Fog" actually provides one of the most detailed descriptions of the city found in poetry.*

*   *   *   *   *   *   *

Fog

Fog falling in on Halifax
leaning wet and windless against the legislature
feeling its way up through the sockets of the city
and emptying the spaces from emptiness
in a soft military parade of completion.

Fog sidling up against the dockyards
and thick and soft on the rat's back
with pearling globes of the sea.
We are with you fog
stalled high up in your forest on the Bridge at night
over the harbour heaped with your awful soft foliage.
To jump tonight would be to dissolve slowly to sweat and salt
and rich pungent ferment
to never reach the concrete of
absolute harbour top
rhymeless tonight without wind
paved rutless by fog.

Fog feeling up the city
up Barrington up Prince up Blowers up Brunswick
up the pant leg of the rumhappy man
drinking too late to make his way to Hope Cottage
or the Salvation Army for sentimental soup and leftovers.

Fog — clean and grey and green and warm
and freezing and collecting like pollen
on nose hairs
burrowing into ears and
drilling out nail holes in tenements
kneeling outside the doors of widows
whose husbands sank beneath your perfect
embrace in your blind efforts at fulfillment.

Fog sucking out sewers of human perfume
scouring the sulfur from
the Power Corporation stacks
and slapping it down like brown chewing gum
on the hoods of rusting Hondas and hatchbacks
and half-ton pickups.
You won't leave us alone
a sinking sky beneath the unseen stars
reminding us of how close we cling to this planet
how easily we might drive stakes through our own hearts
or dream ourselves into holocausts
as we breathe your mix of our own gashouse anaesthesia.

Where there is life on this coast
the fog will dance among the rocks
glazing the graffitti of boulders
at Black Rock Beach
or hounding with seaspit the monuments
to sunken navies and shattered empires.

Carl Sandburg you know nothing of fog
of intoxicating Halifax sea breath
lusting after the land
landlording the night
with mysterious inner light coming from nowhere
but everywhere
complete
consummate

Fog cleaning the shoes of Winston Churchill
frozen in front of The Public Library
fog borrowing alleys to sleep in trash cans
brimful with the hardware of our dreams
fog the great constable of noise
in whose ear the throats of civilization go quiet.
We're with you fog
hiding out in the Public Gardens after dark

locked in between the massive Victorian swing gates
we're with you nibbling at the leaves of trees
planted by English kings and princesses
we're with you crawling out with the mice
from under the gazebo where the music
of two world wars screamed sour in the dawn
we're with you planning designs on the tulips
the roses, the rosaries left on the porch
by dozing nuns across Spring Garden Road.

Fog — in spring you speak forever death
in winter forever life
we believe in the weight of your sleep
your ageless supple spine
your painless powerful jaws
like shark's teeth muffled in angel wings.
For you we define the limits of soft.

We are with you here in Halifax
and linked to the kelp in your breath
tied to the strings of Sable
and tethered to the lip of the Great Shelf.
We can sing like this with the tongues of cod
the ribs of stone
and the bartered symphonies of barnacled whales.
We can trust the rivets of your silence
even here in the riddled city.

I hold your hand
stumbling through the potholes of Water Street.
You make me feel the pulse of my blood
like yours
salted and cool.

GEORGE ELLIOTT CLARKE

* * * * * * *

George Elliott Clarke was born in the Black Loyalist community of Windsor Plains, Nova Scotia in 1960. He was raised and educated in Halifax and later attended the University of Waterloo before completing his M.A. in English at Dalhousie University. One of the major literary voices of Nova Scotia's Black community, he has contributed to a wide variety of regional and national periodicals. His first book of poetry, Saltwater Spirituals and Deeper Blues, *was published in 1983. Clarke presently lives in Ottawa, where he works as an Executive Assistant to the M.P. Howard McCurdy.*

"Campbell Road Church" was first published in the Atlantic poetry journal Germination *(Fall/Winter 1982) and was later collected in* Saltwater Spirituals and Deeper Blues, *forming part of "Soul Songs," a sequence devoted to Nova Scotia's Black churches. While Clarke has written a number of strong poems about Halifax, none surpasses this haunting and angry lament for Africville, the Black community on the edge of Bedford Basin that was destroyed in 1964 as part of Halifax's redevelopment plans. Campbell Road, which no longer appears on maps of Halifax, was the main road into the village.*

* * * * * * *

Campbell Road Church

at negro point, some forget sleep
to catch the fire-and-brimstone sun
rise all gold-glory
over a turquoise harbour
of half-sunken, rusted ships
when it was easy to worship
benin bronze dawns,
to call "hosanna" to archangel gulls...
but none do now.
rather, an ancient, CN porter lusts for africville,
shabby shacktown of
shattered glass and promises,
rats rustling like a girl's loose dress.
he rages to recall
the gutting death of his genealogy,
to protest his home's slaughter
by butcher bulldozers
and city planners molesting statistics.

at negro point, some forgot sleep,
sang "oh freedom over me,"
heard mournful trains cry like blizzards
along blue bedford basin...

none do now.

SPIDER ROBINSON

* * * * * * *

Spider Robinson was born in New York City in 1948. Not long after receiving his B.A. from State University of New York, in 1972, he broke into the science-fiction field. In 1973 he arrived in Nova Scotia, settling in the Annapolis Valley, where he lived until 1978, when he moved to Halifax. The recipient of virtually every major award in the SF genre, he has published six short-story collections and five novels. In 1987 Robinson left Halifax for Vancouver, bidding a bittersweet farewell to his hometown in the June 1987 issue of the Halifax-Dartmouth magazine Cities. *He is presently working with his wife Jeanne on a sequel to their award-winning novel* Stardance.*

The following excerpt is from the opening pages of Robinson's novel Mindkiller *(1982), which is partly set in Halifax during the 1990s. This same passage was earlier published as part of a longer excerpt from the novel, a preview entitled "Reunion," that appeared in the July 1980 issue of* Halifax. *In Robinson's somewhat sardonic vision of the near future, the Angus L. Macdonald Bridge remains a landmark where, for some, life and death decisions are made.*

* * * * * * *

from **Mindkiller**

1994 Halifax Harbor at night is a beautiful sight, and June usually finds the Macdonald Bridge lined with lovers and other appreciators. But in Halifax even June can turn on one with icy claws.

A thermometer sheltered from the brisk wind would have shown a little below Centigrade zero. Norman Kent had the magnificent scenery all to himself.

He was aware of the view; it was before his face, and his eyes were not closed. He was aware of the cold too, because occasionally when he worked his face frozen tears would break and fall from his cheeks. Neither meant anything to him. He was even vaguely aware of the sound of steady traffic behind him, successive dopplers like the rhythmic moaning of some wounded giant. They meant nothing to him either. On careful reflection Norman could think of nothing that did mean anything to him, and so he put one leg over the outer rail.

A voice came out of the night. "Hey, Cap, *don't!*"

He froze for a long moment. Running footsteps approached from the Dartmouth end of the bridge. Norman turned and saw the man coming up fast in the wash of passing headlights, and that decided him. He got the other leg over and stood teetering on the narrow ledge, the wind full in his face. His hat blew off, and insanely he spun around after it and incredibly he caught it, and was caught himself at wrist and forearm by two very strong hands. They dragged him bodily back over the rail again, nearly breaking his arm, and deposited him hard on his back on the pedestrian walkway. His breath left him, and he lay there blinking up at bridge structure and midnight sky for perhaps half a minute.

He became aware that his unwanted rescuer was sitting beside him, back against the rail and to the wind, breathing heavily. Norman rolled his head, felt cold stone bite his cheek, saw a large man in a shabby coat, silhouetted against a pool of light. From the frosted breath he knew that the large man was shaking his head.

Norman lifted himself on his elbows and sat beside the other, lifting his collar against the cold. He fumbled out a pack of Players Light and lit one with a flameless lighter. He held it out to the man, who accepted it silently, and lit another for himself.

"My wife left me," Norman said. "Six years this August, and she left me. Six *years*! Said she married too soon, she had to 'find herself.' And the semester's almost over, I've bitched it all up, nothing at all lined up for the summer, and there's a really good chance I won't be hired back in September. Old MacLeod with his hoary hints about austerity and sacrifices and a department chairman's heavy responsibility, he wouldn't even come right out and tell me! *Find* herself, for Christ's stinking sake! Got herself a nineteen-year-old plumbing student, he's going to help her *find* herself." He broke off and smoked for a while. When he could speak again he said, "Perhaps I could have handled either one, but the two together is … it's only fair to tell you, I'm going to try again, and you can't stop me forever."

The other spoke for the first time. His voice was deep and gravelly and dispassionate. "Don't let me stop you."

Norman turned to stare. "Then why — ?" He stopped then, for the knife picked up the oncoming headlights very well.

"I never meant to *stop* you, Cap," the large man said calmly. "Just, uh — heh, heh — hold you up a little."

He was not even troubling to keep the knife hidden from the traffic. Norman glanced briefly at the oncoming cars; as in a slapstick movie sequence he saw four drivers, one after the other, do the identical single-take and then return their eyes grimly to the road. He yanked his own eyes back to the knife. It was quite large and looked sharp. The large man held it as though he knew how, and all at once it came to Norman that he had cashed a check today, and had two hundred New dollars in twenties in his wallet.

He let go of his cigarette and the wind took it. He put his gloved left hand palm up on his lap. On it he placed his wallet, his cigarettes, a half-empty pack of joints, and the small lighter.

As he peeled the watch from the inside of his wrist he noticed that both hands were shaking badly. Oh, yes, he told himself, that's right, it is very cold. He added the watch to the pile, worked the right glove off against his hip, and took his pocket change in that hand.

"On my lap, brother," the large man directed. "Then go. Back to town or over the side, it's all the same to me."

Norman sighed deeply, and flung everything high and to his right. Nearly all of it went over the rail and into the harbor; a few bills were blown into traffic and toward the other rail.

The large man sat motionless. His eyes did not follow the loot but remained fixed on Norman, who stared back.

At last the large man got to his feet. "Cap," he said, shaking his head again, "you got a lot of hard bark on you." The knife disappeared. "Sorry I bothered you." He turned and began walking back toward Dartmouth, hunching against the wind, still smoking Norman's cigarette.

"You gutless bastard," Norman whispered, and wondered who he was talking to.

Norman Kent was thirty years old. He was one hundred and sixty-five centimeters tall and weighed fifty-five kilograms — although, having been born in America in 1965, he habitually thought of himself as five-five and a hundred and twenty pounds. Despite his actual stature, people usually remembered him as being of average height: there was a solidity to his body and movements. It implied a strength and physical conditioning he had not actually possessed since leaving the United States Army six years before. His face was passable, with wide-set grey eyes, a perfect aquiline nose, and a chin that would have seemed strong if it had not been topped by a mouth a fraction too wide. Overdeveloped folds at each corner of the mouth made it seem, when at rest, to be a faint, smug smile.

One could have flattered him most by calling him elegant. He had shaved for his suicide. The suit was tasteful enough to befit an assistant professor of English — it was his best suit — and the topcoat was pure quality. At thirty his hairline had not yet receded visibly. He wore his hair moderately long; the wind had whipped it into a fantastic sculpture and kept revising the design. The only nonconformist indulgence he permitted himself was his necktie, which looked like a riot in a paint shop.

After a time he put his glove back on, got stiffly to his feet, and left the bridge at the Halifax end, stamping his feet to restore circulation. He had not known genuine physical fear in six years, and he had forgotten the exhilaration that comes with survival. It was a twenty-minute walk home, and he savored every step. The smell of the harbor, the seedy waterfront squalor of Hollis Street, the brave, forlorn hookers too frozen to display their wares, the fake stained glass in the front windows of Skipper's Lounge, the special and inimitable color of leaves backlit by a street light, the clacking sounds of traffic lights and the laboring power plant of Victoria General Hospital — all were brand new again, treasures to be appreciated for the first time. He walked happily, mindless as a child. When he reached his apartment tower on Wellington Street, he was whistling. On the way up in the elevator, he graduated to humming, and by the time he reached his floor he was singing the words too, whereupon he was amused to discover that the tune he had been humming so merrily was the old Tom Lehrer song, "Poisoning Pigeons in the Park."

FURTHER READING

The following list identifies over forty literary works, including children's books, in which Halifax figures as a significant setting or subject. Only the first edition of each work is cited. In addition to these books, readers might want to consult John Robert Colombo's *Canadian Literary Landmarks* (1984) and Albert and Theresa Moritz's *The Oxford Illustrated Literary Guide to Canada* (1987), both of which contain information on Halifax literary personalities and landmarks. Thomas H. Raddall's definitive history of the city, *Halifax, Warden of the North* (1948, revised 1965 and 1971), also contains some useful references to literary figures.

Bell, Lt. Col. F. McKelvey
  A Romance of the Halifax Disaster (Halifax: Royal Print & Litho, 1918) novella combined with non-fiction

Choyce, Lesley
  The Second Season of Jonas MacPherson (Saskatoon: Thistledown Press, 1989) novel

Creighton, Helen
  Helen Creighton: A Life in Folklore (Toronto: McGraw-Hill Ryerson, 1975) memoir

Dyba, Kenneth
  Lucifer & Lucinda (Vancouver: November House, 1977) children's book

Eaton, Arthur Wentworth and Craven Langstroth Betts
  Tales of a Garrison Town (New York and St. Paul: D. D. Merrill, 1892) short story collection

Fowke, Shirley
  Joe, or, The Corduroy Breeches (Halifax: McCurdy, 1971) children's book

Goldsmith, Oliver
The Autobiography of Oliver Goldsmith ed. by Rev. Wilfrid E. Myatt (Toronto: Ryerson, 1943) memoir

Gordon, Mark
Head of the Harbour (Toronto: Groundhog Press, 1983) novel

Gray, Simon
Colmain (London: Faber and Faber, 1963) novel

Herbert, Mary E.
Belinda Dalton; or Scenes in the Life of a Halifax Belle (Halifax: Mary E. Herbert, 1859) novel

Holmes, Jeffrey
Farewell to Nova Scotia (Windsor: Lancelot Press, 1974) novel

James, Janet Craig
Jeremy Gates and the Magic Key (Moonbeam, Ont.: Penumbra Press, 1986) young adult novel

Jones, Alice [Alix John]
The Night-Hawk (New York: Frederick A. Stokes, 1901) novel

Jones, Susan [Helen Milecete]
A Detached Pirate (London: Greening, 1900) novel

Kroll, Robert E.
Intimate Fragments (Halifax: Nimbus, 1985) novel

Lancaster, G. B.
Grand Parade (New York: Reynal & Hitchcock, 1943) novel

Lotz, Jim
The Sixth of December (Markham, Ont.: PaperJacks, 1981) novel

Lunn, Jenni
Gully Goes to Halifax (Bedford, N.S.: Pegasus Publishing, 1986) children's book

McCulloch, Thomas
Colonial Gleanings; William and Melville (Edinburgh: Oliphant, 1826) two short novels

MacLennan, Hugh
Barometer Rising (New York: Duell, Sloan and Pearce, 1941) novel

MacNeil, Robert
Wordstruck: A Memoir (New York: Viking, 1989) memoir

Maitland, Hugh
Brad Forrest's Halifax Adventure (Toronto: Longman's Canada, 1965) young adult novel

Marko, Katherine McGlade
Away to Fundy Bay (New York: Walker, 1985) young adult novel

Merkel, Andrew
Tallahassee; A Ballad of Nova Scotia in the Sixties (Halifax: Imperial Publishing, 1945) long narrative poem

Perkins, Dorothy
Rachel's Revolution (Lancelot Press, 1989) young adult novel

Raddall, Thomas H.
The Governor's Lady (Garden City, N.Y. and Toronto: Doubleday, 1960) novel
Hangman's Beach (Garden City, N.Y. and Toronto: Doubleday, 1966) novel
His Majesty's Yankees (Garden City, N.Y., Doubleday, 1942) novel
In My Time (Toronto: McClelland and Stewart, 1976) memoir
The Nymph and The Lamp (Boston: Little, Brown, 1950) novel
Roger Sudden (Garden City, N.Y.: Doubleday, 1944) novel

Ritchie, Charles
An Appetite for Life; The Education of a Young Diarist, 1924-27 (Toronto: Macmillan, 1977) memoir
My Grandfather's House: Scenes of Childhood and Youth (Toronto: Macmillan, 1987) memoir

Roache, Gordon
A Halifax ABC (Montreal: Tundra Books, 1987) children's book

Robinson, Spider
Mindkiller (New York: Holt, Rinehart and Winston, 1982) novel

Saunders, Marshall
The House of Armour (Philadelphia: Rowland, 1897) novel

Smith, Ray
The Lord Nelson Tavern (Toronto: McClelland and Stewart, 1974) collection of linked short stories

Swede, George
The Case of the Moonlit Gold Dust (Toronto: Three Trees Press, 1979) children's book

Williams, Michael
The Book of the High Romance; A Spiritual Autobiography (New York: Macmillan, 1918) memoir

Wilson, Budge
Breakdown (Richmond Hill, Ont.: Scholastic-TAB, 1988) young adult novel
Thirteen Never Changes (Richmond Hill, Ont.: Scholastic-TAB, 1989) young adult novel

ACKNOWLEDGEMENTS

The excerpt from Will R. Bird's *And We Go On* (Toronto: Hunter-Rose, 1930) is published by permission of Betty Murray.

Earle Birney's "Halifax" first appeared in *New* (December 1968) and is published by permission of the author.

bill bissett's "halifax nova scotia" first appeared in *canada gees mate for life* (Vancouver: Talonbooks, 1985) and is published by permission of the author.

Charles Bruce's "Tide" first appeared in *The Open Gateway* (August 1931) and is published by permission of Harry Bruce.

Lesley Choyce's "Fog" first appeared in *The End of Ice* (Fredericton, N.B.: Fiddlehead Poetry Books and Goose Lane Editions, 1985) and is published by permission of the author.

George Elliott Clarke's "Campbell Road Church" first appeared in *Germination* (Fall/Winter 1982) and is published by permission of the author.

The excerpt from *The Journal of Richard Henry Dana, Jr.; Volume II* edited by Robert F. Lucid is reprinted by permission of the publisher: The Belknap Press of Harvard University Press, Cambridge, Mass. Copyright 1968 by the Mass. Historical Society and the fellows and president of Harvard College. All rights reserved.

The excerpt from Dièreville's *Relation of the Voyage to Port Royal in Acadia or New France* edited by John Clarence Webster; translated by Mrs. Clarence Webster (Toronto: Champlain Society, 1933) is published by permission of the Champlain Society.

The excerpt from Juliana Horatia Ewing's correspondence first appeared in *Canada Home; Juliana Horatia Ewing's Fredericton Letters, 1867-1869* edited by Margaret Howard Blom and Thomas E. Blom (Vancouver: University of British Columbia Press, 1983). Pottersfield Press was unable to identify a copyright holder for this material.